# FIRE ON THE MOUNTAIN

JEAN McNEIL

Legend Press Ltd, 107-111 Fleet Street, London, EC4A 2AB
info@legend-paperbooks.co.uk | www.legendpress.co.uk

 British Library Cataloguing in Publication Data available.

Print ISBN 978-1-7850789-9-6
Ebook ISBN 978-1-7871999-9-6
Set in Times. Printed in Bulgaria by Multiprint
Cover design by Gudrun Jobst www.yotedesign.com
Cover images by Jean McNeil

**Jean McNeil** is the author of twelve books of fiction, non-fiction, poetry, essays and travel. Her book about Antarctica, *Ice Diaries,* won the Banff Mountain Film and Book Festival Grand Prize in 2016 and her work has been nominated for Canada's premier literary prize, The Governor-General's Award, the Journey Prize, for a Canadian National Magazine Award and the Pushcart prize. Her novel *The Dhow House* was published by Legend Press in 2016. She is Reader in Creative Writing at the University of East Anglia in Norwich, Norfolk and lives in London.

Visit Jean at
www.jeanmcneil.co.uk
or
follow Jean on Twitter
@jeanmcneilwrite

I know I will remember the city as a film – a backdrop, somewhere I witnessed rather than lived. The first image, just as the opening credits fade, will be the hot tarmac of its streets smoking after rain, an entire city burning from the ground up. But then there are those things you cannot see: the vegetable smell of kelp mashed on the serrated shore of Ocean Point, the taste of salt on your lips. The light – bleached, peering, as if you were being scrutinised, as if the sun was trying to determine what use it might have for you. For the first week I am blinded by it. The summer gales, the blistering light. The sea is buoyant and cold.

That city is the only place in my life I have ever experienced a nostalgia for when I was still there, as if the days and weeks were destined to be revealed as not real after all. They belonged to a separate dimension, neither past, present nor future. They were being pulled out from under me even as I lived them.

In the film, after the rain-smoked streets, we see Pieter. He is walking toward us across the grass. There is a prowling quality to Pieter's walk, which Riaan inherited, along with his narrow, delicate feet. I am next to Sara, her uncle and her cousin. We are all sitting at a stone table underneath a sculpted shrub, which overhangs in an unnatural oblong. Flies harass the wedges of cheese, the expert courgette and pepper antipasto Sara has prepared.

Only a few nights ago we nearly lost all this – the pool, the sculpted tree, the date palm, the house itself, with its architectural heritage, its price tag in the millions. I remember how darkness filled the kitchen that night as Pieter and I talked, like liquid poured into a glass, both of us so absorbed in the narrowness of our escape we dared not interrupt the moment to light the candles that were our only illumination. How we stepped outside where the flowers – amaryllis, jasmine, bougainvillea – were still blooming. Despite the heat they'd been exposed to they had survived and their scent travelled on the breeze. How after nearly four unanticipated months in the city these reversed skies were becoming my skies. I could read the upside down constellations now, although I've lived all my life in another hemisphere.

Now it is a hot day, a goodbye lunch, and Pieter comes walking barefoot across the grass, past the swimming pool. Patches of sweat soak his sky blue shirt with the small white stitches. He has several buttons open from the neck.

'You're halfway to taking your shirt off,' Sara says.

'Well I would, but I don't want to scare away the ladies,' he says.

'Or we'll fall on you and attack you!' Sara's cousin grins.

'Don't do it,' I say, 'it's not worth the risk.'

The vague air of seduction, of something withheld – do all writers have this? I knew him; I didn't know him. Perhaps that is all I will be able to say about Pieter, in the future. The writer who was tired of writing; who was always on the brink of giving up; who had been left behind by history; who hadn't come into history at the right moment; whose books were considered evasive parables in a time of national crisis; whose works had never found popular acceptance, despite or because of their deadly seriousness. I can see him calculating how long it would be before he could indulge his addiction to contemplation again, how long he would have to serve lemonade to relatives on a heat-staggered day.

But today he is Pieter, slim and winningly arrogant, my friend, the father I never had.

I look up and see he is going to leave us. I know this from the deliberate way he approaches the table. He comes up behind Sara's elderly uncle and hovers. 'I'm going to have to love you and leave you, I have a meeting at the national library.' The uncle with the hearing aid takes no notice of him. I stare at Pieter, giving him what I know it is a plaintive look. This may be the last time I ever see him. My flight leaves in four hours' time.

'Cheers,' Pieter says. His voice is distant, even acrid. He has been this way with me all day. I don't know what I have done. It's as if he has only today discovered or realised something not to his liking.

After he has disappeared into the house and I hear the car pull away I can't hear what anyone is saying. A draining feeling tugs all of my energy from me. Suddenly the heat is oppressive. It ripples through the burnt garden, the tangle of vegetation that used to run rampant without the twice-weekly chop from Lewis the gardener, in a kiln heat, a dead mid-afternoon moment, the swimming pool glistening in the late summer light.

# PART I

# I

'Nice part of town,' the taxi driver said, as soon as I gave him the address. I couldn't read the tone in his voice – envy, rue, contempt. Perhaps all three.

We began the long ascent of the mountain. I craned my neck to look at the city beneath us. I could see where I had come from now, the wide-mouthed harbour flanked by half-finished highways. This was where I'd been marooned for days. Some of the overhead flyways simply stopped abruptly halfway along the roadway, like the highest platform in a diving pool. From up here the gigantic Chinese container ships and oil rigs looked so much smaller. I allowed my eye to skate over the ship, but even so my heart lurched as its green hull flashed at me in the mid-day sun.

We kept ascending, so quickly my ears popped. I could smell jasmine and frangipani through the car windows. We wound through tree-darkened avenues. The houses expanded with each metre climbed until they were full-blown palaces. Finally the taxi delivered me to a sandstone-coloured structure perched on the side of the mountain. It looked like a house you might find in a Dutch village, adapted for life in the subtropics.

'I didn't know it was possible to live this far up,' I said to the taxi driver.

'It is if you've got enough money.'

I buzzed the gate and spoke to a woman's voice – Sara, I supposed. The gate slid open and we glided up the drive, so steep it felt like being in a funicular. Stout plants clambered over the terraced levels on either side of the driveway; they were spiky and bulbous at the same time, with avid, rubbery leaves.

A blond woman with jade green eyes descended the steps to the house. She seemed to float; her sense of ownership was that complete. She was long-legged, dressed in white trousers and a sand-coloured blouse.

'Pieter is out running,' Sara said, as she gave me her hand. 'He's training for the marathon.'

'Oh.' I nearly said, *but I thought he was a writer*. I'd never pictured a writer running a marathon.

'Come in, let me get you some coffee.'

I dropped my bags. I saw her eye glance at them nervously, as if I had brought dogs and not luggage. She motioned for me to sit in the living room.

When I entered the room I couldn't help but stop and stand stock-still. My jaw may even have fallen open.

'Quite the view, isn't it?' Her voice, the cool neutrality of it, told me that many a guest had been similarly stopped in their tracks.

The wide arc of the bay was stretched out before us. In the distance was the low, whale-like back of Garzia Island, which even with my slim knowledge of the city I knew was a former penal colony from when the Portuguese were still loitering on this promontory of the planet, hoping for lucre.

To the right of Garzia Island were blonde hills which gleamed like flax in the sun. The mountain with its strenuous flattened peak filled an entire window. The living room was glass on two sides. The thought entered and exited my mind, too fleeting to matter. People in glass houses.

Sara went to the kitchen. Later she would tell me she asked me to sit down three times that morning but as soon as I sat I stood up again.

I could not tear my eyes away from the mountain. The jagged peak that marked one undulation of its range soared into the sky, piercing a hole in it. Next to the house a date palm towered, its trunk of scaled chocolate bark perfectly offsetting the dark shale of the mountain. Straight ahead was the ocean; off to one side was the harbour, half-hidden behind a headland. My eye rested on it again for a second. The ship, patiently waiting alongside the quay.

I reminded myself it was Saturday. Tomorrow the ship will leave.

'So,' Sara began, when she finally got me off my feet. 'How long are you here for?'

'I'm not sure. I – I've just had a change of plan.'

She nodded, calmly. If she had been English, alarm bells would already have been sounding in her mind: How long will I be stuck with this person? Why does he have so much baggage? Why has a random contact of our niece ended up on our doorstep?

'Well this is as good a place as any to have your plans change.' She smiled easily, warmly, I thought. 'You can certainly stay here as long as you like. We've got no one coming until April.'

It was mid-December. 'It shouldn't be that long, at least I hope not,' I said. 'I'll just make some arrangements for my trip home, and then let you know.'

'That's absolutely fine. It's a pleasure to have a friend of Ruth's here.' Her delivery was unruffled, flawless.

I accepted Sara's invitation to join her on a walk on the mountain behind the house. She met me at the bottom of the steps. She'd changed into trim shorts. She must have been in her late fifties or early sixties but her legs were perfect; there was nothing of the tell-tale bulge of skin at the knees, or those black spidering veins. I stared long enough for her to take my amazement as a compliment, perhaps, because she gave a sudden smile.

We started down the road, which soon ended in a paved cul-de-sac. From it a path led into a sparse forest. It was dry as tinder in areas, the ground parched and weedy. All the trees and flowers we passed were unfamiliar – thick, bulbous flowers. They looked water-hungry but somehow thrived in the seasonally dry climate.

We came to a fissure in the mountain. The sound of water cascading came to meet us. The trees parted to reveal a narrow stream.

'Slaves would come here to wash clothes,' Sara said. Her voice was complex – rich, melodic, but with a tinge of darkness to it, or perhaps this saturnine note was code for her disapproval of the city's history.

I looked up, trying to find the mountain's summit among clouds. I could feel it, somehow, that this shaded bower had once been a place of hardship. Alongside the river were stone steps, knee-worn through hundreds of years of prostrations, and beside them, flat, table-like washing rocks. I could see the interlacing strata of grey mudstone and sandstone, its outer shield dark shale. Then layers of granite: feldspar, quartz, black mica, all glittering in the strange bright light.

Sara smiled. 'You seem transfixed.'

'By the mountain? I guess so. I used to be a geologist.'

'But now you work for a humanitarian relief organisation. How does that fit in?'

I was used to this comment. I can't work you out, people – colleagues, my line manager, strangers met on planes, would say.

'It's complicated.' I offered an apologetic smile.

'Everything's complicated.' Her laugh was itself complex, rueful, rise-above-it-all. 'Pieter should be back about lunchtime. He'll need to take a shower and wind down.'

'Does he often train for marathons?'

'Oh yes, and cycle races, triathlons, endurance contests. Everyone does that here.'

By everyone she couldn't have meant the squatter camps I'd seen on the way in from the airport, their faded tutti-frutti shacks, people inside broiled alive by tin roofs in the summer and congealed in winter. They were enrolled in a different endurance contest.

We arrived back at the house. Sara showed me to their guest flat, which was self-contained but attached to the main house through an internal door. She told me they had designed and built the flat themselves, and that she used to see her clients there while Pieter worked in his basement office.

By then the sun parried the swift ocean clouds for position and shone through, the light bright, carrying within it the promise of a humid heat, should the clouds dissolve. I stood in the light for a minute as Sara undid the three locks and de-activated the house alarm. I registered what was about to happen to me. For a moment, I thought I would be alright. But I could only watch helplessly as the air gathered itself into blackberries, then went dark.

'We thought we'd lost you there.'

It felt like I was lying on concrete. I realised I was. I sat up.

'Hey, take it easy.'

I opened my eyes into the face of a blond-haired man. He was crouching on one knee. His fingers were wrapped around my wrist. He might be a doctor. There was a clinical glint in his gaze. His voice was familiar, somehow, although I'd never seen him before.

'I'm so sorry.'

'Nothing to be sorry about. We'd like you to lie down inside, though. You might find that more comfortable.'

'I haven't been sleeping well,' I said, as the man helped me to my feet. 'I haven't been eating either.'

'Not sleeping and not eating, hey?' His tone was avuncular, but suspicious.

'I've been under a lot of stress – at home.'

'That's fine, Nick, don't worry,' Sara's voice came from somewhere behind me. 'We just want to make sure you're alright. You fainted stone dead, there.'

I realised the man was Pieter. 'We're going to put you in bed and then we'll call Marina, our doctor.'

'No!' I nearly shouted. 'I mean, I don't want to put you to any trouble. Please don't make a fuss. It's just dehydration. I'll take a couple of salt sachets. I'm not concussed. I'll be fine.'

They looked at me in tandem, a double-headed puppet of concern, the same kind-but-wary expressions on their tanned, shining faces. *They don't know you from Adam*, I told myself. *You have to reassure them.*

'I've had some difficult decisions to make recently, and it's left me very strung out. But I'm fine, now.'

Sara gave me the sturdy, professional look psychiatrists likely turn on liars.

'Okay, Nick. But take those salts and get some sleep. We'll check on you in a few hours.'

When I woke it was late afternoon. My bedroom had a patio door. I opened it and was confronted with a garden, two chairs, and the same panoramic view of the harbour and mountain, although the majestic sweep I'd admired in the living room was curtailed by the curve of the house.

The light lay in gold ribbons on the flanks of the mountain. A heat haze had settled over the harbour, blurring the outlines of supertankers. My eye scurried over the quay where the ship was moored but not before I'd seen that it was still there.

I resolved to tell Pieter and Sara the truth, of my fainting spell, why I was here, why I had no idea how long I would stay. They had been kind to me, they deserved to know.

Pieter appeared from around a corner. He wore a crisp white shirt tucked into jeans and a leather belt. He was barefoot and his hair was plastered to his head from his shower. He was very thin – one of those men who are naturally so. You could see the architecture of the bones and muscles in his face.

'How are you feeling?'

'Much better.'

'You haven't got a headache?'

'No, nothing like that. No concussion.'

'That's good. I had one once. I came off my bike, just up there, on the mountain.'

This was the moment in which I would say, Look, I've just made this crazy decision I don't understand. I'm not supposed to be here, but I've got nowhere to go.

We turned our faces in tandem, like sunflowers, toward the setting sun.

'This time of year the sun rises in the sea and sets behind the mountain – we get light all day,' Pieter said. 'The people who live on the other side are spared the wind but they get far less light.'

My confession unravelled itself, or it abandoned me, or I let it be carried away by the moment. I had so little experience with secrets, guilty or otherwise. I'd never liked them; a secret was a dripping overheated greenhouse.

'I've never been anywhere the wind is so fierce in the summer,' I said.

'Not like that in England, is it?'

A dog appeared, a mongrel, or a cross, a bullish dog with a bruiser's face.

'Hello, Lucy.' He turned to me and grinned. 'The name doesn't really fit the face, does it. But she's a sweetheart. Arr! Grrr!' He planted his legs wide apart, a position of mock threat. Lucy went wild with pleasure, charging away, thrilled, then turning on a dime to come back to face the monster.

Behind Pieter I saw a bright light that seemed to zing from inside him in a perfect giant Z, a flash of miniature lightning.

'What was that?'

'Transformer.' Pieter pointed to a sizzling cylinder nestling in a telegraph pole halfway down the road. 'They often explode – too much load on the system. Don't be alarmed if the electricity cuts out. We have candles.'

He turned back to the dog, who rushed at him, growling,

purple gums bared. For a moment I thought she would bite. But she stuck her head between his calves and squealed with delight.

'We have rolling electricity cuts, this time of year,' he went on. 'They announce them in the paper, supposedly, but it can cut out any time.'

'Are there shortages?'

'Ah, if only it were that easy. No, it's corruption, mismanagement. A new government is about to be elected, although we're in a one-party state, effectively. It makes you appreciate how useful it is to have two political parties contesting each other, however bad either of them will be. At least it bestows symmetry if not a chance for historical dialectic.'

His speech reminded me of the policy analysts in our office in London. I wasn't used to athletic, vital men who were also intellectuals, if that's what Pieter was. I lived in a country where a certain kind of man got things done, and a certain kind of man thought about things. Perhaps here they could be one and the same.

'It's not only power, but other infrastructure.' He pointed into the harbour. Along its perimeter, an eight-lane highway conveyed sun-glinted cars into the interior like platelets rushing down an artery. Pieter told me that the diving board freeways I'd seen on my way in had been built in a spasm of economic optimism, which had just expired.

'You *are* English, aren't you?' he peered at me.

'The way you say it, it's not a good thing to be.'

'Well, it might not be, you know. The English don't have a good reputation in this country. They quashed the independence movement, then established a colonial system that set the country back a hundred years.'

'I am,' I conceded. 'But I don't feel very English. I was brought up all over the place – South America, Canada, the Caribbean.'

'Was your father a diplomat?'

'My mother, actually.'

'Ah,' Pieter gave a thin smile. 'I fell into that trap didn't I? Sorry. You know, you don't look English either. You're too dark. In fact you don't look anything.' He smiled. If I had known him better then I would have said I always felt like someone drawn in pencil. A child's drawing of a man, maybe. Anyone could take an eraser and rub me out.

'I'm impressed you still have the energy to play with the dog,' I said. 'After all that running.'

Sara answered for him. She emerged from the patio into the full sun, her hair gleaming. 'Pieter's got amazing energy. You'll see.'

I turned to face Sara. 'It must be so gruelling.'

'Yes, it is sometimes.' Sara smiled.

'No, I didn't mean… I meant the training.'

Sara only laughed. 'Get some sleep, Nick. And don't forget to rehydrate.'

There was something jarring in her voice, not dismissive but rather ironic, as if they still did not believe my story. I turned to look into her eyes. The note in her gaze was evaluative – masculine, I would have said until recently, but I realise now that this is a shorthand for something intangible I associate with men: a streamlining of judgement, an absence of empathy, or perhaps better said, a professionalisation of it. Or maybe just something withheld.

I went to bed in their granny flat. Despite my fatigue I could not get to sleep for a long time. I listened to the night wind, which sliced sideways along the garden. Through a fissure in the curtain I saw the lights of the city stretched around the bay, a semi-circle of distant flickering candles.

I found myself thinking of Sara, of her contained quality. Her jade eyes and heart-shaped face. She was a professional, well-to-do, elegant woman who drove a Mercedes, but I had a sense this version of her was a decoy.

As I fell asleep that night in my new bed I thought, these are the strangest days I have lived in years, possibly in my whole life. Here I am, in the house filled with people I don't know, in a city where I never expected to spend more than a few days, telling lies, or no, that's not quite right: not telling the truth. Why then do I feel such serenity, as if I have come home?

# 11

I wake very late. I feel like I've been on a plane all night, although I'm not sure where I was going. For a long time, a minute perhaps, I don't know where I am. When I remember I put my hands over my face and try to shake the shame out of me.

I go out into the garden wearing only my shorts. Sounds from the distant harbour reach here, all the way up the mountain – clunks, alarm bells, sirens. Three birds fly over, hawking, dusky purple in colour. They have an ear-splitting hawk.

'Nick, you're up.' Sara stands in the doorway of their house. I hadn't realised I could be seen from the step. I leapt back into the shadow of the door. I didn't want her to see my pale body. I'd come from winter into summer. Compared to everyone else, I looked like a ghost.

'We were worried. We were about to check on you.'

From behind the door I said, 'I'm alright. I needed the rest I guess. What time is it?'

'Ten-thirty. I'm going down into town for a meeting. We wondered if you'd like to come to dinner with us tonight?' Her voice fluted at the edge of the question.

'I'd love that,' I said, too quickly. I thought: They know I'm at a loose end.

'Great then, we'll pick you up at seven.'

So began those first weeks when Pieter and Sara absorbed me effortlessly into their lives. There was a steady stream of book launches, drinks parties and barbecues, to which they faithfully invited me without making me feel like a mascot or a temporary son.

These events were attended by voluble, cosmopolitan people, some black, some 'Asian', as people of Indian descent were universally called. The white people, or 'people of European extraction', as I learned it was polite to call them, had a uniformity you never see in Europe anymore. It is not that they came from a single population – the history of immigration was too mixed for that – so I supposed the climate and the life of outdoors bonhomie, surfing, barbecues and physical challenges of increasing extremity – marathons, triathalons, heptathalons – stamped its own code on people, so that they all looked like newly-minted gods. How pale we were in England, I thought, how cowed and trussed into our bodies, compared to these people with their copper skins, their green and blue irises like gems floating in dark water.

One hot afternoon the three of us went to hear a talk on indigenous art at the university. The campus crawled up the other side of the mountain, perched halfway aloft on the slope in a lordly Grecian position, with its Corinthian pillars and Doric columns being slowly consumed by vines, its snaking roads lined with trees with orange flowers bright as flares.

We settled into a lecture theatre panelled in a blood-coloured wood. The audience filed in, followed by the lecturer, a tanned, blond man who looked too young to be delivering such a talk. It was about the serial massacres of the indigenous peoples by those the young-looking man consistently referred to as 'our ancestors'. I surveyed the faces around me for signs of outrage, but they were nodding, their expressions keen, chins held aloft, as if to receive a blow.

After the talk we stood outside. The sun was a shock after the hushed grandeur of the wooden lecture hall.

Pieter peered at me with a half-curious, half-admonitory frown.

'What's wrong, Nick? Are you spinning again?' There was a sharp edge to his voice.

'It's just, my head is full of all these names I never heard.'

'Welcome to our history,' he said.

We were leaving the university in their car when a policeman signalled for us to stop.

'What's this?'

'I don't know.' Pieter called the man over. They had a hushed conversation. He craned his neck to where I sit in the back seat. 'Demonstration. Five people have been murdered here in the last few months.'

'At the university. Why?'

Pieter shrugged. 'Who knows? Robbery probably. I haven't heard much about it.'

'Five people killed, for robbery?'

'You think there should be a more serious reason?' Pieter retorted.

'Well, yes.'

From behind I saw Sara's neck stiffen. 'It's unusual, Nick. The police are looking into it.' Her tone said: *don't worry about it*.

'If I thought much about all the people who are killed in this city I'd never get anything done,' Pieter said.

We waited for half an hour while the procession streamed past us. Students wearing black T-shirts carried homemade signs: *Justice! Make Campus Safe for Students!* They had bright, strident expressions I've only ever seen on the faces of young people in photographs of other eras, in demonstrations against the Vietnam war, or segregation.

I sat back in my seat. My eyes ended up in the rear-view mirror, where they met Pieter's. He did not flick his gaze away, as most people would, after having been caught looking, but kept his eyes on me, a burrowing note in them, so that I felt an instrument digging into my chest, a small drill or corkscrew.

Finally we were let go. We drove through the suburb where the university was located. We glided past scruffy parks dotted with bundles, which turned out to be dozing itinerant workers or homeless people, huddled in pools of shade. The pavements were cracked and choked with weeds. No one walked on them. In fact, I realised I had never seen Pieter and Sara's neighbours walking down the street, I only glimpsed them at the wheels of their cars as they drove through the jaws of their automatic gates.

The mountain filled the windscreen. Pieter drove the highway that wound around its pleats expertly, swinging the car tightly around the curves. The harbour came into view, the indigo taffeta of the ocean, the floodlit docks, the same harbour that so entranced the Portuguese, the Dutch, the English, along with the stony, rectangular God that presided over it. This time my eye did not flinch away from the empty finger of the furthest dock. The ship was gone.

At night the mountain dissolves into the sky. There is a new moon that first week. I sit in the kitchen of Pieter and Sara's granny flat alone with all the lights off, looking for the seam of the mountain against the sky. 'You have to look for where the stars disappear,' Pieter says. 'That's the edge.'

The mountain has floodlights on either side, Pieter has told me, but the city authorities haven't turned them on in months now; they eat too much electricity. 'Unless Parliament is sitting and some foreign dignitary is visiting,' Pieter says. 'Then they suddenly find the wattage.'

When the power cuts come the city shuts off; a switch has been thrown, Pieter tells me, somewhere between here and a coastal nuclear reactor five hundred kilometres away. Thousands of house alarms stagger into automatic shrieks. Dogs wail. This instant darkness is eerie, because it is unwanted. In its dark stealth the mountain is quiet. I hear those birds whose cries sound like someone in pain.

If the blackouts happen in the early evening Pieter appears

at my door. 'Nick, come and sit with us. We're having a glass of wine by candlelight. We can't have you sitting on your own in the dark all night.' I reply that it's okay, that it's not their fault, but Pieter is having none of it. Already he speaks to me with the weary politeness I associate with family. For my part I feel I have always been here, with them, an unnerving, unearned familiarity.

I slink obediently behind him, crossing the threshold of their heavy wooden door, sinking into a giant white sofa, where I sit facing Pieter and Sara on the other side of a trail of candles as we talk and drink Chenin Blanc brewed in chalky fields only ten kilometres from where we sit.

'We're going to a concert tomorrow, would you like to come?' Sara's invitation is issued in a voice both warmly inviting and non-committal. 'We'll need to get you a ticket from somewhere as it's sold out.'

I politely decline. Pieter says, 'Absolutely not, we're not having you sitting here alone like a bloody lump.' He jumps up from the sofa and grabs the telephone. He conducts genial introductions before getting down to the business of securing an extra ticket. I hear my name in his oval, astute tones, and marvel at the familiar syllable of it, how it sounds anointed in his mouth, welcome in the world.

The concert took place in the botanical gardens. The black crag of the mountain hung over fields of rippling, manicured green. As we entered into the lawn I saw people on blankets spread over every inch of the enclosure, drinking wine and eating cheese and grapes.

Pieter and Sara walked ahead, weaving through clots of people standing with tanned bare feet splayed wide apart, swinging children on their hips in time to the music.

As we found a spot, friends of Pieter and Sara's approached us.

'This is Nicholas, a friend of Ruth's. He's visiting from London.'

I rose to my feet to greet them. They shook my hand but angled themselves toward Pieter, their conversations quickly turning conspiratorial in tone. I sat back down and listened to the band.

The air was full of summer. I thought of my colleagues in London, where it had been dark for six hours already. They would soon be heading home to flats they can't afford to heat properly. And then, guilty and fast, I thought of Ernst, of the others on a ship smelling of salt and rust. They would be crossing into the Indian Ocean by now.

In the intermission more people approached us. I began to realise how eminent Pieter was. People asked his opinion on matters that I'd never associated with being a writer. They seemed to want him to tell the future. 'What do you think of the energy crisis Pieter, do you think it will have an effect on foreign investment?' 'What will happen if the local elections don't go the way the nationalists want?' Pieter gave full, paragraph-long answers. I listened attentively at the outskirts of these conversations. It was then I heard his name for the first time – not from Pieter and Sara, but in their friend's mouths.

'Oh, you must be Riaan's friend,' they said, turning to me. 'You met at university.' I explained I was a friend of Ruth's, we worked together, that I lived in London, when I lived anywhere at all. 'Oh Ruth!' they exclaimed. 'Did you know she used to be a film actress in Malanga, before she got her doctorate? So beautiful.' 'No,' I say, 'I never knew that.' Which was true, although she did have one of those exaggerated faces which cameras loved: wide-sprung cheekbones, outsize eyes, like the eyes of babies. Behind these comments was an expectation that I was more than Ruth's friend, and behind that, an expectation that no man could be just a friend to such a stunning woman. But we had never been attracted to each other, Ruth and I. In the last two years of poring over late-night reports and strategy meetings our friendship had warmed. Now, looking from one to the other, Pieter to Sara and their friends with their jade eyes, I realised Ruth looked so much like Pieter and Sara she could be their daughter. Even her temperament was similar. She had Pieter's sly sense of humour, and Sara's lofty calm.

'So what *are* you doing here?' Pieter and Sara's friends asked. I said I was the logistics coordinator for a major humanitarian organisation, that I had been travelling to set up a camp for refugees in Kassala, but had to pull out of the job at the last minute. 'How interesting!' they said this with a conviction that failed to drown out an automatic note in their voices. I'd given them too many place names, all far away, or countries no one in their right mind would ever go to. Their eyes began to dart anxiously over my shoulder, looking for more secure ground.

But mostly they were confused by my connection to the family. I was neither Ruth's lover nor the friend of Pieter and Sara's sons. I was too young to be Pieter and Sara's friend, but not too old to be their child. They had their children young; one of their sons – Riaan I guessed – was my age, thirty-two. The other was younger, perhaps twenty-seven. They both lived far away, Pieter and Sara told me, and that evening at the outdoor concert the names of where they lived were mentioned, places that rang a bell but my geography of the country was still shaky. I got confused as to which son was where. I am used to knowing exactly where I am, to having a map in my head of where water and rice and beans and sterile syringes can be found, having three mobile phones in my hand in addition to a satellite phone, having a plan for that day and the next and for six months ahead, in my capacity as a tour manager for the international salvage experts of poverty and disaster. To be so out of my depth gave me a fugitive pleasure.

I looked into the wary, intelligent eyes of Pieter's friends or acolytes. I sensed it almost as soon as I arrived, how this country installed in its citizens an unusual acuity for sniffing out bad faith. Pieter and Sara's friends smiled, but a wince in their eye told me they knew something was wrong – with my presence, with my backstory, with my very being, cold and pale, the smell of the killing regularity, the sober arrogance of my country, which lingered on my clothes, my body.

It is late when we leave and I struggle to keep awake in the back seat of the car as Pieter takes the turns of the highway so fast I slide along the upholstery. We round the corner of the mountain where the harbour comes into view. I stare at the docks. Floodlights cast pools of white light on them. Two oil rigs rest in the bay, their legs tucked under them like giant cranes.

'What's the matter Nick?' I meet Pieter's eye in the rear-view mirror. 'You look like you've lost something.'

'This is the most beautiful harbour I've ever seen.'

Pieter flicks his eyes back to the road. 'I don't believe in beauty.'

'Pieter,' Sara sighs, 'Nick didn't ask you whether you *believed* in it.' Yet in the mirror I see her slide her eyes toward the harbour and give it a distrustful look.

That night I wake from a dead sleep. The sound comes again: a breathy recoil, then a jolt, like the house is being hit by a battering ram. I get up and look out the window into the garden. The palm trees tear at the sky. The thud comes again, a sickening sound that I begin to worry is going to shatter the glass doors of the flat. It's feels like a clawed animal is trying to get into the house. Then I realise what it is: the wind ricocheting off the mountain and then slamming into the back of the house.

The next day more summer gales take hold. The harbour churns with whitecaps. This was the return of the wind we had on the ship, the kind of wind I have never felt anywhere else. It blows slabs of hot air into my face, unseats café awnings that billow like parachutes. An unanchored feeling comes over the city. The mountain seems to shrink in the wind.

The wind blows for three days. Then, all of a sudden, it stops. I stand in the garden, alert to its absence. I wait for another gust, but it never comes.

The days become separated by languor. They no longer have to be pried apart from the slab of time and summoned into existence. I have no Skype conferences to organise, no Air France tickets to book or container shipments of emergency winter-proof tents to broker.

The house plays its part. In Pieter and Sara's house I begin to feel an ease I haven't felt in so long. It is all so familiar somehow – the lanolin smell of the dark wood furniture, that humid smell of warm places where the temperature never dips very low, even the baleful masks that eye me from the living room cabinet, the towering artisan pottery Sara has bought, the severe blue sky and mysterious birds and bloated flowers all lean toward me, as if bearing a message.

Pieter and Sara never ask how long will I stay, what will I do next. They must know something is wrong, or strange. Pieter is a writer, Sara is a psychologist; I may as well be staying with a couple of intelligence agents. How can a man like me with a responsible job simply have nowhere to go, nothing to do?

More than that, they can see I am not animated by the ragged energies they usually encounter in people – ego or sex or whatever you want to call them. They give me glances that suggest they could interrogate me if they choose, but they are letting me off the hook, for now.

# III

I was fifteen years old when I realised my mother was a spy. My mother was – still is, although she has retired now – a tall woman veering toward plumpness in middle age with an entirely ordinary English face: blue eyes, a fuller lower lip than an upper, an un-placeable, democratic accent.

I came home late one night to our apartment in Copacabana. We lived in Rio for four years, where my mother was Consul General (later, when I was at school in Canada, she would become Deputy Head of Mission, one rank below Ambassador, in Brasilia). She was at the kitchen table, where the maid had produced a midnight supper for her. My father was away on business, in London. He worked in oil. I saw him even more rarely than I glimpsed my mother. Even now, when I try to conjure up his face it slides away from my mind's grasp.

I sat down. She slid her eyes toward me. 'What have you been up to, then?'

I told her I had been out with friends, eating pizza in Botafogo, which was true.

'Such a good boy, always telling the truth.' The look she gave me then was conspiratorial, but also admonitory. The cast in her eye was one she had never treated me to before. And suddenly I knew. It was like a something was being rearranged inside me and placed where it should always have been – a re-alignment. She had always told me that her job required *absolute tact*, which even at fifteen I knew was a byword for secrecy. She'd told me I was old enough now to understand that sometimes she would not be able to tell me where she was travelling, or why.

For the moment I sat and watched her eat. She cut her food – I don't remember the dish – into tiny pieces, spearing them individually and chewing slowly. She'd been taught this trick by the Brazilian equivalent of Weight Watchers. She went to weekly meetings there, in a building located in a row of boutique malls in Ipanema. She'd even taken me with her once. I remember a row of very thin Brazilian women, all there to cleave ounces off their bodies. My mother was the only woman who was genuinely overweight.

My suspicion rattled around inside me. I felt afraid, I think, that she would come to some harm, or – if I'm honest – that I would. I began to have paranoid fantasies of kidnappings, of James Bond-style rescues. Such things actually happened in Brazil in those days in any case.

I started to rifle through her diary, the papers she brought home in a locked case but sometimes left open in her office, her rolodex and telephone book – this was before email – but her diary was bland, studded with *meeting with Chef de Mission or call London, 2.30 local*. Her most important documents she kept in a small black safe that had to be installed in the apartment when we moved in. This had a combination key and I knew she would never have written it down. I even followed her, twice. Both times she went to her office in the business district and stayed there. I was so bored I came home.

I took to asking semi-clandestine questions about the detail of her work. She parried effectively but evasively until that day when I was fifteen and she revealed that she could not divulge certain aspects of her job and that it was important I did not feel excluded. I remember how she finished her explanation: 'It's very, very important that I keep my counsel.' That was the word she used, counsel, not secret, and I preferred it, with its legal ring, its sense of a conversation between two parts of the self, like a priest and confessor wrapped up in one person, or a spy and her informant, locked in a universe of secrets and danger.

'Let me show you my study.'

Pieter issued me the invitation at breakfast. I'd taken to having a croissant and coffee with him about nine, after he'd returned from his training session; most days Pieter was out the door by six-thirty for a two hour run. I lingered in bed, drugged by the morning heat and humidity. In London I was an early riser, but here if I tried to get out of bed before eight my bones felt lead-heavy.

I liked the way Pieter spoke, the way everyone in this country did – decorous, with a forgotten courtly quality, a sense of obligation. *Must I accompany you down the stairs? Allow me to fetch you some coffee*. The *must* instead of *shall* gave their speech a pleasing sense of oversight, or ownership, perhaps. Even though I had known him for only a few days I already knew Pieter might be someone I would consent to be led by, if not owned.

I followed him downstairs, the air cooling as we descended. The walls on the stairway and those of the study as we entered were carpeted with framed photographs: Pieter and Sara at functions in black tie and evening gowns, Pieter and Sara at a dinner table with thirty-odd people, all of them with pale, serious expressions, with their two sons, I supposed, although as we passed they were only a blur of tanned faces, Pieter running a marathon, leaning across the finish line, political cartoons whose jokes I wanted to understand but escaped me, collages of photos taken at awards ceremonies, barbecues, sailing trips.

'I love your office. It's so full' – I wanted to say, *of life* – but instead said, 'of important things.'

'Isn't yours?'

'No, mine's rather impersonal.' I thought of my office, languishing off a corridor in a converted warehouse in

Clerkenwell, a sliver of St Paul's visible from my window, its walls showered with a few photographs of myself in the field and a poster of the periodic table of elements, left over from my former career.

'Well we must fix that,' Pieter said, as if he would have a hand in changing the decor of an office six thousand miles away.

My eye was attracted to a small painting – a watercolour, although faded. It was tacked on Pieter's bulletin board and showed a man standing beside a truck against a wide, empty road. Not Pieter, I supposed; this man had darker hair. The truck was a white pickup, just like the one I drove when I was working, *UN* emblazoned on its doors in blocky black. I peered at the photo, the man's dark eyes. He had a drastic, quite beautiful face. There was something familiar about him.

'Oh, Riaan was always drawing that man. We never met him.' Pieter laughed. 'He did that when he was twelve, that's him there.' He pointed to a photo. The print was now faded, but I could make out the once-ripe hues of a tanned boy with hair the colour of light pine and bright blue eyes.

Pieter plucked a postcard off the crowded bulletin board and handed it to me. It showed a lizard, some sort of chameleon that looked like a miniature dragon with dark grey scales, ridged eyebrows. I flipped the postcard over and read *The earth is rust. At night the wind soothes the land. I keep reaching for a way to describe this place and I end up in a dream, in a fixture, in a kind of fiction.*

Pieter gave a wry smile. 'Not a conventional missive, is it?'

'It's from Riaan?'

'Yes, he never signs his name. It's as if he thinks it's still the bad old days when the censor read your letters.'

I put the postcard back in its place. I was drawn back to Riaan's picture. It looked like someone seen in a magazine, *National Geographic*, maybe, with its rigid panorama of rose-coloured sky. Perhaps he'd copied it from there.

Pieter was staring at it too. He looked from the drawing to my face.

'It looks like we've finally met him.'

My mouth went dry, suddenly. 'It does look like me.' I had to sit down.

'What's wrong? Not another fainting spell?'

I put my head in my hands, my elbows propped up on my thighs. 'I don't know.'

Pieter towered above me, glasses perched on his forehead, his hands on his hips, a cartoon of concern. 'We should really get you checked out, you know.'

'It's nothing,' I said. 'The heat, maybe.'

Pieter nodded. 'It's going to be thirty-six degrees today. You'd better stay in the shade.'

Sara's voice reached us. There was someone at the door for him, could he come.

'Stay put,' Pieter instructed as he bounded up the stairs, taking them two at a time.

I remained in the chair, absorbing the quietude Pieter's absence created. He was electric, he charged any space he inhabited with a spiralling energy. But anything could entrap his attention and take him away from you. With Pieter I was aware of working harder than with others to retain his interest, to say sharp, enlivened things, collecting ambiguities, saving up intriguing daily ironies to serve to him, later, as if for dessert.

While I waited I looked at the books that lined his office. Two entire shelves were devoted to his novels, lined up with their slim spines of bright tropics colours and spare, cunning titles. *Shame*, *Mercy Street*, *The Glass House*. I realised many were foreign editions of each novel in English: American, British, Canadian, Australian, then the translations: Spanish, French, German, Portuguese, Italian.

I pulled out a copy of *Shame*, which I would learn was his first great success. Its cover showed storm-harassed palms on a dimly lit boulevard. I imagined the orphic glamour of the world encased in that slim spine: affairs, desolation, corruption, but everything exquisitely beautiful. I opened a page at random and read.

*He is driving the road back to the city. It will take him forty minutes to return, winding through mountains that stray into the ocean, then dissolve into the cold sea.*

*He has seen her, so the thirst has been slaked. For now.*

*The days when he does not see her are like thin migrants. They shuttle back and forth in time, searching for work, a place to live. It is summer and marine shadows soak these days whose dimensions are so strange; billowing jellyfish or drying like scars. He is bored. Life is only a beautiful censor.*

I heard steps, bounding down the stairs too fast for me to snap the book shut and return it to the shelf.

'What are you looking at?' There was no accusation in his voice, but another, indefinite, query.

'I have to confess I haven't read any of your books. Where should I start? Which one is your favourite?'

'Books are like children. You don't have favourites. You like them all for different reasons.'

I tried another tack. 'What are you writing now?'

'A short book, a novella.'

'I've always wondered, what's the difference between a novella and a short novel?'

'They have completely different energies and emotional intents,' Pieter answered, so quickly I wondered if he had been asked this many times before. 'Novellas are one-note stories, like an extended short story but curiously expansive. They're usually about passion, in some form, either won or lost. Mostly lost, in fact. A good form for an elegy, or a requiem.'

'Why are they about passion?'

Pieter shoved his reading glasses onto his head – a gesture,

I would come to learn, of impatience. 'Passion is usually short and intense, don't you think?'

'Is that enough of a subject for a novel, even a short one?'

'That depends on how important a force you think it is in life. And whether you've experienced it, no doubt.'

'This book you're writing now, where is it set?'

'Here. The mountain catches fire, if that's enough of an event for you. But really that's just a backdrop.'

'Does that happen often, forest fires?'

'Every few years. The vegetation here actually needs fire in order to regenerate. They say the mountain has always been burning, usually sparked by a lightning strike. These days though it's people who start the fires, either deliberately or through stupidity.'

'It must be frightening, with the mountain so close.'

His posture, which had been tense, even defensive, relaxed. He did this, I noticed – lurched from his normal keyed-up energy to languor with no warning.

'It's bloody terrifying. One year for two nights running I slept up on the roof. Dousing it with the hose all night, watching the fire come closer and closer.'

A picture installed itself in my mind, of flames fizzing in the glass walls of their living room.

When I looked back at Pieter he looked troubled. His face, so alert and thin, even gaunt, looked sluggish. He peered at me with that way of his, as if he were tacking you on a bulletin board like a postcard. 'Why did you study geology?'

'Because it's the history of the planet. A history that has nothing to do with people.'

'What have you got against people?'

'I'd rather we weren't here sometimes, that's all. And then the planet could just live happily.'

Pieter folded his arms across his chest. 'Did you write books, when you were a geologist?'

'No, I wrote papers with titles like "Phanerozoic glaciation during the Carboniferous – Permian on the Southern Hemisphere Gondwana supercontinent".'

'And you actually understand this stuff?'

'No, I just wrote it.'

This provoked a laugh so sharp I jumped in my chair.

'That's a good line.' Pieter was still laughing.

'Why do you ask? Are you interested in geology?'

'I might…' Pieter hesitated. His bravado seemed to have deserted him. 'I might write something about it.'

'About geology?'

'No, about a geologist.'

I understood I had already become a character. I couldn't fault him. Part of me wanted to see myself reflected in the mirror of his mind.

*'…told you he doesn't think of us.'*

*'That's not true.'*

*'Why doesn't he bloody come to visit?'*

*'He's building his own life. He doesn't want to see us. It would throw him off track.'*

I couldn't help but hear them. They were in the garden, not arguing, but their voices held a strident, anguished note that carried into the flat.

I went into the bedroom and shut the door. I couldn't bear the thought of eavesdropping on them, the betrayal of it, although I suspected they would have carried on with their conversation in front of me, even taken me into their confidence.

I guessed they were talking about Riaan. They rarely said his name. I heard the name of their other son, Stephen, more often. I had seen no more of Riaan than the painting he had made of the man who looked like me and the postcard Pieter had shown me, yet I felt an allegiance toward him.

By the time I returned to the kitchen they had dropped their voices. I heard the word 'Christmas'. I had forgotten it was December. There were no clues of the winter I had become accustomed to in nearly twenty years in England and the months had spiralled off into irrelevance.

In the days leading up to Christmas I make several visits to the National Library. It is housed in a white stucco building with dark wooden shutters. Spidery palms edge its grandiose entrance. Inside there is no air-conditioning; instead in each aisle of reading desks standing fans whirr.

Here I work my way through the titles Pieter has written down for me and which he says I must read if I want to understand this country: *The Slaughter of Innocents, Wounded Civilization, The Ethics of Nostalgia, Empire of the Wind.*

The latter tells me the winds that come to this city with rain are called the Black Wind. There is a Black Province and a White Cape. The city is thick with Portuguese and French and Dutch names: *herenhuis, praia grande, le pic du diable*. As the names attest, everyone – even the English – came here at intervals, chasing gold, slaves, diamonds. When they overlapped they fought and ransacked the city. Now, fearing an internal revolution that seems perpetually imminent but which never arrives, their descendants are desperate to leave, planning escapes to winterless places in the same hemisphere such as Australia, New Zealand and Argentina.

Books cannot be borrowed from libraries here as no one trusts you will bring them back. So I request Pieter's suggestions, a process involving three listless assistants. I wait, cooling my heels in front of a fan, thinking how I can no longer read my intentions. There is someone else inside me, suddenly. *Who are you?* I ask this interloper, but either there is no reply or I can't understand it. I pray, with poor concentration and little belief, for direction, for understanding. *Why did I do it?* But who am I asking absolution from?

But at the same time I'm happy, I realise as I trade glances with the other queue inhabitants, graduate students, probably, hunting for obscure volumes their university libraries don't stock, our hair struck around our faces by the fan so that we become a line of despondent medusas. I don't understand why I feel such joy in this city. I've heard of it for years of course, with its modest yet romantic name that carries a clue to its position on the rim of the world. The skies are wild and empty of contrails. I still can't identify the dark grape-coloured birds that shoot between the trees and the succulent flowers. The feeling of waiting hangs in the air – waiting to gather the courage to leave, yes, but also for something else.

Through the books I try to anchor myself in history. I read about this country's discovery by Europeans and the disastrous fate of the indigenous peoples. Dank portraits of the country's first burghers watch over us library readers, along with giant landscapes of the city before it was a city, showing the thatch huts of the original inhabitants, smoke curling from their roofs. Other oily canvases are of the slave market in the city centre, castles, cannons, the remains of the auctioning block. The hot trade winds of history has blown shame, wealth, disgust and despair over this city, so sultry in its summer incarnation, so ruled by the empty sea.

'Would you like to come to Cabo Frio with us for Christmas?'

I hesitated. Christmas had been looming in my mind, a solid month when, people told me, the country stopped in its tracks. No business was conducted and the president and his ministers anchored their yachts on the Mozambique coast or descended upon the arcades of Dubai. Going back to London was impossible. When I checked I found the airfares were triple the price my employer had paid to send me out here.

I knew Pieter and Sara were planning to go to their beach house but I didn't expect to spend the holidays with them. We had just met. Who would want to fold a stranger of two week's acquaintance into their Christmas?

'Are you sure?'

'We're certainly not going to leave you here to go a bit doolally on your own for two weeks.'

Pieter's no-nonsense tone spared me the embarrassment

of begging their hospitality. In that moment I wanted to say so many things to him: *You've been so kind. No one has ever taken me in as you have done. For the first time in my life, I don't know what to do with myself.* But the words refused to leave my head.

'Riaan' – the narrowest of pauses followed his name – 'will come at some point for the week.'

'What about Stephen?' I asked.

'It's high season for him. He can't get away from work.'

'What does Riaan do again?'

'He runs a charity for schoolchildren.'

'I guess neither of your sons was interested in being a writer.'

'I think they thought I had that territory occupied already and they'd have to push me out to do it,' Pieter answered lightly. 'But they weren't that interested, either. That's the truth. From the beginning they were both fascinated by nature.'

'This is a good place to live if that's what you're interested in,' I replied.

'Yes, well, think it over. Christmas can be quite lonely, wherever you are.'

We stood for a moment, absorbing his sons' rejection of him, or of his territory of the human. He said nothing, his gaze fixed on the floor. An unhappy current emanated from him. His explanation of his son's ambition sounded a flat note, a kind of lie, but which was not.

'Be warned. It's a real beach house,' he rallied. 'Quite basic in other words. There's no television or internet.'

'That's a relief.'

Pieter raised his eyebrows. 'I thought no-one of your generation could be enthusiastic about the prospect of no internet.'

'Well you've just met one.'

I hadn't told him about the emails that arrive every day now in my inbox. Human Resources; three-step grievance procedure; sick leave; counselling. Then, only yesterday, an email titled FINAL WARNING, its capitals blazing in my inbox. My salary may not be paid at the end of the month. There will be no Christmas bonus this year. No one in London knows where I am. I realise that part of me – the functional me, the decider of things – is still on the ship. I don't know where to look for myself; in the past, present, future. All my life I have been in a rush to catch up to myself. Now I must stay in the present, that fictional time we are always being badgered to live in, but which anyone who thinks about it knows does not exist.

# IV

*It was February. He'd always thought of the heat at that time of year as a cruel parliament, an arena where sentences were passed. Summers in the city stretched for four, five months, into April, when finally the mornings crisped and the tangerine heat thinned.*

*He drove to the technical college, a thick concrete structure, more a conference centre than a university, that squatted beside the motorway that followed the shoreline.*

*Class started at 11am. He would be in the room and talking to his new class of girls, some brazen, some collected and intelligent. They were mostly girls, now. He could still remember how fifteen years ago he faced a room full of lanky, flop-headed boys.*

*In an hour he would meet her, and his life would be changed. At this moment in time though, driving through the heat-haze of the city, he thought there would be only a continuum – his wife, their visits to their in-laws who lived in tidy, heat stunned towns in the mountains, a feast of stability and reassurance.*

*Only two weeks before they'd been found, Malcolm and Louis, slumped on the black seat of their little white car, crimson lakes expanding beneath their chests. 'They bled for such a long time before they died,' Ingeborg, his secretary, had said, more than once or twice. They were twenty-three.*

*Now the college flag slumped at half-mast. It would remain there for a month, or a similar seemly period of time.*

*He parked his car as he always did, recklessly, sliding into a space and leaving the rear wheel propped on the kerb. 'Bank robber parking', Crystal called it.*

*Yes, now everyone knew someone who had been murdered, you were only ever one degree away from that form of enforced separation. Murders became necessary, like trinkets that were traded between children:* Did you know Mark was killed coming out of the mall? Shot for a bag of groceries. That's nothing, Ilse told me that an entire family was killed on the coast, they were on holiday when the robbers just walked in.

*Everyone was down at the shooting range taking marksman training, or buying fat black puppies to train up into monsters. He ought to look into this himself, he thought, as the doors of the college flew open for him, inviting him into a wash of cool air. He ought to be better protected.*

*He saw his outline reflected in the glass panel doors. He felt its presence, even when he could not see it. It was behind him, the mountain that loomed like a solid wave over the city.*

Pieter was nowhere to be seen but sheets of paper peppered with angry marks in red ink covered the breakfast table. I stepped around them on my way to the coffee maker.

He did all his work in his office. I'd never seen his papers or a book anywhere else in the house. I wondered if he'd been revising when called away suddenly, or if the red pen marks had driven him away in disgust. I could feel something of the spell these pages exerted over him. I had seen flashes of his addiction to concentration, how his temper quickly frayed if his writing were interrupted by the gate intercom or a telephone call and had to attend to the clamour of the real.

As I made coffee for us both, in case he came back, I considered how I'd never given much thought to writers. Now I wondered what compelled them to spend – part of me said waste – their lives constructing imaginary castles in their minds when life itself was so compelling. Writing a novel must be like constructing a set for films that had to be abandoned. An image came to me then, of the many emergency camps I had constructed on plains or fields of lava or beaches, row on row of white tents.

I heard his step on the stairs. 'There you are.' He sat at the table and gathered up the pages. 'So what do you think?'

'Of what?'

His eyes moved to the pages, then back to me. 'Of what I've written.'

'How do you know I've read them?'

He held my gaze. 'Have you?'

'It's intriguing,' I offered. 'There's the story of the murdered boys –'

Pieter cut me off. 'Yes well every story now has to have murdered boys in it, or girls.'

'Surely there's more than one story you can write.'

'When I started out as a writer you had to deny crime existed. Now you're not a writer of any conscience or purpose unless your book includes at least one murder. Otherwise you're not keeping step with the national reality.' Pieter paused, his mouth tight.

'If you're not happy with it, then change it. Write something different.'

'That's what I've been doing all my life. They wanted me to write apolitical books, I wrote political ones. They wanted me to take the temperature of the nation, I wrote about small town love affairs. They wanted a book set in the intellectual hub of the city, I set one in a game park. They wanted the rawness of real wilderness, I set a novel in the blandest suburb on the coast…' He lapsed into another troubled silence.

'You were a rebel.'

'No, I was just very successful at being out of step.'

'The quote on the back of *Mercy Street* says your books are quietly subversive.'

‘That’s what I was aiming for, that the poor reader would wake up in the middle of the night, feeling vulnerable, alien in their own skin, but also galvanised, human.’

‘It sounds like you knew what you were doing.’

‘But it’s best when you don’t have a clue. Now I know – ’ here he sighed heavily – ‘everything. I can write my own reviews, I can write the letters foreign editors send me querying details of their precious translations, I can write the essays by critics in universities up to its eyeballs in snow in New York or Norway, the critics who said I was a puppet of the government. Actually one used the word “megaphone”. How would you like to be accused of that? Or the critic who said I was a lapdog of the regime.’

‘Megaphones and lapdogs,’ I whistled.

‘Quite, no? Then there was the critic who said I was playing at being a visionary radical whose novels were a conservative manifesto in disguise.’ He drew a breath. His speech had deflated him. The man who sat in front of me now, while still vital, looked smaller than the rectilinear, taut Pieter I’d met two weeks before.

‘I’m too aware, that’s the issue,’ he said. ‘I could write the book that would get me the most acclaim tomorrow; in fact I could write it by numbers. Or even better, it could write itself.’ He gave a flat bark of a laugh. ‘Yes, I can see it now: boy brought up on the farm collides with his childhood friend, they meet and discover one has become rich and one poor. One is black and one is white. But aha, before you think you know the story – ’ Pieter leaned forward in his chair, pointing his index finger at my nose – ‘you find that the rich boy is not the race you expected him to be.’

He sat back on his chair, pleased. ‘I can even award myself the Varley prize at the end of it.’

I nodded reasonably through this, but it was a secretive tirade. Listening to it, I thought the world of writers might be surprisingly small and insular. They cared only for themselves and their art, but as well as this they were self-torturers, too, measuring themselves ruthlessly against dead men and women who'd had the vast advantage of living and writing in coach-and-horses times when there hadn't been much of a life to lead, or marketplace competition.

'Whatever is happening, it's not working, this book.'

'Why not?'

'It's always the same problem. Not enough *life*.' He hissed the last word. 'The life used to be there from the beginning. I never had to make things happen, I never had to calculate. I knew animated people, what they cared about – love, the freedom to dream, to build a country that is the best reflection of those dreams. Now I have no idea what people care about. Money, probably. Sex.' The word dripped from his lips. 'Now everything I write seems a calculation. I've become too aware. Or too old. There might be a connection. I keep feeling I need to tear away a mist or veil,' he brought his hands up in front of his face and mimed ripping something away, 'and that if I were young and writing my first book, I would see everything clearly again.'

Something called him away, then, the phone, or the security gate, or the frantic barking of the dog that might signal intruders in the back perimeter where the garden dissolved into the wilderness of the mountain. I sat in the kitchen for a while, accompanied by the vortex of Pieter's energy – an unhappy, even tormented presence, nearly as alive as the man himself.

I had never tried to get through to somewhere, as Pieter did. I'd never set myself such an opaque struggle. I'd gone here, gone there, I'd set up communications systems and encampments and had been indirectly responsible for people's lives being saved and sometimes, possibly, being spent. Pieter had passed so many years in his office downstairs, stalking the corridors of that collapsible writer's castle, when he could have been experiencing things. Where was he trying to get through to? What lay there, on the other side of nowhere, that could be more compelling than life?

Those last few days before we leave for the coast I cross paths several times with Pieter, although he is always preoccupied and I feel every pleasantry I muster to try to detain him, or lighten his mood, is a burden.

I take myself for walks on the mountain. Pieter makes me take Lucy with me, for protection. We tread the access roads the firefighting crews use to pare back vegetation or to put out blazes. We see small ochre antelope bounding up the mountain through the swollen flowers and the shale, and one day even a cobra, which Lucy to my horror tries to chase. On the mountain the forest fire alert dial has been switched to the deep russet of Severe Danger. At night the gale batters my flat. I go outside into the garden terrace and its lordly view of the city. From here I watch the orange carpet of streetlights flicker and am sure I see some pattern and meaning in the movement, a message in code to outer space.

# V

The drive took us through blond-pated mountains which gave way to limestone flatlands. Ostrich grazed in battered clumps under a severe sun and white farmhouses sheltered beside veins of water. The sea and the coast were visible long before you could actually see them; on the horizon the sky was drained of blue and was pearly and milk-coloured where the sea sucked at it.

Cabo Frio – Cold Cape – was aptly named, Pieter told me. The sea was freezing on one side of the cape, where the Atlantic collided with Africa. But on the other side, where Pieter and Sara's house stood, the sea was a full ten degrees warmer. Cabo Frio was the last stop for the Indian Ocean, that vast sea which connects Tanzania to the Philippines. 'It ends here,' Pieter said, and it was clear that something about the finality of an ocean's terminus pleased him. His mouth was a beacon for his feelings, I've noticed, and it made a particular shape, hard and satisfied, when considering an unalterable fact, as if he were throwing himself against it as the ocean hurls itself against this land.

Pieter kept up a steady commentary through the drive about the history of the area: displacement of native peoples by early settlers, herding them into mission towns, the clearing of the land for cattle, so that there was hardly a tree in a hundred miles. Cabo Frio had always been a place of fishermen. The collision between the two currents, one frigid and one warm, created acres of krill, which attracted sharks. Fur seals leapt through the waves and into the jaws of yawning great whites. The sharks hardly need to hunt, he said, they just waited with their mouths open.

'Do you swim there?' I asked.

'Of course we do,' he said.

'What about the sharks?' I pressed.

'If you worried about sharks you'd never go in the ocean. They're too well fed on fur seals in any case.'

Sara turned and looked at her husband. From behind I saw the questioning note in her gaze. Perhaps Pieter had just uttered a fact so accepted and true she had always known it. It occurred to me they were discovering their country anew, by having to describe it to the stranger who had washed up on their doorstep.

On the way we stopped in a well-stocked supermarket because in Cabo Frio itself there was not a single shop, Sara said, although milk and bread could sometimes be bought from the one hotel.

Ten minutes before we arrived in town the soil became grainy and dry, then towering caramel-coloured sand dunes began to appear. We pulled to a stop on a street, which terminated in the sea. 'Here we are,' Pieter announced.

Pieter let Lucy off the leash and she immediately bounded toward the ocean. A stiff wind ripped the words from our mouths. 'You get the trailer open,' Pieter instructed. He headed toward a towering dark-wood door in a white wall. I followed him through the door into the cool interior. On the other side of a panel of windows I saw a courtyard and in the middle of it, a single tree with some kind of fruit hanging pendulous on its branches.

The smell of the house – cool but warm, musty but also dry – alerted me to something I could not remember. It was like seeing the shadow of an animal disappear around the corner of a house.

Sara saw me stop in my tracks. 'What is it Nick?'

'It's so familiar, the smell. I've stayed in houses just like yours, but I can't remember where.'

Sara showed me the bedrooms and told me I could take my pick. I walked up and down the passageway, looking through louvered doors, trying to think where the smell reminded me of. Cuba, maybe, its storm-tossed coasts. My mother had taken us all on holiday to the north coast of the island in the years when she was posted to Jamaica. Or Jamaica itself, maybe, although we had never had a holiday there.

'Well, we hope you will feel at home here,' Sara said, with that light note in her voice that means I shouldn't take her too seriously.

I did feel at home, but simultaneously abandoned. I'd felt this since I had arrived in the country. It was as if I'd come to a place I had forgotten and the memory was being returned to me only now, so far away from where the memories belonged.

I have to lean against the door frame. The realisation falls on me. I do know this country, even if I have not been here before. It has been waiting for me. It is trying to speak to me. It says, *Finally you've come*.

Those nights, before Riaan arrives, Pieter and I stay up late talking by the fire, the dog at our feet. Sara had gone to bed at 10pm on the dot, a pile of photocopied articles from psychology journals tucked under her arm.

I've met many psychologists through work. They are deployed after I build the tents and commandeer the mobile homes that house and connect them: child psychiatrists, trauma specialists, very often Manhattan or Hampstead therapists on a Red Cross voluntary rota. Sara is one of this tribe, outwardly empathetic people, as perhaps they need to be, but elevated above mere mortals by their analytical power. I am intimidated by their X-ray eyes, the shadow of their diagnosis suspended there: *narcissistic, dreamy only child. Fills his otherwise empty tanks on making himself important to the world. Seeks some kind of world-weary knowledge to disguise his fear of being a lightweight, a fraud. Enjoys roughing it but has the thin-skinnedness of the fundamentally privileged.*

Those nights Pieter sinks back into his chair, leaning toward the stone fireplace, as big as a small theatre. He tells me he comes from Malanga. He grew up there but was born in France; his mother was French, his father Dutch. His family emigrated when he was only three, and he has no memory of dark winter cities. Pieter went to the best private school and university in the country. He has two brothers, one is a cardiologist in Australia, the other a chiropractor in Virginia. 'They're rich, by the standards of this country,' Pieter says. 'They got out.'

'Why did you stay?'

He rolls his head back. 'Ah, the million dollar question. You've been in the country less than a month and you've asked it. So bravo.' He closes his eyes and I think he will not say any more, that he has delivered me a rebuke. But then he props his head forward and fixes me with a rigid look. 'What would be your guess?'

'Because it's home? Because writers have a vocation to be the conscience of their country, at least in some countries.' I say. 'Because to write in exile you would be doubly irrelevant – here and wherever you chose to live?'

He gives me a severe look. 'Because I couldn't bear to live in that parallel reality, writing incessantly about this country while living in the kinds of suburbs my brothers live in, getting coffee in air-conditioned malls and walking on the streets without fear for my life, writing about a reality that becomes more distant with each day.

'Or because I couldn't face exile. Because I didn't have enough confidence to make it in a bigger arena. Because I had become comfortable being the great home-grown writer who wins prizes abroad but who if he moved to London suddenly wouldn't be able to compete.'

'What about Sara, where does she come from?'

She is from a Portuguese family, he tells me, which is a surprise; she is as blond and direct as a Scandinavian. Sara's family were import-export magnates in Mozambique, where she grew up, although she attended the British school there and so her English is unaccented.

In those days before Riaan arrives I leave Pieter and Sara to their reading and writing and mount expeditions to the coast. I go running on the hot limestone plateau leading into the interior, into the horizon, beyond the farthest headland where I encounter a foaming sea. This is the edge of both a country and a continent.

I walk back along the coastal road. Smoke from a hundred beach barbecues hangs over the dunes. Trucks pass with tanned children hanging off the back of truck tailgates, their eyes green jewels in a sea of butterscotch skin. The children here don't look like children at all but like wizened spirits.

I try to put aside my fear of sharks and go swimming. The sea is warmer than in the city, Pieter is right. But I find I can't go in further than waist-deep. The ocean is turbulent, as if dark clouds have installed themselves inside it. When I return to the house after these expeditions I feel protected. It's something in its architecture and also its spirit: it is a stark, romantic house, the sort of house where you could take your lover early on in the relationship, when you are still besotted with each other, when everything they do casts a golden light around them and even the wind cannot prise you apart.

# VI

Two sand-coloured dogs poured out of the truck. Then a man emerged, limb by limb: a leg, two legs, a tanned arm, a hat. His face was in shadow. The hat was khaki felt and triangular, the kind worn by Bavarian farmers; it only needed a feather. The hat turned toward us and I saw Pieter's face, perhaps more ovoid in shape.

He stepped down from the truck, gave us a half-wave, then dove back into his cab to rummage for something, which turned out to be a pack of cigarettes. We all kept a respectful distance; we could see he was dusty, tired.

'I did a lot of it on cruise control,' he yelled to us, although we are not far away. His Landcruiser was like an airplane. I would discover it practically drove itself courtesy of Sat Nav and a video screen for reversing or taking tricky corners. It even had a built-in television.

His dogs entwined themselves around our legs. He called two unintelligible names to them, his voice gruff, and the dogs exploded toward him to stand panting at his feet. Stuffing the cigarettes into his jeans, he walked toward us with a clipped, elastic stride.

He was tall, taller than Pieter, and while thin his body emanated a certain power. He wore a dark green shirt and jeans, secured by a belt of a black and white animal hide, like zebra.

He gripped my hand. 'I've heard about you, man. I hear my parents rescued you. Good stuff!' He gave his mother and father a quick hug. Pieter and Sara looked amazed, I thought, also perturbed. We backed away, involuntarily holding our cheeks or hands where he had touched them, as if we had just been anointed.

I wanted to absent myself. I thought they should be left to be a family, it's the first time they have seen each other in a year. But no one would hear of it. 'I'm not having you wandering off into the bloody night,' Pieter barked. Pieter's being was newly invigorated by the arrival of his son. His voice was louder, gestures more emphatic.

I went outside to sit in the courtyard, to give them some space. After a while Riaan emerged. He shook a cigarette from the package. 'Want one?'

'No thanks.'

'Smart move. I'm always trying to give up. I might have given up on giving up, come to think of it.'

I studied him as he lit up. One fingertip, I'd noticed when he offered me the cigarette, had been crushed. It was completely flat, a miniature paddle. He had very fine hands: long, tapering fingers buttressed by knuckles, like candlesticks. His hair, released from the hat, was darker than his father's. He wore it short. In the pictures Pieter had shown me Riaan appeared as a regulation surfer guy, blond and long-haired. Now his hair was a woody colour, somewhere between driftwood and shale. He had an intelligent face, which is to say one capable of registering many expressions – flexible, alert.

He exhaled a thin stream of smoke and turned those careful eyes on me. 'How do you like Cabo Frio?'

'It's so beautiful I find it hard to believe,' I replied. 'I've been running as far as I can make myself go, over the dunes. I've found beaches with no one on them.'

He nodded. 'Yes, you can get that here. When I was a kid Cabo Frio was paradise. I'll show you some places I know.'

'I'd like that.'

We watched each other for just a second too long. Then he slid his gaze away. For a second he looked almost bashful.

Perhaps he was not as hail-fellow-well-met as he seemed. Or perhaps it was just fatigue. He had driven for two days, after all.

'Where did you stay?' I asked. 'On the way down?'

'I camped. I just pull off the road in what looks like a nice place and put the tent up. Or sleep in the truck.'

'Is it safe?'

'Well I've got those two.' He pointed to the dogs. 'They look dumb, but they'd rip you from limb to limb if I told them to.'

'Well I hope it won't come to that.'

He laughed. 'I hope so too. It would upset my parents. It seems you're part of the family now.'

There was no malice or resentment in his voice. Still, I felt a shiver at the back of my neck. He had identified my greatest strength and weakness in one shot, this expert archer: his parents had taken a shine to me, and I had no family of my own. Which is to say, no protection.

Sara emerged from her room just as I was opening the door to the house. 'Where are you going?' she asked.

'Just out running over the dunes. I want to see the sunset.'

Riaan's voice came from the kitchen. 'I'll come with you man. But let's walk, hey? We can take the dogs.'

'Sure,' I said. Sara smiled at me. She understood I had meant to be by myself. I had become used to my long solo explorations on which I would meet other lone men walking aimlessly through rocky shallows and tide pools, dressed in striped shirts, torn jeans and knitted hats.

We set off down the sandy lane that led to the sea. It wound through beach houses made of wood or white stone. Children in wetsuits with miniature surfboards hustled past us like outsized penguins. I thought for a moment to share this image with Riaan, but he was looking in the other direction, waving at someone he recognised but who was too far away to approach.

I was careful not to transmit to Riaan my resentment of having to make talk. We walked easily together. His dogs came bounding up to me from time to time. 'They like you,' Riaan said. 'They need a second father. I'm often distracted.' They were hunting dogs, a popular breed where he lived, Riaan told me. They were almost identical and they looked just like him: fawn-coloured, rangy.

'What do they hunt?' I asked.

'Nothing, now. But if I let them they'd bring down a kudu.' Riaan sniffed the air and took a gulp. 'Smell the *wetness*. It's dry and cold where I live. This is what I miss, more than anything. Moisture.'

'Yes, it's too hot in the city.' Suddenly everything that came out of my mouth sounded bland. I couldn't say what I meant. Something of Riaan's person was siphoning me of what I had taken to be my originality, my singularity. Next to him, I became just another guy. Although it was pleasing, this erasure. Maybe now I could stop trying so hard.

His face settled into a slight frown. 'But it's very lonely. I always think carefully about coming here. What state of mind I'm in. It can really tip the balance.'

'At times this past week I've felt incredibly alone,' I admitted. 'But I couldn't figure out why. Your parents are such good company.'

'No, man, it's the place. When I was a kid I thought I'd die from loneliness here. Although it taught me I could withstand being alone. Empty places are valuable that way. It's as if they draw this line inside you – ' his hand and the cigarette gripped within it sliced the air in front of us – 'a horizon. Although if you stare too long at the horizon you go a bit strange.'

'When did you move up country?'

'About ten years ago. But I went for the first time long ago. In the war. The Annexation war,' he clarified. I'd heard of the Annexation war of course – for twenty years, until the mid-1990s, a separatist movement in the northern strip had threatened to secede and form their own country, taking the bulk of the nation's diamond and copper reserves with them.

'Weren't you too young?'

'From eighteen to twenty-one I was conscripted.' He looked at me and I saw it again, a rigid conviction that seemed an organic part of his eyes. Riaan had eyes I have only ever seen in this country: the luminous light blue of swimming pools. Within them, his pupils were very dark, blacker than usual, and pinprick small.

'Did you want to go into the Army?'

He laughed. 'Do I look like I want to die?' His smile vanished and the sideways, almost bashful expression took its place. 'Very few guys wanted to. But it was necessary. Or so it seemed at the time.'

I studied him as we walked. He was thin but not too thin, tall but not commandingly so – he was perhaps three inches taller but seemed to loom over me.

The dogs raced away from us. 'They're going up there,' he indicated with an incline of his head. The dune was much taller than the others, something you'd see in the Sahara.

Riaan was off, and before I knew it he was running up it, flanked by his dogs. He stopped on its cusp, a distant silhouette, the outline of his body hard against the sky. The dogs had disappeared over the edge. I could hear him calling for them. He waved, he seemed to be beckoning me. I shrugged apologetically.

The truth was, I wanted to see him from a distance. He was difficult to evaluate close up. In Riaan I could see what an impressive character Pieter must have been at that age. I made a note to stop comparing him to his father.

He came down from the dune, trailed by his dogs. His expression was jubilant.

'My parents told me about your work. You've seen some pretty terrible shit, haven't you?'

'I don't know, it's hard to tell after a while, what's terrible and what's normal.'

Riaan shook his head. 'Even in the Army, I never lost sight of that.'

'Well maybe you're a better mortal than me.'

A small door closed, very delicately, behind his eyes. They narrowed. 'What were you doing, in all those places?'

'I worked in oil exploration after I graduated,' I said. 'I just got very good at getting to remote places, setting up camp, fixing a generator, rigging up a satellite connection. But it was too… rough,' I settled for the word. 'Not the work, but the people, the world. So I moved into logistics. My first job was with the Red Cross in Mauritania. Lots of sand. That's what your logistics consists of, in the Sahara: how to get through the sand, how to survive on the sand, how to get the sand out of the power drills and incubators and tyre wells. I had dreams I was drowning in sand. Which is pretty predictable, really.' I tried a laugh but it came out as a rasp.

'And now?'

'Now I'm considered one of the top guys in Europe, apparently. Or I was, until recently.'

There was a sharp note in his gaze. I could almost hear a brittle grinding coming from within his mind, like flint.

'You seem very calm,' he said.

'I am…' I laughed. 'Calm.'

'Why do you do it?'

'I thought I was being altruistic, for a long time. Then I realised I was using experience to mould myself into someone I wanted to be, could be proud of being.'

'Who would that be?'

'Someone experienced. A serious person.'

Riaan gave me a look that made me stop short of confessing – what? It was on the tip of my tongue, but I had no idea what I was about to say. I couldn't locate the usual coherent story in the tangle of emotions inside me. How I was trying to teach myself something through exposure to disaster, something fundamental about the arbitrariness of life, the sheer danger of being alive. How in organised, comfortable countries we delude ourselves that we are in control, switching mortgages, calculating pensions, taking out insurance policies, comparing mobile phone contracts – plotting, always, to get the best deal, and the system colludes, drugging us with the delusion our choices are unique and precious. It turns us into children, no, spoiled children who, when something goes wrong in their lives, take it as an affront to their dignity, much as they treat any emotion they can't control or understand. I didn't want to be that child.

The wind blew fine hairs into his eyes. He swished them away. 'What's the saddest thing you've ever seen?'

I shied away from this question. I'd been asked it before. It was salacious, vaguely obscene. I hadn't expected it from him.

'I have to think,' I said. 'But I'll tell you when I've decided.'

He seemed happy with this answer. But also resolute. He would not forget.

We walked on, across dunes, through the spiky resinous grass that grew from their hollows and crests, across beds of half-dried kelp, its ruched edges black ribbons scattered across the beach. We walked through the car park in front of the beach with its solitary ice cream van, an apparition in such a wild place. All the way back to the house the dogs loped up and down the dunes, their shadows torn by the flutes of sand.

'They look like wolves,' Riaan said, so quietly I nearly did not hear. 'Don't you think? Not that I've ever seen a wolf.'

'You haven't?'

'I've never been to a cold country.'

'Oh, well. You haven't missed much.'

'No, I have, man. I want travel. That's what I want most now, more than anything, to see snow and ice. Rivers and rivers of ice. It must be so beautiful. You've been there, haven't you? My parents told me. The Arctic.'

'Yes, I did my doctoral research there.'

He shook his head. 'I would give anything to go.' He walked on, then, he held himself slightly away from me.

He'd inherited something else from his father: how his spirit plumed in his vicinity, like a warning system. I had known him for only one day but already I could read his moods by the air around him. He was one of those people who give off a lot of heat but not much warmth. He would require you either to move away, out of his aura, or be stripped bare, until your purpose and destiny were nothing more than to warm yourself at his flame.

I woke from a dreamless sleep. Somewhere dogs were baying. I could hear the slip of saliva in their bark.

I found my glasses and torch and was outside in my underwear when I saw Riaan, pacing the long corridor of the house. Underneath his arm was an unmistakable silhouette.

'Nick, man, go to the back of the house. I've got the front.'

'What's going on?'

'The dogs are onto something.' He lowered his voice. 'Someone's tried to get in.'

'Where are your parents?'

'In their bedroom.' He brought the rifle in his hand up to his shoulder. 'If you hear a shot, stay where you are.'

I collected the keys to the kitchen from their hiding place in the bedroom. Even in this sleepy town every room had a separate lock. The keychain was as heavy as a jailor's.

I managed to unlock the kitchen and turn on the lights. I crept round corners. What did I expect to see in the living room – men in balaclavas with 9mm pistols? It wouldn't be the first time I had faced gunmen unarmed, but I'd had more clothes on, then.

'Nobody,' I shouted to Riaan.

'Okay,' he shouted back, his voice lingering on the vowel.

Pieter and Sara appeared. The first thing I noticed was that they were not afraid. They wore matching bathrobes, black with silver tracing.

'You two made more noise than the dogs,' Pieter said. 'Let's have a cup of tea. And unload that bloody thing before you leave it in the house,' Pieter barked at Riaan.

'Okay, Pa, take it easy. I haven't chambered a round. You might want it to be loaded, one day.'

'This is not one of your hunting trips,' Pieter retorted. 'A loaded gun means someone is very likely to get hurt. Or haven't you learned that yet?'

Even his black bathrobe and bare feet, Pieter emanated anger. Pieter had been in some sort of situation involving a gun. This came to me in a flash. Riaan didn't know, I guessed. Whatever had happened, his father hadn't told him.

I looked at the rifle, now leaning up against the wall, its muzzle pointed to the ceiling. I was familiar with guns from working in militarised zones, in civil wars, in police states. But I wasn't used to having one in the living room. In this country everyone had one – the security men at the shopping mall, the airport guards, the police, private citizens who went hunting rabbits or kudu on the weekends.

Riaan stacked wood in the fireplace. 'The bloody dogs don't go berserk for nothing.'

'We've had it before. Lucy's scared them away,' Sara said.

'You'd think in this backwater at Christmas they'd leave off,' Pieter grumbled.

'Now's the only time anyone's here, Pa. It's bonanza season for them.'

'Who is "they"?' I asked.

Three sets of eyes in those swimming pool shades gave me a startled stare.

'Who do you think?' Riaan said.

'I don't know.'

I made myself busy in the kitchen making tea. My neck was hot. What a stupid question, too. I knew perfectly well that 'they' were the poor disenfranchised masses. Also the 'they' were a different race. But for a moment I had run out of patience with so many *they's*.

Pieter and Sara went back to bed. It was three-thirty in the morning. 'Nick and I will stay up for a bit to keep an eye on things,' Riaan said, and threw me a collusive look.

Riaan stoked the fire. Bent over the wood, his body made a slender question mark. Pieter looked young for his age; Riaan had lived in the desert north for years, and the climate must have sharpened the angles of his face. They looked more like brothers than father and son.

'I hate scaring my parents, but better safe than sorry,' he said.

'Your father doesn't like guns.'

'Hah,' he snorted. 'That's an understatement. No, he's against them on principle. He was sure I was going to be killed by one, that's for sure.'

'You mean in the army?'

He sat down on the sofa abruptly, so his hair fell over his eyes. He swatted it back. 'Yes, although there's my work.'

I sat opposite him. The fire leapt to life. 'Are you threatened?'

His smile was thin, evasive. 'That's one way of putting it. What about your folks?'

I was bewildered by the change of subject. 'My parents? What do you want to know?'

'You haven't said anything about your family. Not a word.'

I shrugged. 'My parents know where I am. I've sent them an email.'

'Yes, but what are they like?'

'My parents are witty, charming, amoral people.'

He gave me a sharp look. I lowered myself into the sofa and moved close to the fire.

'Here, take this.' Riaan lobbed something at me. I picked it out of my fingers – a shirt. I put it on, grateful for it, even if it smelled of wood smoke.

His gaze was cool, evaluative. Then it vanished, as if he'd pulled a trigger. 'I've never heard anyone speak about their parents that way,' he said. 'Maybe in novels. Maybe in my father's novels, come to think of it.'

'I don't think about them much. Is that – ungrateful?'

'You tell me.'

'My parents are like a minor political party whose views I've never sympathised with but can't quite get round to condemning.'

'It's not for me to judge.' A distracted look came into his eyes. I had lost him.

'Do you like Pieter – your father's books?'

'I don't know about *like*. I've never *liked* books. It's beyond liking. Either they're necessary or they're not.'

'You're a purist.'

He seemed to be about to retort, then stopped. 'I can't read his books anyway, although I have. I only see *him*.'

'Which him do you see?'

'It's strange, isn't it – millions of bloody people all over the world, for all I know, investing in these people my father created and who say things like you've just said. That insight, or acuity, or whatever you call it. I've never had that with people. To me, people are like the wind or the sea. It's a good day or a bad day. It's rough or calm.'

'I think you don't believe in your father's books because you know he wrote them.'

He was silent for a moment. Behind us, the fire spat. 'Of course I know he wrote them.'

'I don't know, for me writers are necessary impostors. We are all that, but only writers have the guts to remind us that there's no core self, really. We are just a collection of personas.'

'Sure,' he said, breezily, as if this were obvious. 'I'm relying on you to tell me who he is. Who they both are.'

The solitude of the house had surrounded us. For the first time since I met Pieter and Sara, I began to feel out of my depth. It was a feeling of subtle vertigo. Not unpleasant, but so far from the reassurance I'd felt in my first fugitive days in their house.

'To have a father who's a writer is not to have a father at all,' he said. 'Or at least if he becomes a national figure.'

'Is that what he is?'

'Absolutely. Although he's gone through several incarnations: friend of the state, enemy of the state. That's all writers were, in this country, for a long time, one or the other. It's not like being a writer in England, where all you have to do is tell a story and make money.'

The fire exploded, shooting a small piece of coal which lay smouldering on the stone floor at my feet.

'I was ten years old before I realised who my father was and I had to look at him with everyone else's eyes,' Riaan said. 'He was always about to flee into exile like all the other writers did. He was like an exotic animal, maybe the last of his kind. By tomorrow, he might be extinct.'

We let the fire burn down. The subject of Pieter – his fame, his profession, the burden of him – melted away. I can't remember what we talked about for the rest of the night. Riaan was not a person for pleasantries or banter. He'd rather sit in silence than talk about the weather, something he'd seen on television, his friends – in fact he hadn't yet mentioned friends or a girlfriend. Everything we said to each other was a kind of test or consecration. He elicited a brutality from me. Perhaps I had always known it was there, and was only waiting for the person who could name it and set it free.

A rhythm settled between us for the rest of the holiday. Sara and Pieter went to the beach and Riaan and I took the dogs for long, vaguely punishing walks. The coast was monumental; it went on and on. I pushed myself to keep up with Riaan, who always wanted to go further. 'Just another few minutes, Nicklaas.' He almost always used my full name, dragging the final 'a' out. 'I'll show you the most incredible tidal pool.' He was always promising something amazing to show me.

For the first kilometre or so the beaches were lined with fishermen standing beside their rods and staring out to sea like prophets. Behind them, families barbecuing, dune-buggy drivers tearing through the sand. But after a mile or two these all petered out and we were left on our own. When the sun is out it was impossible to look at the ocean, the glare was too bright. When there was cloud the sea and sky became jade. We trudged through patches of gelatinous kelp, up and down dunes which crumpled beneath our feet. We passed more lone black men dressed in striped shirts and knitted hats, seemingly come out of nowhere, who did not smile or speak. I never asked them where they had come from, or where they were going, nor did Riaan, although he sometimes greeted them, and they greeted him back. Clouds moved low and fast over the ocean.

# VII

This is how we encounter new countries now, from 35,000 feet. We watch them descend into visual puzzles, the boa constrictor rivers, flaxen trapezoid fields, miles and miles of ceramic pieces of earth, broken into pieces like a shattered urn.

I always book a window seat, but not for the reasons most people do. This might be the only chance – other than satellite imagery – I get to see the ground I will have to tame for human habitation. Where the pyroclastic flows have stopped, where the earthquake has fissured the ground, or the burnt villages that signal the retreat of war.

We flew over the north of the country and slowly watched it turn green as we headed south. I didn't pay attention as I usually did. I watched the news – now one-day old – on the screen instead. There was nothing to suggest this country would be anything other than a transit lounge for me. I was scheduled to be here for three days, perhaps four or five at a stretch, if something went wrong – if our equipment hadn't arrived on the cargo ship, or weather, although in the summer what could go wrong with the weather?

From the window of the plane I could see the mountain. Faint at first, then its outline hardened. Its crown was flat. It looked more like a tectonic plate, as if land had levered itself out of the ocean and come to meet the sky as a single entity.

The airport was located behind the mountain – I knew that much from Google Maps. But instead of heading straight for it the plane banked out to sea. We flew right by the mountain and out into the open ocean, which foamed underneath us with angry white horses. I scanned the other passengers for signs of alarm at our deviation. Everyone looked out the window; those on the ocean side of the plane craned their necks to see the mountain better.

The sun was overtaken by a cloud. A storm, or squall, loomed ahead of us – this was the reason for our detour – casting the inside of the plane in a throbbing, purple darkness.

Then we were on the ground and I was in the harbour we had seen from the air with its toytown ships and fingers of docks, being driven in a minibus toward the ship, tied at one of the furthest of those long concrete fingers, the one reserved for the white wedges of cruise ships.

This was also familiar: the drive to unknown airports or harbours, before I knew it being handed a clipboard and a hardhat, a high-vis vest, having my luggage stowed away by a porter who had materialised from nowhere. I was to start counting boxes and loading containers within minutes of arrival, even if I didn't understand the local language and the heady smell of this particular ocean – so cold and clean – made me dizzy.

Few coastal cities in the world sit on the skirts of a mountain, I suppose because mountains usually occur inland, and they present a major challenge to buildings and roads. Rio, for example, snakes along the littoral of a chain of ancient basalt plugs. Those mountains were impressive, but they lacked the single-minded intensity of this one.

The mountain was there, always; even if I turned my back on it and looked out to sea I could feel its presence, daring me not to look at it. I would catch it out of the corner of my eye and stop my pacing between the cargo hold and my cabin. It was often covered by a flat cloud which fell over it, tumbling over its edge, before vaporising.

The wind was fierce and hot. On the day after my arrival we had to suspend loading of the ship.

‘There goes our departure date,’ the first officer said, when we gathered for our first briefing on the bridge that evening. This was also routine: a logistics conference held in the largest space on the ship. In the monumental windows of the bridge we saw the static planet of the mountain.

‘This is the bad news,’ he went on. The wind was forecast to blow for three days. An announcement came over the tannoy. We heard the captain’s crisp voice. ‘All cargoing is suspended until further notice.’ Until then it had been just the container ships. Now we’d have to stop the forklifts and manual loading. We couldn’t risk someone being blown off the docks and into the cold black sea.

Our departure date receded. But our organisation went ahead with the departure reception that night. Whichever country we were in, these were always the same: canapés, more juice than wine – alcohol was kept to a minimum – Embassy people, usually second-rung spooks masquerading as commercial liaison officers, Red Cross and UN logisticians, delegates from the deputy prime minister’s office and one or two military types. Before diving into the marathon of hand-shaking the maintaining of serious, committed expressions, I braved the wind and went out on deck.

The sun had disappeared behind the mountain, which was still draped in the vaporous cloud cloth. In the harbour strings of lights were being turned on, forming a chain necklace which reflected on the water. Yachts and powerboats huddled in the harbour.

I looked at the bowlines that held the ship fast to the dead men pillars on the dock, thinking how when berthed ships look extra-terrestrial, like a mock-up of a sci-fi craft. Soon – although we didn’t know when – we would cast these off, leave this city and the mountain behind, to live its own life without us. I usually relished this feeling about ship life, the thrill of rootlessness; we could turn up in a town, sample its flavours with the arrogance of people who knew they did not have to commit to its dank alleyways, its steam-drenched afternoons, its bureaucracy and traffic codes. The places I had visited by ship seemed to treat all of us ship-bound creatures as unreliable lovers, resenting our lack of commitment but in thrall to our independence. We acquired the sullen glamour of those who are always about to leave.

This time, however, I could feel a reluctance. *Why are you tugging at me?* I addressed the mountain.

'Talking to yourself already? We haven't even left harbour yet.'

Carlos appeared at my elbow and took up a similar position, draped over the railing. He had joined us from the Spanish Red Cross only a month previously. We'd worked together in the office in London for only ten days before coming on mission. His Spanish was almost unaccented. The only way you would know he was not English was the burnt cherry complexion and the narrow goatee.

'Just limbering up for full-on craziness.'

'Yes, weeks to go, or who knows how many, with the usual misfits.' Carlos smiled, perhaps to show me he did not count me among them.

We both had to steady ourselves with our arms on the railing. This wind did not blow around people, but made straight for you, hitting you like a slab.

'Is it your first time here?' I asked.

He nodded. 'I'm not sure I like it.'

'You mean the city?'

He gestured toward the mountain. 'It's like an alien. Nature didn't make this mountain, I think. How can it be so perfect?'

'Millennia of erosion, very typical of sandstone. Three hundred million years ago it was under the ice sheets. They flattened it, and when the ocean receded it retained its shape because it's supported by granite underneath.'

'How do you know all this?'

'I used to be a geologist.'

Carlos gave a smile. 'Everybody here used to be something

else. Annika was a ski instructor and Justine was a doctor. Well, she still is, I guess.'

'It's the ideal second career. If you didn't manage to kill yourself with whatever you were doing the first time around, you can always try again with this one.'

He gave me a look that was difficult to read. He was not English enough to agree to the appeal of gallows humour. Perhaps he thought I might be one of the many amongst us who were washed-up adrenalin junkies, living on a free-fall diet of uncertainty, risk and duty-free whisky.

'Did you say three hundred million?' His frame was already twisting to see if the party had begun.

'That's right.'

'Human beings didn't even exist then, did they? I realise it's not cool to say this, but I have no interest in the natural world.'

Carlos was younger than me, although not by much. He had an unhappy, unstable energy, the kind that feeds on feuds, resentments. I wondered how he had ended up in the aid industry – that fantastic oxymoron – and how long he would last. I had a sense his time here was short. His edges were blurring, as if he was already fading out of the picture.

He became aware of my scrutiny. 'You've been in the business a long time.'

'Only six years. I did a couple of years as a mining geologist after my PhD.'

'You must have started young. I mean, you must have had your doctorate by, what, twenty-four?'

'Twenty-five.'

He looked thoughtful for a moment, then his head jerked up straight. It was as if he had received an internal signal. 'Well, time to meet the big shots. I guess we'll be seeing a lot of each other. Lots of time to fill in the blanks.' He gave a rueful smile and slid through one of the doors that led from the top deck down the long narrow passageway to the cabins.

It was time for me to return to the reception too. If I stayed much longer my absence would be noticed. I looked around me at the deck, which bristled with anemometers, the VHF tower, a V-Sat dome. These antennae would be our only communication with the outside world for weeks.

I prised open the same door Carlos had walked through. The ship was an ex-German navy ice-breaker, put to peculiar use in the tropics. My cabin was number 106. The day before I had met my cabin-mate, a young German communications specialist called Ernst. We would share a cabin together all the way there and back. I remember thinking that he was friendly and accommodating, but that he, like Carlos, refused to cohere somehow.

The ship was full of busy, purposeful people, people like me. I knew a few of them from previous missions: there was Laura from the New York office, Maeve from UNICEF and a towering Dutch counterintelligence expert I had met once in Kurdistan but whose name I could not remember. When I asked the Dutch expert how he had been since we'd last seen each other he grimaced and said, 'We'll have plenty of time to talk in the next seven weeks' and stalked down the corridor.

I stored my suitcase in the locker, I took my laptop to the radio officer to be networked, I unwound my flak jacket and hung it on the door of the cabin, settling my toothbrush into its holder. Ships were designed for motion, right down to the details; all drawers and doors had safety catches, to keep them from swinging open and shut. My desk was fitted with a rubber mat for my laptop, my wheeled office chair had brakes, like a child's buggy.

All this was familiar now. I'd done three previous ship-based missions, I looked forward to our two weeks at sea, which would be a hiatus before our rendezvous with danger. Most people find time spent on ships stupendously boring – cramped quarters, always bumping into the same people, evening entertainment limited to telling stories of near escapes in the bar or watching whatever DVDs you had managed to pack on your laptop in your cabin.

But I liked the slow approach to the conflict, how being at sea gave me time to confront the coming ordeal. We would see the low, green coast of Mozambique, garlanded with mother-of-pearl tropical islands. We would cross the squally Indian ocean before turning to the shores of Kisamu and its hot coast scissored by sharks.

This ship would be my home for many weeks while I directed the ship-based operation to ensure the entry of the medical and logistics teams to the fallen coastal city of Kassala. *This is what I have come here to do. I always get the job done.*

Yet as these rehearsed reassurances floated through my mind I had the sensation, passing through the decks on the staircase, walking through the bar with its smoked-chrome windows, that something was wrong. It was a minor kink in my perception, like waking up on a Wednesday when you think it is actually Tuesday, or forgetting your date of birth or bank card PIN for a split second.

I joined the party on the afterdeck. I got a G&T from the bar and ploughed into the crowd. 'Nick,' a tall man in a black suit pulled me aside. 'Just the man I wanted to introduce to our friend here.'

I angled myself to shake the hand, which the man held out, ramrod straight. Army, no doubt, uncomfortably trussed into civvies.

'This is Major Porteous. He will be your liaison.'

'You're flying in?'

He nodded. 'Tomorrow. Beats the slow boat. That's if we don't get shot down.' His face had that blank, let's-do-it expression they specialise in producing in the military. We said enough to each other to determine that we did not detest each other on sight – always a relief – and shook hands again.

He peered at me. 'Why aren't you flying? It's safer, you know, disregard my comment about being shot down.

They don't do that anymore, not since Dag Hammarskjold anyway.' He sounded almost disappointed.

'I prefer ships, believe it or not.'

'I think I'd choose hitting the dust at 500k an hour over being beheaded by pirates.'

'Tough choice, I agree.' I smiled.

I didn't tell him how much of my life I've spent in airports wearing a rumpled shirt, clutching a carry-on bag with another rumpled shirt inside, having received the call and my e-ticket with only a couple of hours' notice. Dili, Luanda, Tegucigalpa. I used to find them exciting places. I would always be susceptible to beauty but only ever be attracted to some element of disorder or danger. Without it, beauty became complacent, even obscene.

For years I had loved the moment of uplift, when the aircraft wheels left the ground and I felt the pure thrust of the engines defy gravity. It felt like the future. I loved the cruise, when I would read briefings generated by our policy unit and watch the moving map on the entertainment system obsessively, zeroing in on places I had been deployed to, scouring the satellite imaging of their terrain for memories. I even loved the careening descent in thunderstorms, the way the air fell away underneath you.

Now each moment I spend flying is a dark lake that threatens to draw me down to the dimension where I belong. I take beta blockers and still drink G&Ts but now they exist to drown my fear. I used to believe in the physics, I used to have confidence in the air, that it was a solid enough dimension to support my progress through space. My problem is with air, not mechanical failure or terrorism or hijackings. I've ceased to believe it can keep me aloft and so for the whole flight I think I am taking part in a dangerous fiction. I wonder why I've been taking the air for granted all my life.

# VIII

On Christmas Eve we had a quiet dinner, just the four of us. Sara grilled salmon on the barbecue and made a couscous salad. Three candles stalked the dinner table and the butter light of candles drew a conspiratorial angle on the scene. It was curious. Even though I had been aware from my second day in Pieter and Sara's house that they had two sons – that they had a family – as a couple they had a self-sufficiency about them that made me disregard that they were parents to other beings.

Now, for the first time I saw them as a continuum, as involved. I thought, but of course they are kin. The sculpted outline of Riaan's face was Pieter's, although the expressive eyes, or their shape if not their colour, were his mother's. He was a perfect amalgam of the two, with his soulful face, his watchful eyes.

We finished dinner. 'I love Christmas in the tropics,' I declared.

'The subtropics,' Pieter corrected.

'Whatever. It's warm.' I smiled. I had drunk two glasses of wine.

At one point Sara put her hand on Pieter's arm, as if to steady herself. They went to bed early, wishing us happy Christmas in subdued voices. I tried not to look at Riaan for the answers to the questions mustering in my mind. Did they have a fight? Did I say something wrong? I couldn't trace the moment of rupture.

Riaan and I sat beside the fire. I took in the living room,

trying to locate its familiarity. It had a certain international beach house décor: pieces of driftwood crawling along the mantelpiece, seashells hanging from the walls in macramé spirals, dusty games of Scrabble, no television, only a pile out-dated papers in the kindling basket.

'Lost in thought, Nicklaas?'

I turned to find his eyes on me. 'I was just thinking how time passed in houses like these feels more real, somehow.'

'I remember every summer we spent here as a kid. As if they sunk into my bones.'

I had noticed he often spoke as if he was completely alone as a child, as if he had no brother at all.

'Do you see much of your brother?' I wanted to use his name, Stephen, but I had never met him, and it seemed too familiar, to utter his name.

'Not anymore, not since I moved away.' He stood. 'Time to hit the sack, all this sea air tires me out.'

I said I would extinguish the fire, put out the lights. The dogs looked at Riaan's retreating back, then at me, as if to say: *What did you say? I don't know*, I muttered in reply. *I only asked him about his brother.*

Stephen was six or seven years younger than Riaan, Pieter had told me; he would be only twenty-six. I didn't know anything about him, other than what Pieter and Sara had told me when I first arrived. He had rung twice when I'd been with them and Sara had spoken to him without handing Pieter the phone.

The room seemed to close around me. It was Christmas Eve – Christmas Day, now – and I was alone. My parents were in their condominium in St Lucia, that much I knew from an email they had sent, before I became too afraid to open my inbox.

Riaan's unhappiness left a wake of turbulence in the room. I waited for it to dissipate. I recognised him now as the kind of person I would normally avoid at work in the office, or in the field. He was unpredictable, he had a lax ferocity which was waiting to be ignited. If I hit one wrong note – as I had just done – I might be banished from his friendship. Such people exhaust me, normally. But in leaving the ship and abandoning my job I had relinquished whatever power I had to choose where I was, or with whom. Now I was just a leaf. I had to rely on the wind to take me to where I was supposed to be.

I sat alone with the dogs for an hour, the fire muttering, going over our conversation. Before I had mentioned his brother, Riaan had told me about his girlfriend, Tanya. She was spending Christmas with her family in a town ten hours' drive from Cabo Frio. Then he turned the question around.

*'Have you got anyone at home?'*

*'Not at the moment. I meet people all the time, in my work. But then she's posted to Kazakhstan, and I'm sent to London and, well.'*

*'That's tough.'*

*'It's a good way of life if you can take lots of intense relationships of short duration.'*

*'Is that what you like?'*

*'I've learned to like it.'*

'Still up!' Pieter appeared in the doorway, dressed in a sarong. Through the window I saw light tugging at the edges of the sky.

I sat up straight. The dogs were still there, in front of the fire. 'I must have fallen asleep.'

'I thought so. Merry Christmas.'

'Oh, yes.' I'd completely forgotten it was Christmas. Birds sang in the trees outside. The first ray of sunlight penetrated the house. 'Merry Christmas to you too.'

'Where's Riaan?' Pieter asked.

'Here he is.' Riaan appeared behind his father. He was already dressed in a T-shirt and shorts. We both looked at him. 'Well, it's Christmas morning. Good to get up early and score a nice spot on the beach. Aren't you going to put on some clothes, Pa?' In his mouth the word, *Pa*, sounded so sweet and capitulating.

'This is what happens when you get old,' Pieter said to me. 'Your children start treating you like an imbecile.'

Pieter went to make us coffee. Riaan sat opposite and gave me a perplexed, almost guilty, look. He could see I had fallen asleep where he'd left me.

'Nicholas came with us to Claus and Michaela's for dinner the other night,' I heard Pieter say, from the kitchen.

'Oh yes?' Riaan's voice was wary.

'And we discovered Nick isn't interested in politics at all.'

'It was literature I wasn't interested in,' I called, hoping to make a joke of it.

Pieter called 'Everything is political.'

He came into the living room bearing a small tray with three cups. This he set down, delicately, on the coffee table. 'Wait until someone invades your country. Then you find out how political you really are.'

'I don't have a country,' I said.

'Well isn't that convenient for you.'

I didn't understand why Pieter had turned on me, but I had seen from the moment he entered the room that morning he was spoiling for some kind of fight.

'But here you talk about politics only in terms of what has been done in the past, but actually it's the future that is upsetting everyone.'

At this, Riaan sat up with a crack. Pieter gathered his sarong around his waist and tied it tighter. 'Who knows if there's a future in this country?'

'It's very unstable,' I agreed. 'But also invigorating. I feel alive here.'

'That's because you don't live here all the time.'

'Pa, it's seven o'clock on Christmas morning,' Riaan said. 'Let's not talk politics.'

'What better time than the birthday of someone who was killed by ignorance and lust for power?'

It took me a moment to realise Pieter was talking about Christ.

'I'm trying to figure out what our visitor here,' Pieter flung his hand in my direction – 'stands for.'

Riaan and I glanced at each other. He gave me a look that might have said, *What can you do?*

'Okay, Pa. But let's save the interrogation for after we've had coffee at least.'

Without saying anything more, Pieter left to shower. I intended to say something grateful to Riaan, but his gaze had fallen on me with that cool, evaluating look of his. In such moments his eyes were covered by a thin glass frame; more windows than eyes. 'So why have you come here?'

'Because your father asked me to.'

'Not Cabo Frio. Why did you come to this country?'

'I was sent here, for my job. I was supposed to take a ship. But I pulled out, at the last minute. I don't know why.'

Riaan was silent for a moment. 'We all do things we can't explain.'

'Do we?'

'Don't be so hard on yourself, man. I'd like to hear about it, if you want to talk. But if not, no pressure.'

The word, *pressure,* ricocheted in my mind. I felt a venting, a bottle being uncorked, the effervescence of relief, or its beginning.

'I'm going for a long walk,' I said. 'I'll take the dogs if you like. You might like a day off.'

His eyes brushed over me as I stood up. 'Sure man, take them with you. They'll be ecstatic.'

I walked over the dunes that Christmas morning, sleepless but more awake than I had been in years, walking along four or five beaches until I was worried the dogs and I would be cut off by the tide on our return. *You don't know this place or these people*, I reminded myself, speaking to myself as if I were another person, as I always do when I am angry with myself. *You don't know where you are going*.

We spent Christmas day at the beach. Pieter and Sara brought lunch in the same large basket they'd brought to the botanical gardens concert. They lay on the towel with their trim, muscular bodies. Sara wore a green bikini. She had none of the blancmange midriff that women in their fifties and sixties often have. Her skin was alabaster yet duskily tanned at the same time, the skin of someone who had spent a lifetime in furtive angles, avoiding the sun.

'It's so great not to be sitting in an overheated dining room being force-fed goose and jelly.'

'Is that really what you do?' Sara asked from beneath her straw hat.

'I've only spent a few in England, actually. I hate Christmas there. The whole country goes into a kind of mass hysteria.' I took in the scene in front of us – children pummelling the waves on min-surfboards, sea-foam, the jade sky. 'It's so quiet here.'

Just then a fine rain began to fall from the cloudless sky. I craned my neck, looking for the source.

'Monkey's Wedding,' Riaan said.

'What?'

'When rain falls out of a clear sky it's a monkey's wedding. Where I work it's called the jackal married the donkey.'

'Something that shouldn't happen. Something unnatural,' I say.

'Bingo.'

There was a distant note in Riaan's voice, not unlike the wind whistling through a small crack in a door. His eyes scanned the beach. I followed his gaze. All the women on the beach had tanned, planar bodies. The men were thick, their salt-coated hair stood straight up from their skulls. The sea met the sky in a rigid turquoise line. On its lip a ship ploughed into the horizon. For a second I believed it was our ship. But I knew they would be at Kassala by now, at anchor off the coast. It was on the schedule: Arrival, December 25th. There would be no Christmas on board, other than radio messages and rapid, hushed calls made on satellite phones to families at home.

Lately a constant videostream of the life I had jettisoned

had unspooled inside me. This was not an internal guilt cinema or even an imagined scene; I was convinced it was real, that I was following the path I broke away from and was simultaneously there on the beach in Cabo Frio, just like those dreams we all seem to have, when we are both inside a plane and at the same time watching its departure. In this alternate life I discussed the tender of cargo to the shore with Ernst, how to avoid theft of the emergency supplies on shore – basically, send an armed escort – I ate the cauliflower cheese of the canteen, smelled the salt of the ocean, stared at the rust coastline through binoculars and saw black flags flying there, their slim scripts guttering in the breeze – a warning to us, the infidel in their midst.

That afternoon Riaan and I went for a drive into town to buy beer and supplies. Because it was the high season everything was open, even on Christmas Day. We drove out of town through the have-not area: Cabo Frio was beach mansions to the south of the hotel and poor fishermen's cottages to the north; on first inspection these looked pretty, fringed with neat flowerbeds, but clapped-out cars huddled in the driveways and snarling dogs flung themselves at you if you tried to approach.

'They've been living here for centuries, fishing happily,' Riaan threw his arm out the window in the direction of the cottages. 'And then we rock up in our Mercedes and start building houses five times the size of theirs.'

'There are two worlds here,' I said. 'I'm not even sure they see each other.'

'That's what everyone says, but it's not quite that simple.'

I accepted his admonishment in silence, waiting to see if he would elaborate, but he carried on driving.

We drove with the windows open, watching the flatlands stretch from the coast into the breadloaf interior, where they foamed with fields of wheat. Ostriches clattered over the limestone plain. We passed the air force base used for test launching missiles, which was announced by many warning signs and barbed wire.

Riaan looked relieved, I thought, as we left the dunes behind. He wore a brown leather bush hat encircled by a braid of leather and a faded khaki shirt. 'You look like you're on safari,' I said.

'I am. It's called the visiting my parents safari. All sorts of wildlife here – the town burghers, distant relations, rich people from up the coast, travelling minstrels.'

He was referring to a sort of opera production we'd seen in the village church the night before. Two men sung German *lieder* and it was strange to hear those songs and their Mitteleuropean melancholy in this wild place.

I hung my face out of the open window and drank the slipstream.

'Don't get me wrong,' he said. 'I like to see my parents. We get along fine. But it's always the same at Christmas. Somehow the atmosphere always becomes… I don't know. Heavy. If we're unlucky it sours.'

'I know. I've felt it too.' I felt guilty as soon as I said it. Why was I betraying Pieter and Sara with my commiserations?

'I've asked them what's wrong but they say it's nothing,' he said. 'Just the fact that they get a rest from work and can finally stop and think. But I think there's something they're not telling me. It's as if they go into mourning at this time every year. They'll come out of it before New Years'. Listen, I'll show you somewhere, before we get supplies. There's no rush is there?'

We left the limestone plain and took a road that rose into the coastal mountains. The sky clouded over and a cool mist penetrated the car. After a few kilometres we pulled into an identikit village; all the buildings were grey with thatched roofs. A couple of rusted gas pumps stood, as narrow and contorted as Giacometti sculptures, in the forecourt of what once would have been a store. There was no one around at all.

We got out. Riaan lit a cigarette and wagged it at me. I haven't smoked in ten years, but I took it.

'Bit of a ghost town,' I said.

'This place was built by missionaries. They were the only settlers to take an interest in the local people.'

'But nobody lives here anymore.'

'Yes, it's a kind of live museum. Everyone lives in town now.'

We stood among the deserted cottages, the ex-store, the old mill, listening to birdsong. Before long a fine rain began to fall.

'It's nearly New Years already.' There was a wistful note in Riaan's voice. 'I'm glad to say goodbye.' He exhaled a stream of smoke, then threw his cigarette to the ground. 'It's been a lonely year.' His eyes wanted something from me. He might have expected me to ask him what he meant. I was thinking of my own year, which had taken a smooth and predictable path, until recently.

'That was a bloody intelligent thing you said to my father. About us being afraid of the future.'

'I'm not on anyone's side you know.'

'I know, man.' He gave me a long, slow look. 'You're one of life's non-partisans.'

'Your father thinks I'm apolitical but the truth is I've seen too much politics. Now I call it by a different name. Or several.'

'What would they be?'

'Greed, corruption, ego, mismanagement, power masquerading as religion – it's a useful front. Then again, I only work in countries where politics have failed so badly people have taken to killing each other.' I offered a wry smile. 'So I'm not well placed to judge the good stuff – institutionalised responsibility, social welfare, policy-making, trust.'

'Why did you take on such a depressing career?'

'It's not – it's uplifting. When I'm in these places of chaos and death, I feel I am being leant an unusual clarity, if only for a while. The time will come when I have to return it. But while it's there I have these moments of perception.' I looked at him, but he wouldn't look at me. 'I can see *everything*. I feel alive.'

He was quiet for a minute. 'To feel alive you have to fling yourself at something. Like throwing yourself into the jaws of a shark and hoping you'll come out intact. You should come and see my project. I live in paradise.'

*Paradise*. The word echoed uneasily in my head.

Riaan leant against the truck, waiting for a response. I had been mentally preparing myself for never seeing Riaan again, after New Years was over and our holiday dispersed. Normally I wouldn't have allowed the word to enter my thoughts until the person was long gone: *never.*

'Sure,' I said. 'Your father mentioned your work but in passing. What's it about?'

'Education. We run a bursary scheme. We send village children who show ability to High School in town, then to university. Their parents can't afford school fees, so we pay them.'

'How long have you been doing this?'

'Since I first moved. You'll never believe what I did before that.'

'Let me guess, a venture capitalist in Shanghai.'

He managed a grim smile. 'So much worse. I taught geography in High School.'

'No!'

'I don't look like much of a teacher, do I? I wasn't sure what to do after university; a Bachelors in Earth Sciences, a Masters in Geography. I didn't think I had it in me to go into research, so I taught.'

I tried to picture Riaan's body trussed into a shirt and tie. Radicals often ended up as teachers, it happened all over the world. He had the presence and command. I didn't doubt he could hold a room rapt simply by counting from one to ten.

'I liked the job, actually, it was a good subject, we took

field trips, that was the best part, getting those kids out into the world. But too many rules and regulations, inevitably. So I decided to do something more grassroots. Quite the do-gooder, no?'

'There's nothing wrong with that,' I said.

'Maybe I just didn't know who I was. Or am. Who are we, really?'

We were still standing by the truck in the strange town. But now I saw it wasn't empty at all. Rather men in blue overalls were watching us, from around the corners of houses. They hadn't been there when we arrived.

I darted my eyes from these men to Riaan. He was daring me to answer his question.

'Everyone is entranced by the notion of the true self, but actually there are just selves you can live with, and those you can't.'

I felt suddenly unmoored. This might be a tactic of his, I considered, to shake people up, make them question their beliefs, how they were living their lives. One minute you are perfectly content with your life and the next you are riven with doubt.

'Riaan,' I said. My voice was hoarse. 'There are these men in blue overalls watching us.'

He jerked to attention. 'Where?'

'Around the corners of the houses. They don't want us to know they're here.'

'Okay,' he said. 'Let's hit the road. Ma and Pa will be wondering where we've got to.'

Half an hour later we were on the outskirts of Cabo Frio. The road ascended the belt of dunes that encircled the town, studded with saltbush. The sky was no longer slack with mysterious rain but alert. Velvet dunes shimmered on the horizon.

I thought of our return now to the empty beaches and diamond horizon, the lonely seas that converged at its feet, one a warm ocean and the other cold, the battleship mountain that backed Pieter and Sara's house, whose gaze I was relieved to be free of in those weeks, but which called to me, as if I had flown off course and needed to return home. Why did this place move me so much? It was an edge country, and perhaps I needed to align the landscape with the feeling inside me, as if I were teetering on a precipice, my life completely open, which is to say empty.

A line from *Mercy Street* loiters in my mind: *Edges are necessary, exciting*, Pieter writes. The main character says this to a friend of his. The novel takes place in a coastal town raked by cold waves. The main character has no name. He's a wild man, not a people pleaser. He does what he wants to do and that's that. He is the kind of man who easily acquires acolytes and who shuns those people whom he intuits he cannot influence. He is always looking for somewhere more wild, bigger skies, more people packed into a pickup truck. *Edges are there for a reason*, Pieter writes: *but if you're not careful you can cut yourself.*

# IX

'Happy New Year!'

The cries reach us in the courtyard where we are having dinner. It is a balmy night and we sit by candlelight under the stars. After dinner, Riaan and I leave Pieter and Sara playing Scrabble and we go down to the hotel bar to have a New Year's drink.

The hotel stands white and mute in front of the ocean. It is full of people who have come from the city to spend New Year's at the beach. We walk through the lobby into the bar, which has a nautical theme – a ship's searchlight is welded to the edge of a wood-panelled interior. In the corner a flatscreen TV blares rugby.

Riaan strides across the room and orders a beer quickly. Even though they have their backs to us, the women arranged around the bar seem to have received a signal to sit up straighter at his approach. We align ourselves to a group of men a few years younger than us and watch the rugby on television. The women, who are blond and tanned as if by decree and who have the slightly infantile faces many women have here with huge, seemingly guileless eyes and plump lips, shoot us looks. I see them register something. They glance at each other, the set of their shoulders hardens and they go back to talking to the younger men.

A rocket goes off outside the restaurant. We realise it's midnight. The entire bar files outside to watch the beachside fireworks and the traditional skinny dipping. As soon as I realise this I fall back.

Riaan tugs at my shirt. 'Come on.' Dozens of men are heading down to the beach in front of what looks to be the entire town who watch from above. No women come with us. The men ahead of me are shedding their clothes as they go.

I follow Riaan, shrugging off my shirt and trousers. I can't see him anymore in the throng. We are only a sea of tanned forearms and blistering white bottoms, as white as the moon.

The sea is so cold I struggle for breath. It feels lighter in the darkness. Just beyond Riaan's head, out of a pool of darkness in the water, blue and green ribbons shimmer. I open and shut my eyes, but they remain.

Riaan sees it too. 'Bioluminescence,' he shouts.

The water shimmers with this marine aurora. It's rare to see it at the surface. I try to remember what I learned at university; how bioluminescence is produced in the depths of the ocean where no light ever penetrates but where squid and octopi and other small creatures, burning with their own power source, flash on and off like Christmas lights in the darkness. These creatures withstand extremes of pressure and temperature, their gelatine limbs expanding and compressing, hunting nearly blind in complete darkness.

His head bobs near me. 'Look up, man!'

I can't see the skies because above the beach people have turned on the high beams of their trucks to see us better. But when the headlights are suddenly extinguished the blackness reveals more creatures, this time in the sky. I see the Milky Way, the small and large Magellanic Clouds. When I worked in Iraq my translator and I would sit on the outskirts of the camp at night. He taught me that the Sumerians, the ancient civilisation of southern Iraq, had called the stars 'the shining herd'. Now I saw they did look like horses or gazelles or the stout golden eland, the ox-deer which flourishes in the north, where Riaan lives, all running across the tilting plain of the sky, tipping over its edge into infinity.

On our return, Pieter was still up. We broke out the ritual New Year bottle of single malt scotch, procured by Pieter in some Duty Free on an overseas trip.

From the town we heard isolated puffs of explosions, screeches. In the house it was quiet, apart from the hungry lapping of the fire. Pieter sat in a chair across from us, twirling a tumbler of scotch.

He was in an expansive, page-turning mood. 'It never comes to you the same way twice. With most of my books it's as if someone was dictating them to me. All I had to do was transcribe them. It was effortless.'

'What's different about this one, Pa?' Riaan asked.

'The story can't settle. It doesn't know what it wants to be.' He gave us a beseeching look.

'But surely you're in control of that,' I said. 'It's your story, after all.'

Pieter turned his gaze to me. 'How do you know it's my story?'

'I mean, you're writing it.'

'That doesn't make it my story.'

'I'm sorry, I don't know anything about writing,' I conceded. 'But isn't it just a matter of making a decision?'

His piercing gaze took in Riaan and I in a single glance, implicating us in something – our ignorance of what it is like to be a writer, perhaps. 'I'm just a conduit. The story comes to me. You could say it chooses me, if you want to be fanciful.'

I was confused. It hadn't occurred to me that writing a book was anything other than a sustained act of will.

'It was easier when I first started,' Pieter went on. 'There were so many stories that weren't allowed. You just had to choose one. It was your duty, in fact. Then, there was a

Publications Board. All books had to be submitted. And the worst thing was, it was my colleagues, even my friends who were censoring me.'

I glanced at Riaan, who was only half paying attention. Perhaps he had heard these stories before, although he'd told me his father didn't like to talk about his work. I remembered something Pieter had said to me, the first time we spoke in his office and I had asked him about his books: *serious writers never talk about their work*. Those writers who did were dilettantes or egoists, he had gone on to say.

'Anna, you remember her? That nice academic from the English department, she was one of them.'

'No!' Riaan said. 'She even went to the street demos.'

'Yes, it was all an elaborate ruse. She had to agree to it, if she wanted to keep her job. That was how it was in those days, you had to choose between friends and your work.' His voice was suddenly strident. It could be the scotch, I thought. He didn't often drink.

'I didn't set out to be controversial. I did an interview with the BBC, and that's what started it. I said that writers were being put in impossible positions, which was true. All those nice academics and minor writers we thought were our friends accused me of betraying my country.'

As I heard his clipped logical sentences, I wondered again at the unabashed sensuality of his work. 'But your work is so…' here I wanted to say sexual, but changed my mind at the last minute. 'Emotional.'

'That was the problem,' Pieter answered. 'They kept looking for a political message and not finding it. They were enraged. By not finding it they suspected me of pulling the wool over their eyes, of being cleverer than them. But the state was everywhere; in your bedroom, even your bathroom. There were separate bathrooms, beaches. Even benches.'

'I know,' I said. 'I've seen the photographs.'

'It was neurotic,' Pieter said. 'It made people so, too. I still see them sometimes, the signs for whites, for blacks. I look at the walls of train stations and they're there. Except it's a hallucination. Then, when I was formally banned suddenly everybody cared,' Pieter leaned forward at the word. 'Can you image it? I had notes from the Swedish ambassador, delivered to me by some apparatchik in decoded cabled gobbledygook. The BBC sent a man to interview me disguised as a telephone repair man. I had letters from ladies in Oklahoma. I have never felt so connected.' He shook his head, dazed by memory. 'I almost enjoyed it, provoking so much hatred.' The word seemed to stop him in his tracks. He turned to me, or turned on me. 'You Europeans don't know much about all this.'

'All what?'

'Civil war. Living in a police state.'

'Have you heard of terrorism?'

'Yes, I have. We invented it.'

Pieter sat very still and silent, perhaps absorbing the scotch. He went to bed soon after, leaving Riaan and I to smother the fire.

'I've just figured it out,' Riaan said.

'What?'

'You still don't know who my father is.'

'Who is he?'

He shook the question away. 'You talk to him as if he is anyone. He likes that.'

'You resent what you see as your father's intellectual vanity, but if he didn't have that he'd never write anything.'

Riaan's response was immediate. 'And would that be such a loss?'

*He'd felt this desolation before but never this malign twist in the centre of it, like a snake coiling up a spine. How would you describe loneliness? That's a better word than nostalgia, than regret, for that lost state of innocence and ardour with people, before everything must become about sex, or wantings of other kinds.*

I am reading *Mercy Street* in bed at night. It is as if Pieter is addressing me, personally. I feel shamed by this intimacy.

*Only gratified people talk about their desires*. Pieter had said this at some point in our conversation that first evening of the new year. I struggled to reconcile these bitter pronouncements with his persona. Pieter could be such a *bonvivant*, with his taste for expensive shirts and marinated artichoke. There was a tarnished seam inside him and he mined it in the name of art. Yet his life was happy, as far as I could tell. He did not live out the ambiguity he generated with his mind.

Halfway through the novel Pieter shifts the point of view and we hear the character speak in his own voice. Until this point the story has been narrated by someone I assume is Pieter, but I am wrong. I feel surprised, but more than that, betrayed.

All night the wind is brash. A squall howls through the louvered windows. Other sounds keep me awake: the tick-tock call of an owl, leaves falling on the roof, the creak of a gate. I think *they* have come. *They* are trying to get in.

Something is coming. I can just make out its shape on the horizon. When we were at the strange missionary village sharing a cigarette Riaan turned to me. His eyes shone from the shadowed penumbra cast by his hat. 'I am so relieved you are here.' At the time I basked in his admission, but I also thought, what have I done to earn your relief? I had only been company, someone to do things with. With him I felt myself playing the role of the dull relation, the well-intentioned but boring cousin. At the time I was so pleased with his admission that only later did I realise he did not say happy. He was relieved. Another line from *Mercy Street* jumps out at me: *he was not certain about life but no day passed in which he was not relieved to be alive*.

These are the things I remember about those final days in Cabo Frio: the wild cranberry bush at the entrance to their house, its wafting smells of sweet and sour. Riaan teaching me the names of the flowers: the amaryllis, strelitzia, several types of aloes. There are few trees on this wind-blasted coast but he hunts out a specimen of three species, the stinkwood, black ironwood and yellowwood.

We go to the beach where fishermen buck and strain against the catch on their lines, we pluck stranded sunfish off the beach and throw them back in. We drive the dunes, sand spitting from the wheels, Riaan whipping the truck expertly through the dense sand, hauling us from side to side. We go to Danger Point and watch great whites surf the breakers. We see two sharks, they are unmistakeable – their pewter backs rising out of the water like submarines.

We sit in silence there and look at each other shyly, from time to time. It is an impressive thing, the birth of a friendship.

In the morning of the day Riaan left, Rodrigo, a neighbour who owned a beach house one block away, dropped in to visit. Pieter and Sara entertained him in the courtyard; Riaan took me aside in the kitchen.

'That guy,' he whispered stagily, darting his eyes at the man sipping coffee outside, what do you think he did for a living?'

'What do you mean *did*?'

'Look at him. He looks, what, fifty?'

I stole another glance. Rodrigo was wiry, very fit. His hair was dark. 'I get the sense you're about to tell me he's seventy.'

'Seventy-bloody-five. That man ran the navy.'

'No.'

'Yes. Killed thousands in the annexation war. Now here he is, nice as pie.'

'Riaan, no one says "nice as pie anymore". Possibly no one ever said it.'

He licked the icing sugar off the border of one of the brioches Sara was about to serve Rodrigo. 'Mark my words, that man is a mass murderer.'

Rodrigo told no stories about gunning down innocent civilians. Instead he bemoaned his failed horticultural project, the cultivation of roses in this wild, salty place – 'the infernal heat always kills them' – and how much his grandchildren had disappointed him by moving to Hong Kong. Then, before he left, he suddenly offered to take our picture. 'Look,' he brandished a bag none of us had quite clocked. 'I've got this new camera, Canon something or other. Cost me the earth. Let me try it out.'

We all waved our hands in horror, but finally we gave in and arranged ourselves near the front of the door to the house, underneath the tree that produced clouds of wild pink blossoms. Pieter and Sara stood flanking Riaan, who towered over his mother. The sun was in their eyes, so Rodrigo asked them to turn around. They adjusted themselves, then resumed grinning at the camera.

Riaan called to me. 'Come, Nicklaas, and have your photo taken.'

'No, it's a family shot. You carry on.'

Suddenly, I know what will happen next. I know with absolute certainty that Riaan will prop his sunglasses on top of his head and look at me with concern, tenderness, ballasted by an uncertainty or rather vulnerability masquerading as uncertainty. He will expose himself totally.

We look at each other, Riaan and I, for one long arrested moment.

I drop my bag and go to stand with them, Sara in between Riaan and I, Pieter by his side, our arms draped over each other's shoulders. We smile at the camera: four tanned, salt-scrubbed faces. This remains the only photograph I have of all of us together.

Riaan reverses out of the driveway so fast two black rubber burn marks are instantly imprinted on the concrete driveway. The wheels say words like *hunger, lean, never*. Words Pieter deploys in his novels.

His rough laugh. *It's time to go.*

The world falls silent again. The only sound the emerald sea.

We were supposed to return to the city the day after Riaan left. But Pieter and Sara made phone calls. 'We can stay a few days longer,' Pieter announced. The relief on their faces was so graphic I wondered what they were avoiding. It felt more than mere pressures of work.

In those days I can't seem to settle. I go for long walks as we did, trying to emulate Riaan's swinging stride, his racehorse ankles. An unhappiness crashes onto me and I sit down in a heap in the sand, a pain at the base of my spine. I walk back ignoring the landscape which only a few days ago so entranced me, the wild coastal roses, the soaring sand dunes, the salt-scrubbed sky.

On my last night in the house I can't sleep. Outside the waves come ashore, punching and punching their way into the land. I wake up, my heart pounding. At dawn I get up and raid the kitchen. I imagine Riaan there, up already, reading the newspaper, just as when he first arrived. On one of those mornings at the beginning of his visit he had looked up at me and said, 'I know you think my parents are cosseted. They've always had each other and you hold that against them.' He slid his eyes away from my stare. 'I like you,' he said. 'But you want something from my parents. I wonder what it is?'

# X

We returned to the city and rare summer days with no wind. We woke in the mornings to a fine haze settled in the streets. Guinea fowl trotted down the driveway, looking for water. Twice we found them congregated around Pieter and Sara's pool, a gaggle of teenagers wetting their feathers and preening.

I went for walks on the mountain and passed the forest fire alert dial, a billboard with a moveable arrow on it and a pie chart in segments coloured green, yellow, orange and red. The arrow pointed to the red segment, titled Maximum Danger.

After a couple of these walks I returned dizzy from the heat. I took to venturing out only at dusk. It was too hot to go running on the mountain. I'd been warned, too, by a neighbour of Pieter and Sara's, about the cobras. They were emerging from the bush desperate to find water, it seemed. You could easily step across one on the path, so quick you wouldn't realise it, but if it bit you could be dead in a matter of minutes. I couldn't believe cobras would be lounging underfoot only a few metres from the house. It took seeing two of them in quick succession, their hooded heads raised periscope-like above the spindled grass, to convince me.

Instead I went running around the giant reservoir. There herons made Concorde landings on the surface. The concrete pavements that encircled it were encrusted with rotting banana tree leaves and chocolate-coloured seed pods that looked like boomerangs.

I was just getting around to booking my ticket home. It was still high season and seats were hard to find. I'd settled on a date the following week, but when it was time to pay my finger hovered on the mouse, itself floating over the 'pay now' button, and I let the booking lapse.

The page glared at me. The title appeared in capitals. *THE PERMIAN ERA*.

*The geologist came to stay with them in late November. She was a friend of their daughter's, that was all they knew. They were accustomed to receiving visitors from abroad. His eminence as an archaeologist assured him of a steady stream of visiting professors, graduate students, foreign experts who came for reasons he soon sniffed out – fact-finding missions, divorce evasions, northern hemisphere fatigue.*

*This one was not so easy to dissect. She said she was in town on an academic exchange programme, for an 'indefinite period of time'. The phrase hooked in his ear. Who came on an academic exchange indefinitely? Visas, university bureaucracy saw to it that no such dimension existed.*

*On an obscure impulse – what else did he have to show her – he took her to see his office on the day after she arrived.*

*'It's so full' – she paused for a moment. 'Of important things.'*

*'Isn't yours?'*

*'No, mine's – rather impersonal.'*

*'Well we must fix that,' he said, as if he would have a hand in changing the atmosphere of an office nine thousand miles away.*

*He wondered again about the real reason this young woman had washed up on their shores. There was a lie within her, or if not a lie then an evasion. It intrigued and unsettled him. He told himself he had no interest in secrets, but when they were harboured by young women a strange animal instinct was sparked within him.*

*She didn't seem to know what to do with herself next. There was something of the vortex around her, as if she had no past, and no future. He felt the urge to give her that – a future – but what price he would charge, he didn't know. He felt that peculiar frisson that came from being around a person who, for whatever reason, reminded you that there is no protection in life, no guarantees. As if her vulnerability would infect him like a disease.*

Upstairs the door opened. Pieter and Sara clattered into the hallway in a rush of keys and purses. I had no good reason to be in his office; there was nowhere I could hide.

I bounded up the stairs. My only hope was to say I came in looking for them about something urgent – I could not find the dog anywhere, I decided this was the worry, and had come downstairs to Pieter's study to look for her.

I emerged. Surprise and then annoyance flickered through their eyes. I launched into a volley of explanations: dog, worry, company. 'Oh', is all Pieter said. Then he smiled – an automatic, flickering smile.

Later, there was a knock at the door. I could see through the glass that it was Pieter. I opened the door.

'Why have you turned me into a woman?'

He gave me the strangest look. Puzzlement mixed with affront. A parental look.

'I've become a woman and you've become a scientist.'

'There is no *me* and *you*,' he said levelly. 'There is only fiction. It's not real.' His voice said: *get over it*.

I waited a suitable amount of time, then went out and got in the car I had rented for my last few days in the city, so I could get to know it before I left. I coasted down the driveway in neutral, hoping they would not hear me leave. I drove up to the road that snakes around the mountain, parked the car under two tall trees and got out. In front of me the city lay bathed in that late evening light of mauve and dusty silver.

I had gone for years and years without feeling shame. Now it was my constant companion. Behind it was a desire to find favour – with Pieter, more than Sara, who did not trouble me in the same way her husband did. The story he was writing confirmed my suspicion that Pieter saw me as a son, a protégé, a student. This was his due; he was thirty years older than me, he was a national figure. He had hacked through an emotional undergrowth I would never dare venture into. He had done that lethal moral arithmetic, beliefs versus safety, conscience versus family, freedom versus guilt. He knew what he valued in this life. Why shouldn't he take a pastoral attitude to me? What more did I want?

I sat there for a long time, until it was dark, watching the car headlights curl around the headland on the opposite side of the harbour. Eventually a security car showed up and a man shouted out the window. 'I'd go now if I were you. It's not safe here.'

The next day two emails arrive. One is from Riaan, the other from my employer. Riaan's email is titled *INVITATION TO PARADISE*. I read it quickly. *It should take two weeks, max, but why not come for three or four? This place gets under your skin*.

As I read Riaan's email I begin to see the desert as just that: skin, a pink-ochre hand, fingers of dunes gripping an inconsolable sea.

It is not difficult to explain my professional interest in Riaan's project to Pieter and Sara. I've worked in NGOs for six years now, I say. I may need to soon change direction in my career. Plus I'd like to see the desert, it's geology.

Their faces are open, delighted. Go, they say, go, and I am reminded they are honest people, they have been good to me, better than my own family. They may even be family. I tell them I'll miss them but I'll be back within the month.

You'll be amazed by where he lives, Pieter says. You'll come back a different person.

But I sense Pieter is unhappy with me. There is a suspicious curve to his gaze.

The other message crouches underneath Riaan's in my inbox. I assume it is another threat, or at least a confirmation of my suspension without pay. In its subject line are the words *CONFIDENTIAL: Kassala Mission*. I know what it contains, but do not want to know it for real, to have it imprinted upon me, forever. I close my eyes, as if steeling myself for a rough landing in a plane, and click.

# Part II

# I

The plane keeled in over a cold ocean. We landed in a sandstorm, with what the pilot helpfully informed us was only two miles visibility. For a while there was a question if we would be able to land at all – sand can stall aircraft engines – or if we would be diverted to the capital. *Don't worry*, the pilot said over the intercom, his voice drawling with easy command. *The engines can take it*.

If the wheels of a plane leaving the ground was once my favourite feeling, it's now when they meet the ground. I breathed once more as gravity grabbed us out of the air.

Rose-coloured sand stretched to all horizons. A single airport official wearing a high-vis jacket and a knitted hat appeared on the left wing of the plane. The sea fog and moist sand left an instant smudge on the window. I had read that the sea off the coast came directly from Antarctica and was chilled by melting ice. Somewhere beyond the perimeter of sea fog, the sun pounded into the desert. I could just make out its pewter halo.

I switched on my phone and a text from Riaan appeared on the screen: *Gone up country to project, sorry, emergency. Take a taxi and I'll catch up with you tomorrow*.

It was forty minutes into Nova Friburgo, the town where he lived. Before I knew it I was speeding through a corridor of lordly sand dunes. From the air they had looked uniform, a flat carpet of sand, but now that I was moving among them they towered over the taxi. There were the dunes that moved with the wind, and those that were so big they remained, like mountains. These dunes had numbers: Dune 5, Dune 8. Petrol tankers and long-distance trucks streamed by, coating the windshield with sand. The driver flicked the wipers over the screen dry. 'If you use the window-cleaning fluid the sand gums in your wipers,' he said. Between the dunes I saw flashes of the cold Atlantic rolling ashore in long unbroken waves.

Suddenly we were in a town. Between the desert and the town there was no boundary. The sand ran into the streets, thinning, until eventually asphalt emerged beneath its blanket. The houses were squat and built of wood. One was a bright pink and blue, its paint blistering in the sun. They looked like solid structures, yet I had the impression they could be packed up, folded away and the desert would encroach. By the following day there would be only sand.

We slowed to drive over a hump. 'What's that?'

'The pipeline,' the driver said, swerving to avoid hitting a single horned goat that had wandered out from the front yard of one of the wooden mansions. 'It brings water to the town. It's the only supply.'

'Where does it come from?'

'The uranium mine.'

'And where is that?'

'Two hundred kilometres inland. Not much water around in a desert, as it turns out.'

'Do you mean a town of some forty thousand people relies on a single pipeline for water?'

'That's about it, yes.'

'What happens if it breaks?'

The driver shrugged. 'Then there is no water.'

After I checked in to the hotel – a gloomy Teutonic guesthouse which could easily be in Salzburg or Munich – I went for a walk. Riaan had warned me about the climate. The sun was somewhere behind clouds but I could feel it corkscrewing through my head. The town was notorious for bestowing the worst sunburn of peoples' lives, he'd told me: 'It's so cold people don't feel themselves frying.'

Palm trees formed a kind of causeway up the centre of the main street, drooping with dust and cold. People dressed in parkas, hoods up, hands shoved in pockets, passed. I searched for their faces inside their hoods. Some of them were white, all with a curious consistency to their skin, brittle, caramel at the edges, like overcooked puff pastry. I passed hardware shops with black cooking pots and barbecues in their windows. On each street corner buff-coloured businesses flogged Desert Adventures.

I turned and looked down the main avenue, away from the sea, to an astonishing sight. At the edges of the town the suburban houses of pale peach or rose ended and the desert began. There, in the direction of the airport, a dune brooded over the town, throbbing with gold. I couldn't see the sunset – it was lost in a blanket of coastal fog – but the sand mountain caught its reflection and threw an amber light back onto the town.

*Where have I come to?* I thought. The voice that answered was mine, ostensibly, but also Riaan's. Even though he was absent, I could feel the town speaking for him. It said, *welcome to the moon.*

The next day there was still no news from Riaan. He was out of cellphone range, I supposed. There were whole swathes of the north without electricity, running water or mobile phone masts, I knew. Still, I worried he had forgotten about me.

I decided to go for a walk on the beach. I discovered a pier, the kind you see in south coast cities in England. But this pier was small and constructed of greying wood. I found the staircase and stood at the railing above.

The sea rolled ashore in long muscular waves. They broke, kelp-laden, pummelling the wooden pier so hard it felt it would snap in two. There was a promenade along the oceanfront, lined by beach houses painted in faded tutti-frutti colours, but which were all closed. I clambered down the stairs to the beach. From above it had looked inviting. But now I could see it sloped precipitously. I tried to walk next to the shore but the tug of the wet sand and the incline pulled me toward the sea. Birds – gulls? Arctic terns? – dive bombed me. I struggled up the shore in thick wet sand. For a second I worried I wouldn't make it.

'Hey,' I felt a hand on my shoulder. 'You can fall in here you know.'

I stumbled and turned. There was dust in his hair. I stared at its grains, how the sun was filtered through it. 'How did you find me?'

'There's not a lot of places to be in this town. I looked in the supermarket, the café, and then came here. Third time lucky.' Riaan tugged me up the beach. 'The slope here is a killer. Before you know it you're in the sea and getting wrecked by waves. When did you arrive?'

'When I told you I would.'

He heard the hurt in my voice. 'I'm sorry I couldn't be here. I had to go up to the project, one of my staff was sick. I had no choice. Believe me, if I could have been here to meet you I would have.'

I swallowed. I had no idea I'd been so angry he wasn't here to meet me. The thought careening, as if I were drunk: *Get a grip, Nick.*

'Come on, I'll walk you back to the hotel.'

We walked along the promenade in front of the boarded-up beach houses. Men patrolled the avenue selling carved conkers. On them were carved miniature elephants and rhinoceroses. Sandy trucks, their yellow fog lights illuminated, crawled through the streets. Tourists emerged from the town's hotels and pulled their coats around their shoulders.

'So, what do you think?'

'It's the strangest place I've ever been,' I say. 'Hands down.'

'It is, isn't it? To think I've spent seven years of my life here.'

A presence made its impress on me in an abstract way. I

felt I might be crushed, walking down that street, the Atlantic on one side and a desert on the other, trapped between two immensities.

Riaan was changed, if only subtly, since I had seen him only weeks ago in Cabo Frio. He was tanned and slightly thinner. He walked with that clipped purposeful stride I remembered, a moving exclamation mark.

He caught me studying him. There was a perplexed look on his face, and within it, something unstable, a fleet definitive flicker.

'You know, at first I thought you were some kind of impostor.'

I stopped in my tracks. 'Why?'

'My parents were so impressed with you. It's been years since they've felt that way about anyone.'

'And that made you think I was some sort of interloper?'

'No, it was that they couldn't get a handle on you. In emails or phone calls they would say, "We have this man staying with us. He's Spanish. No, English. No. Canadian. Actually we don't know where he's from." What did you expect me to think?'

'That they had met an interesting person who had grown up all over the world. Someone you might like.'

'They did say that. They said, you'll like him, he's in the same line of work.'

'But we're not at all.'

'My parents think charity is all the same, whether you're saving refugees or cheetahs.'

'I think you need to give them more credit.'

'There's one thing you need to know about my parents: they are not political. It's just not in their nature. They pretend to be, but they're in the wrong country. Wrong time, wrong place.'

'But your father is a writer. Of course he's political. And anyway, what does it matter to you if they are or aren't?'

He peered at me. 'You love them.'

The sea wind clawed at my hair. We had been together only a few minutes and already I wondered if I were up to whatever challenge Riaan would set me, set us. Somehow, in Riaan's company, everything became a drama of choice, of black and white, of courage or cowardice. I should just go back to the city, to Pieter and Sara's house, I thought, the sundowner drinks over the harbour, the air-conditioned shopping malls selling sourdough bread and blueberry smoothies.

'I do,' I faced up to him. 'I have never met kinder people.'

'It's easy to be kind to strangers.'

'Yes of course. All families are like that – kind to strangers, unkind to themselves.' I felt a surge of impatience. 'What's this about, Riaan?'

'My parents respect us, people like you and me. But they feel bested by us.'

'You don't have to turn it into an us and them.'

He was impassioned now, or angry. In him they looked the same. 'Their worlds are all about self-expression, feelings. I think they wonder if there's anything there, really. I wonder if they know that action is character. If you never do anything, you never become anyone.' His voice trotted, a strange stuttering gait. I would come to know this happened whenever Riaan was speaking of something he wanted to believe in absolutely but of which he was ultimately not convinced. 'On some level my father realises his books have never benefited anyone, not in the real world.'

'But how can you know that – how can he – how can *anyone* – know that?'

'I can't stand the way he grasps at everything you say and takes it inside himself to be ground into meaning until there's nothing left. No bloody *life*! You realise you're just material for him, don't you?'

'Would that be so terrible?'

He did not reply. I felt a pang of a sadness on Pieter and Sara's behalf. Did they know their son held them in disdain? Perhaps they did, and that was why they kept their distance from him while at the same time orbiting him, pulled in by his gravity, two satellite moons.

We stopped talking. The sun had disappeared behind a milky film of cloud. Without it the wind was instantly cold. We stood in silence, leaning into the wind.

'I had this feeling, you know, the night before I met you,' Riaan said. 'It just came to me. I said to myself, something's going to change.'

'But then you met me and you thought I was an *impostor*.'

'Impostors can be exciting.'

His eyes were flat and cool, like the sea. The gathering dusk had the effect of smoothing out its edges into long contours, like giant oxbow rivers. It might have had the same effect on Riaan over the years he had lived here, sculpting his mind as much as his body in these same shapes, his sickle-shaped calves, those slim, surprisingly delicate fingers, the sandbars of his shoulders.

We stared out to sea, watching as night colonised the sky and the waves dashed their heads on the shore.

The next day is a blur, the shock of what happened between us has carved it into separate slices of memory.

He delivers me to my hotel with a promise to meet me the following afternoon. I will meet his girlfriend, his friends. Then in two days we will drive into the desert. Riaan will take me to a school his project runs in the far north, near the border.

Beyond this, I don't know what will happen. I feel alarmed, to be so totally under the power of circumstance. My job may require me to face chaos but I am the one in charge, it is my role to command the situation. Here, there is a headlong quality to people's lives. I felt that even in Pieter and Sara's house, it is even in the muscular hedonism of their city. They throw themselves into the swimming pool of life, rather than standing on the edges, filling out insurance claim forms, calculating career moves and pensions.

In my hotel room I wait for whatever will happen next. Strange sounds fill my ears at night. The air is very dry and the sea a distant grumble. Some sort of nightjar trills in the hour before dawn. I wonder again, where I have come to? I know well enough, I can find it on the map: Nova Friburgo, a coastal town nearly a thousand kilometres north from Pieter and Sara's house. Here we are closer to the tropics, but it is as if I've come to Mongolia, or the Sudan. This place grafted from some other reality onto this country. Apart from the indestructible German mansions, the town could be folded away in minutes and shipped somewhere else.

As for Riaan, in Cabo Frio I felt bested by him but not vulnerable to him, because his parents stood between him and me and I knew they would protect me, even though he was their son. Now that distinction has been sewn shut.

That night I wake up out of nowhere at three in the morning and go to stand at the window. Small arrow-shaped bodies fly from the eaves to the tree in the courtyard and back, as if on a reconnaissance mission – bats. I look up just in time to see a shooting star tear a streak in the sky.

*Nox* – Latin for night. I like its shuttered, claustrophobic sound. It has something of the vigil in it. How many nights have I spent like this, in a torn mountain towns in the Balkans or in the brackish capitals of West Africa, standing next to a window or a door or even the opening of a tent, unable to sleep. There is an ancient summons in these jolt awakenings, surely, a call to vigilance, like spells which have the power to turn back the sun.

# 11

'It will be like Libya, only worse.' Major Porteous was clutching his drink. I noticed his knuckles were white. He gave the glass a suspicious look before upending its contents into his mouth.

'Do you mean a crazed dictator with teenaged sex slaves in his basement and female bodyguards?' I asked.

'I'm serious. Watch out for the cripples in the dock. There's a band of them. Don't let the wheelchairs and crutches fool you. They've got machetes, grenades, even AKs. There's even a legless guy on a skateboard. They drop their crutches and that's your signal to run. It's like Mad Max there.'

His eye snagged on a glamorous woman in a black halter neck dress with a severe, over-made up face. He turned and, without saying goodbye, followed her.

I went out onto the afterdeck and remained there for the rest of the reception, conspicuously companionless. The bar was inside a mini-marquee but the tables were under the stars, which burned in an oceanic night sky. There was no moon. A wedge was cut out of the stars; this was the seam of the mountain against the sky.

We awoke the next morning to the sight of containers still lined up on the pier. The cargo holds were half-filled. It was gusting to 45 knots and the container vessel which had brought the food and tents from Europe could not come alongside the docks to be unloaded. In this wind the cranes that winch cargo from the ship to shore were unreliable, and the last thing you wanted was a container weighing several tons swinging above your head.

The purser came on the tannoy and summoned us all to a briefing. The first officer told us that delays aboard the ship were extremely rare. Every day we spent in port was a day when people were dying. 'You can imagine, my head is full of red crosses right now.'

I turned to Ernst. 'You think he means *black* crosses?'

Ernst frowned. 'I don't know.'

We would be in port for at least another two days, the first officer told us. To pass the time Ernst and I went shopping in the warren-like quayside shopping mall, buying months of toiletries to add to our stash, just in case we were mandated to stay at Kisamu into the summer – a distinct possibility, if what we heard about the relief effort was true. Then we queued in the hold of the ship, buying mineral water and beer for our fridges from the purser's assistant.

Even now, odd details come back to me from those days: the purser's assistant wore white Birkenstocks; the captain, an unusually thin man, for a ship's captain (all that physical confinement and good food); going running on the promenade snaking along Ocean Point and thinking it was the last time I would run for many weeks.

It began the first day of our delay, the day I went shopping and running. At first it was a sense of dislocation, nothing more serious. My eye was drawn again and again to the mountain. I turned toward it no matter where I was in the city, a compass needle seeking direction. Through my binoculars I watched black eagles launch themselves from its ramparts. I thought how, if we had more time, I would have gone for a walk on the hiking trails that wound up and down it. *But you do have time*, a voice said – the voice I would come to associate with what was about to happen to me. The immigration authorities have stamped me out of the country, I replied. It's too much hassle to exit, then get a re-entry visa.

I had that feeling which had struck me when I spoke to Carlos that first night aboard, only now it had focussed on me. I felt myself fading out of the picture with each minute that passed. People who I met only the day before greeted me blankly in the corridors. Even the ship didn't recognise me. I got lost on the way to my cabin, then realised I was on the wrong deck.

I caught a snippet of conversation from an open cabin as I passed between a worried voice and a resolute one. 'Six days up a coast studded with pirates,' the worried voice said.

'I still don't understand why then can't fly us in.'

'You want to get shot down? They've not RPGs. Believe me, this was the only way.'

'We're just doing our job,' a resolute voice said.

I thought of our office, so far away now, a distant Mother Ship pirouetting in space. It was located in one of those regenerated London neighbourhoods, formerly empty Victorian office buildings and eel and mash shops now being slowly devoured by organic supermarkets. It was a hushed citadel of endeavour where we watched as a digital river of messages coursed down the computer screen: lunchtime seminars, workshops on human dignity, safety in the field seminars.

Gemma was there, her dark gloss of hair, her gossamer neck. She was a policy analyst with degrees from Cambridge and Yale, a killer duo if there ever was one. She was one of those effortlessly cool Englishwomen who are reared hydroponically somewhere in limp shires studded with bohemian private schools and wedding marquees. Her emotions rattled like cutlery in drawers. No amount of beguilement deafened me to the fact that I could hear whether she'd decided a knife, fork or spoon should be deployed. She had an unerring instinct for how to apportion her affections – who would prove useful to her if they thought they had a chance, who could be manipulated, who could be frozen out.

She seemed to think I was worth talking to – 'Well, you're the best-looking guy on the floor,' said Hassan, the Algerian country officer, with a shrug in his voice, when I asked his advice as to why. I watched as Gemma stalked the purple corridors of our department. She was too beautiful to work for us. We are the sort of organisation that quickly turns attractive young women into older women with deep frown lines and frizzy hair. Outside our office eyes electronic watched us like guard dogs on swivel rotate. We were frequently the target of terrorist attack; at least various groups we had enraged by saving their victims kept announcing they would bomb the building, but it never happened. Perhaps they got waylaid in the organic supermarkets on the way.

I'd been with the organisation five years, and based back in the headquarters for two, running logistics in the field only when there was no one else available. I'd become fond of my London life, of its regularity and predictability: my commute on the Piccadilly line, my boxed lunches from the Mexican food stall at the outdoor market.

The organisation dealt only in the evils of the world: war, poverty, arms dealing, female genital mutilation, discrimination, genocide, surveillance. Coming to work every day was like waking up to new iterations of dystopia: bioweapons, iris scans, superbugs. Each day I went to work to find the future already installed at my desk. It was time I went back to the field, I decided. Life was simpler there: a satellite phone, instant coffee and dried milk, AK47s waved in my face. All very routine.

Two days later, the email arrived: *mission head required, Kassala*. Gemma deigned to speak to me that day and came to stand tantalisingly near me, over my right shoulder.

'Nice place,' she said, her voice easy with knowledge. 'Before the war. At least I've seen photos – jade green swimming pools, palm trees. A lot of sharks, though. They used to butcher camels on the beach and the sharks got a taste for the meat.'

She had an exceptional voice – like smooth-running caramel, poised but not over-schooled or arched, as those well-bred Englishwomen often are. 'Thanks. That's all very reassuring.'

'If it's reassurance you want,' she laughed, 'you're in the wrong business.'

She made her exit then, perfectly timed. I watched her walk down the hallway. She was wearing a halter necked top – it was an unusually warm autumn day, and the heat always rose to our fourth-floor office area. Her shoulder muscles rippled.

Some women had the effortless ability to communicate impossibility. It was like a metal taste in your mouth, the fact that you would never – or at least it was very unlikely – possess them. I wasn't talking about sexual possession, more that you would never ignite that cold fire at the heart of their being. Gemma's nickname among the male researchers was Thin White Duchess, after David Bowie's Aryan nation persona in the Seventies. She had a hint of the planar otherworldliness of Bowie's face.

'She likes you,' Hassan whispered from across the screen that divided our desks. 'It's your air of mysterious hurt.' He winked.

Enough time had passed now – two years – that some people, Hassan included, would make these oblique references to how my last relationship had ended. How she had ended. I hadn't displayed any outward signs of distress. I hadn't had time off work, or gone to counselling. I suppose they thought I was safe.

# III

The bar was called Las Brisas. It was mostly outside, surrounded by thatched windbreaks, perched on the beach. Over the tops of the windbreaks the setting sun hovered above the ocean. I watched its progression. It started out as a familiar force, but by the time it touched the ocean it looked like a meteor, striped with red and yellow bands. What I witnessed then was like no sunset I'd ever seen. The departure of the sun felt like a desertion, a terminal abandonment. When it plunged into the Atlantic I wondered if it really would return.

'Nick, Tanya. Tanya, Nick.'

I found myself grasping a woman's hand before I even knew it was there.

Concern flashed across her face. 'Are you alright?'

'Just a muscle spasm, sorry.' I sat down next to Riaan, still dazed by the spectacle I had just witnessed. The bar was full of versions of Riaan – who he might have been, or yet become: leonine men with hair down to their shoulders, beefy men of fifty, so tanned their skin was nearly black, staring with tourmaline eyes, roaring at each other over the distant-traffic sound of the sea.

'So you know Pieter and Sara,' Tanya began. I realised Riaan hadn't told her how we met. He may not have told her anything of Cabo Frio at all. I had imagined him talking about me all the time.

'That's right. Riaan and I met in Cabo Frio at Christmas,' I said. At this, Riaan stood up with a jolt. He hadn't been listening, I thought – he was talking to someone else as Tanya and I greeted to each other. 'I'm going to get a beer. You want anything?' His eyes fell on the square of table in front of Tanya.

Tanya turned her eyes on me, extending the offer Riaan failed to make. 'Nick? Something to drink?'

'No, I'll get my own in a bit.'

'No thanks. I'm off the booze, you know that.' After he had left she gave me another seamless smile. 'He's careless sometimes,' she said. 'Don't worry about it.'

The pain I felt when I first took Tanya's hand shot through my heart again, as if carried on an arrow. *He has deliberately not asked me if I would like a drink. But why?* Then, quickly, a hardening. The wound closed.

More friends of Riaan and Tanya's – tall, tanned people like them – arrived. Riaan ensconced himself with them while Tanya was left to mind me.

Everything I noticed about him that evening at Las Brisas I had perceived before in Cabo Frio, but now there was a cast of loss to them: the over-vigorous way he gripped his glass, the restlessness that gathered at the core of him, the reckless disdain in his gaze, which travelled freely. When it alighted on something or someone he liked he made no effort to disguise it. Such people are hunters, never satisfied with what fate delivers to them. Yet his hands were those of a more recalcitrant person – a pianist, a surgeon: thoughtful fingers, capable of repair.

I turned back to Tanya. She was beautiful, in a salt-scrubbed way. There were fine lines around her eyes, which were the same radical blue as Pieter's. Her hair was dark blonde. She was wearing a shawl which slipped from her shoulders from time to time. They were powerful, like a man's. She looked like a surfer, or some supremely capable female athlete.

'How did you meet?' I asked.

'Oh, so long ago it hardly matters.' She smiled. She had

clever, lovely teeth with a gap in the middle of the two front incisors. 'At high school.'

'Oh yes, I went there with Pieter and Sara. For a concert.'

'It has a great auditorium. And fantastic views. I took it for granted, seeing the ocean every day from the classroom.'

I thought of the night Pieter and Sara and I had gone to hear chamber music. Even though it was a public school, Pieter told me that you only went to that school if your father was in the government, or the Army, or important, as Pieter was, even if he was technically of the wrong political stripe. Now, he said, the school was a liberal, multi-racial school, a whitewashed three-storey structure, surrounded by hacked-at banana plants that grew at a supernatural speed and defeated the army of gardeners the school governors employed on breadline wages.

'What was he like, then?'

'Very different. He's much calmer now.'

I thought of the younger version of Riaan I had seen tacked up on Pieter's office bulletin board: his hair longer and lighter. The way he stared the camera down in the photo, as if it were an adversary.

Riaan held up his cellphone to us all assembled around the table. 'Our table's ready,' he shouted. I walked with Tanya to their truck. Their friends piled in before we arrived and with Tanya there, there was no room in the cab. 'I'll walk,' I said. 'I'll catch you up.'

'No, don't be stupid,' Riaan said, instead of *silly*, as one would say in England. 'It's too far to walk. Hop up in the flatbed. It's a long walk but a short drive.'

Tanya smiled encouragingly as she slid into the passenger seat. 'Hop on the back Nick,' she said. 'Everyone does it here.' As she said the words I heard the voice which spoke to me only when I was working, in those quicksilver moments when circumstances can shift to reveal danger. It asked me, *what's going on, here?*

We drove through town, me hanging onto the rim of the

flatbed. The people in the cab did not look back to make sure I was still there. I suppose they thought it was safe – as Tanya said, everyone rode like this here, although when you saw a white person in the back of a truck it was a lark while black people in the backs of trucks were almost always being carted to work.

At the restaurant we took our places around a large round table. Riaan sat on the other side, too far from me to speak to comfortably. But then we all shifted seats so that Tanya and a friend could talk, and he and I ended up next to each other. He leant away from me; a subtle list, like a boat into the wind. To my right was his friend Richard, who worked as a wildlife guide. He told me the dramatic stories he likely reserved for such occasions as this – dinners with impressionable strangers from effete countries. 'Once, a lioness stalked me,' he said. He did not see her until she was ready to spring. Once a brown hyena stole his lunch from under his nose on the beach.

Richard answered my questions in a friendly way, without expectation. Riaan's banishment began to feel all the more brutal. I'd taken far, far tougher medicine than what he was dishing out, of course. I'd been ignored by dignitaries and the celebrities who came to visit my camps, I'd been shot at enough times I no longer bothered to count, I'd even been gouged with a homemade bayonet once. I'd learned I had an odd relationship to violence; physical violence made less an impression on me than its emotional strain.

As soon as our plates were cleared, I pleaded a headache. I said goodbye to everyone at once, not lingering on anyone's face. From the corner of my eye I saw Riaan inclined away, talking to the waitress.

Tanya looked at me – evenly, I would have said. She must have been wondering what kind of friends we really were.

I walked out of the restaurant and into a cold night. The smashed kelp smell on the wind, the sea fog knitting itself between palm fronds, the limbs of those hunched figures who walked down the street, hoods over their heads in defence against the cold – why had I been brought to this place?

I thought back to Cabo Frio, the drastic loneliness of that coast. In our fireside conversations at Cabo Frio Riaan had spoken of this place as a hard paradise. How it felt less real than imaginary, even while you were living here, created from an idea only to be later abandoned, a place of rumour and exile to where people moved reluctantly or shuttled through, searching for solace of a category they might not recognise when they found it.

Now I was here I could see it was a solemn, elemental, yes, and that this would suit him, how in its reduced nature – sand, sea, the sky, the moon, the precious rain – there could be a kind of succour.

Yes, tomorrow I would leave this place, and never return.

'Hey!'

It was Riaan, loping after me.

'Hey!' he said again, when I did not turn.

A hand gripped my shoulder.

'I'm sorry.'

'What about?' My voice was tight.

'Tanya and I – we're going through a hard time. We have been, for the past year. That's what I said to you in Cabo Frio – it's been lonely. She's been – we've been – trying to get pregnant.'

The genuine chord in his voice disarmed me. Still, his explanation was a kind of lie. 'Your problem isn't with her, it's with me.'

'No, that's not true.' He had the good grace to look down. 'She's very unhappy. I just can't tell anyone. So I thrust it onto you. I'm sorry.'

'Don't mistake me for your *girlfriend*.' I heard the bite in my own voice.

Shock simmered in his eyes like a low blue flame. A small nod – an acknowledgement to himself, maybe. Then he turned on his heel. The sand actually flew from underneath his boot, he'd moved so fast.

I watched him walk away with his quick martinet gait. I could have salvaged the situation, but I chose not to. That was how Riaan learned there were some things I did not forgive.

As it turned out I couldn't get a flight home – there was no space on the plane for the next two days, something about every available seat being taken up by the employees of a mining multinational travelling to a regional conference. To drive back to the coast would have taken me two days minimum over lonely desert roads. I would need jerrycans of fuel and water and international driver's insurance. So I had to stay and wait for a place on the daily flight.

I spent most of the next day in the town's one bookshop, hiding from the sun. The owner had skin the same crème caramel colour I'd seen on other whites in town.

'What brings you here?' he asked. 'Are you going up to the game park?'

'No, I'm here to visit a friend. He works here.'

'Who's that? Riaan Lisson?'

I must have looked surprised.

He shrugged. 'It's a small town.'

'Do you know him?'

'Yes, of course. He is one of our best customers. I'm always ordering books from Europe for him.'

'What sort of books?' I tried to keep my voice as neutral as possible. I didn't want him to think I was spying. 'I mean, what sort of books can't you get here?'

'Well if you want hunting manuals and wildlife guides, this is definitely your place. But literature – Riaan reads very off-the-beaten-track stuff. He has great taste.'

'His father is a writer,' I said.

'Yes, sure. Everyone knows who his father is.'

'Well, I'll have a look around.'

The man made a sweeping gesture. 'It's all yours.'

And it was. No customer entered the shop in the hour I stayed. I bought four books and took them to my hotel to read. At eight o'clock in the evening hunger drove me out onto the streets. I couldn't afford the hotel restaurant and the only thing I could find to eat were warmed-over pasties in the 24-hour gas station. I bought one, a bag of crisps and a bottle of coke and retreated to my room, passing through the lobby of fake and real palms, of women just flown in from Germany with their blonde hair and gold sandals. The following day these women would appear in the lobby, draped in Ralph Lauren safari gear.

At ten o'clock there was a knock on my door. Riaan's voice reached me, muffled, through it. 'Nick.'

'Yes.'

'Could you open the door?'

I swung it open, the blood in my throat. 'Don't come here sounding exasperated when I don't open the door quickly enough.'

He dropped his gaze. 'Look, I'm sorry. I shouldn't drink. I'd had too many.'

'That's not true, Riaan.'

His eyes scanned the hallway on either side of him, as if he were afraid of being seen. 'Can I come in?'

I held the door open for him. He went straight to the mini-bar, grabbed a beer and sat on the bed. 'I don't know what to tell you, man.' He ran a hand through his hair. 'I was always volatile, I remember my father telling me that. But I haven't been, not for a long time. I know how that must have been for you last night. I invite you all the way up here and you pay the money to come and then – then.'

'Then you push me away.'

I sat down opposite him. I leaned forward, put my hands on my knees – a negotiating position I had learned and used for great effect in my job.

'Look Riaan, maybe it's for the best. It's time for me to stop drifting forward in my life. I've got to pick up the pieces of what's happened and go home. I realise that now. I've booked a seat for tomorrow.'

He put his beer down. 'No, no, man. You can't do that. You've come all this way and now you're going to go back without seeing this place?'

It occurred to me that he was worried about what his parents would say. They would realise something had gone wrong between us, and this would confirm a suspicion they had long harboured about their son.

'I won't tell Pieter and Sara. I'll make something up. Emergency back in Europe. That sort of thing. I'm good at flying off at short notice to deal with emergencies.'

His face looked thinner, somehow, than even the day before. No-one lost weight that quickly. It must have been the light. Or, under the desert sun, we were all diminishing, shrinking from its blare.

'So you're decided, then.'

'You didn't give me any choice.'

He stood up. I realised he was going to leave, with nothing more said between us.

'Look Riaan, we're not children. I've been the head of logistics for a major aid agency for years. I am – I was – a capable, responsible person. I'm regressing, somehow, here. I want to go back to being myself.'

'And what does that mean? Being in control all the time?'

'I guess.' This sounded too hesitant, so I added, in as firm a voice as I could muster, 'Yes.'

'Let me show you where I work. But you won't be able to control much. Even I won't, and I've lived here for years. You're going to have to just let things happen. Let yourself live, for once.'

'I've done more living than you think.'

'Stay here, with me.' He countered.

If he'd said, only, *stay here*, I would have left.

I didn't move, or say anything. That was how he knew I'd accepted.

'I'll pick you up tomorrow.' His voice had lightened.

'I need to change my flight again.'

'That's easy. We can pass by the office on our way out of town.'

We stood facing each other in that strange resort hotel which doubled as a casino, the *ching* of the one-armed-bandits below my room ringing in our ears.

After he'd left I saw his beer on the floor. I picked it up, turned it around and around. The pulse of a foreign hope moved through me. I set the bottle on the table, lay down on the bed and stared at it until I fell asleep.

I am twenty-seven and working in Brazzaville, my first posting of any length, a six-month stint which turns effortlessly into two years. There is something about the Congo that attracts extreme itinerants. I have already become aware of an emptiness in how I am living but which I am not prepared to forsake for a more settled, comfortable life. England makes me feel as if someone is throttling me, constantly, squeezing the air out of my lungs.

Over the years my aversion to normal templates of existence turns into a kind of addiction to desperation and turmoil. It fuels me with conviction and enough energy to deliver me to the next temporary obsession.

The people I work with are cut from the same cloth – they fall into two neat camps: young, elaborately educated cosmopolitans, or forty-something women with no children and an identifiable source of money behind them – parents with flats in New York, farmhouses in northern Italy. It was in these they stay, when they are not sorting out the calamity of Africa.

I accompany these women to ethnic drumming classes, to overpriced restaurants near the giant river. I might be ardently desired by some of them, but there is so little interest on my side I never give it any thought. In the bars they watch me closely for signs of vice. But I only ever drink two beers a night. This is unusual; many of my peers are addicted to something – Valium, painkillers, weed, alcohol.

I drive roads that bristle with bandits, smoking with evaporated rain, rain that the second it hits the tarmac becomes steam. I used to pull over to the side to watch the rain vanish in between the thirty or forty roadblocks I would have to negotiate on a typical trip, my currency of cheap Scotch clinking on the back seat.

All the time I feel I am being conveyed through this experience by an impersonal force. What most people refer to as choice and desire are for me only a series of storms gathering and dispersing. As for love, I only want someone who can unite the past and the future, who can assuage the desolation of having to live without faith in a typical God and without roots in any country. I want too much.

There is Elise, the ten year-old girl whom I informally adopt for the two years I work in Brazzaville. I discover her through the non-governmental organisation working on HIV whose operations I helped set up. She is not HIV positive but her mother is. Within a month of my meeting Elise her mother is dead.

I give Elise a stuffed elephant and she carries it everywhere. It is her only toy. Elise's uncle and aunts look at the toy with such wariness I eventually ask them what is wrong. It turns out that her father had been killed by a forest elephant while out on a hunting trip, leaving Elise, her mother and baby sister and brother alone.

I think I can solve the problem – or at least help – by feeding Elise, buying her clothes and medicines, helping her to take care of her younger siblings. At twelve years old, as I leave her, she is a capable mother to them.

When I hear I am to be transferred out of the country I go to see her in her uncle's compound. I will not tell her I am leaving – whether to protect her or me from despair, I don't know.

I find her sitting on the step in a Socratic pose, her elbow on her knee and chin cupped in her hand. She wears a green shirt and a pair of shorts I have bought for her at a street market. The elephant peeks out at me from between her calves. What's the matter, Elise, I ask. Today I am sad, she says. I don't know why.

She looks up at me and I can see the knowledge in her eyes. She knows, somehow, she will not see me again. There is no betrayal in her gaze, no taking me to task, just a loneliness. I can feel it, as clearly as if she has spoken. I am becoming a memory before her eyes. This will happen over and over again in her life, people will fade out of the picture: her mother, her father, me. She will be *toute seule*.

That first night in my Nova Friburgo hotel room I had stayed up, watching the bats commute back and forth on their mysterious missions, wondering if it would have been less cruel for her never to have known me, the food I bought her, the clothes, never to have known satiety.

What could I do? I could have left the aunts and uncles money but I didn't trust them; they'd sooner spend the money on a television than feed their niece. Eventually I left her in the care of a colleague, a woman who would stay for another year. But after that, then what? Elise had seen the photographs on my laptop of my home in London. She'd eaten well for a year and a half. She had a vision of an alternate life, a possible yet impossible existence she may yet live, when I return to rescue her.

When I look into it I find that formal adoption would be a nightmare of red tape and Home Office bureaucracy. I consult a lawyer and discover that as a single man, my claim to adopt a pre-pubescent girl would be viewed with suspicion. Only if I married would I have a chance. I write to my colleague in Brazzaville who is by this time in her parents' farmhouse in upstate New York digging her parents out of snowdrifts after her father had a heart attack wielding the same shovel. She made sure Elise was okay, she said, but when I write back for more information she never responds.

Elise has become an artefact of memory, a fetish of my guilt. When I picture her in my mind I see her on the step, as if she has never moved, grown older, or become herself: her desolation held in check, green plastic sandals on her feet, her dusty elephant giving me the reproachful look she had the dignity to spare me.

This is the story I tell Riaan one of those nights we stay up talking until dawn in Cabo Frio, the story he asked me for and which, if I did not deliver it, he would not forget, of the saddest thing I have ever seen.

# IV

The road was a platinum river. It flowed through sand and khaki scrub bush, telegraph poles sailing by as we dipped into the washaways and sand rivers that criss-crossed the land.

Half an hour after turning inland from the coast we began to see signs of habitation: people sitting outside shacks, legs thrown out ramrod straight in front of them, the backs of their knees touching the ground. The shacks were made of poles stuck in the ground at crazy angles. These huts were metres from the road, open to all the world; any snake or predator could simply wander in. Sometimes hubcaps or pieces of plywood had been used to plug the gaps.

A truck speeding in the other direction started beeping long before it came upon us. As we sailed by a face stuck itself out the window and grinned.

'Hey, Silas!' Riaan called in the rear-view mirror to the reflection of the vehicle speeding away in the other direction, gravel spitting from the wheels 'That's my director of operations.'

'He drives fast.'

'Everyone drives fast here. He'll join us later on. He's just gone back to town to get some provisions.'

'You mean he's going to drive three hours to town and three hours back?'

'Of course,' Riaan gave me a look – *so*?

In the desert the edges of the field of vision liquefy. I remembered the mirages I'd seen in Mauritania – oil rigs, entire sea-going ships, regiments of horses or men walking lone and unaided from the blasted interior. After a while I got used to these apparitions. I wondered if, as with dreams, the images I saw could be a kind of code for what I was really thinking.

'Does it ever rain here?' I asked.

'When the rains come it's like the end of the world. You can feel the pressure drop in your bones. Ever been in a white-out? Well here it's a sand-out. You can't see a thing. Worse than a sandstorm. Then it starts raining.' He whistled. 'Never seen anything like it, before I came here.'

I looked out to the batter-thick hills that rose and fell against the horizon. 'I can't believe you came here –' I searched for the word – 'willingly.'

He did not answer right away. I stole a sideways look. His brow was furrowed, in thought or in concentration on the gravel sway of the road.

'My parents thought I was turning my back on everything important,' he said, after a while. 'But only on the things that were important to them.'

A gust of loneliness passed through me. I thought of my weeks with Pieter and Sara, our outings to the sushi restaurant in the harbour, to the art house cinema on the university campus, the summer concert in the botanical gardens under the platinum sky. How at home I felt in their company. Why had I put myself in Riaan's power, I wondered, again. He was a door that blew open on the wind, then blew shut. He wouldn't care who might get caught, how badly their fingers were hurt.

After an hour a low line emerged out of the horizon; hazy, irresolute. It grew as we drove into a lone massif, garbed in sky.

'What's that?'

'Its local name means Fire Mountain.'

'It's all on its own.'

'That's right, there's not another mountain for thousands of kilometres in all directions. Strange, isn't it? It's a good landmark – you're not going to get lost. You'll see, at sunset. It actually looks as if it catches fire.'

At the mountain's base was a perimeter of olive green scrub which gave way to copper flanks. The sun struck it with a metallic glint. I had seen photos of Uluru in Australia, but apart from that I'd never seen a mountain like it, how it grew out of the landscape without any warning, no foothills or undulations at all, a jagged dome dropped by some careless god.

We stopped in a hamlet which had what Riaan told me was the only supermarket and petrol pump for three hundred kilometres.

At the supermarket we hauled a giant cooler out of the back of the truck and packed it full of ice. Riaan disappeared into the darkened storage room to fetch the week's meat. It would keep, he'd reassured me, despite the forty-degree heat during the day, as long as we didn't open the cooler any more than necessary.

From the parking lot I saw the silver carcass of a mining rig, the squat water towers encircling it, and a structure like a giant truncated escalator ascending into the sky. We were in the middle of aluminium seams, but they had been mined dry a decade before. Stringy young men loitered in the shadows, eyeing us.

I waited for Riaan to pay. The town, of only one or two streets, was not unpretty: whitewashed houses with bougainvillea draped over fences. There was even a thatched mushroom cottage, as in an English village.

'Come on, let's get the cooler in the back.' We hauled it in, me in the flatbed and Riaan on the ground, because he was the stronger. The cooler stored, we wiped our hands on our trousers. 'Let's grab a beer.'

We ambled across the town's empty main road to a guesthouse. Inside it was very dark. My eyes adjusted slowly to see hunting trophies studding the walls: an antelope, his dark shining eyes, a sagging rhinoceros head.

Two Chinese men sat at a table in the corner. Sweat coursed from their temples.

'Check them out,' Riaan gave a low whistle.

'Who are they?'

'Investors.' He leaned on the word.

'What are they investing in?'

'Anything that moves. Land, crops, copper. Probably cattle, although I doubt they're getting anywhere with that. People here will sell their grandmothers before they'll sell their cows.'

Riaan approached them. The men looked up, their eyelids flickered, startled to be spoken to. I couldn't hear what he said. He walked back.

'What did you say?'

'I told them to watch their step around here. I told them traffic accidents were frequent, and there were never any witnesses. It was a message on behalf of my neighbours, whose land these men are trying to buy with unconventional tactics, should we say.' His eyes hardened.

'You threatened them?'

'I just let them know where they are. In case they think they're in Shanghai where they can rely on blackmail and graft.' He saw my face. 'Relax. I'm not going to have these guys wasted. At least not yet.'

I wanted to smile, to indulge his joke, then I understood it was no such thing. 'I'm just going to get some air,' I said.

His gaze followed me out the door. Something about the moment, the whole cocktail of impressions: the way the air had closed around us in the bar, the sleepy-eyed men, their undoubted campaign to fleece this land of something and Riaan's stony gaze, was very familiar, as was the feeling that the situation could turn on a dime. Instinct told me the Chinese men might be armed, under the table. I'd experienced similar situations, even if I could not remember where or when. My working life was full of these blackouts: moments of violence or near-violence I forgot, or half-remembered, so that it felt as if they'd happened to someone else.

I breathed slowly and counted my breaths. This was a tactic I relied on in moments of stress. I tried to take my cue from the landscape, whether it could tell me anything, but it was silent. The land rippled with flat-topped mesas. In the afternoon light they were the greasy white of chestnut flesh.

After a while I heard the crunch of gravel behind me and Riaan's voice. 'You okay?'

'Fine.'

'Let's go. We've got another couple of hours before we reach camp.'

In the car he did not ask me why I'd left. His manner seemed to soften. He offered me a cold diet coke, which I drank gratefully.

After a while we turned off the main road onto a sandy road that wound up and down over hillocks crowned by huge amber stones. We bumped down this for what felt like another hour. 'Well this is definitely off the beaten track,' I said.

'I used to come out here when I was leading hunts. That's how I found it.'

'What kind of hunts?'

'Sometimes for the Ministry of the Environment, to cull overpopulation. If you don't shoot some of the animals, the ecosystem collapses. Then once I knew the place and had the right permits I'd take clients, hunters from overseas, into the bush to shoot a particular animal.' He shot me a quick look. 'They were more plentiful then.'

'How can you be a conservationist and a hunter?'

'Hunting is part of conservation here.' Riaan kept his eyes on the track. We were driving the dark now. From time to time the glint of eyes appeared in the grass on the side of the road. 'I did it for the money. I was trying to raise funds to start up the bursary scheme. You don't approve?'

'Of hunting? I don't know enough about it.'

My answer was an evasion, to a degree. I knew I never

wanted to line up another creature in the sights of a weapon and take its life. And also – the realisation came to me then, on the track with Riaan, for the first time in my life – that if it came to it, I'd be more able to kill a human being than an animal.

'Does Pieter know?'

'About me hunting for a living? Yes, he didn't like it much either.'

We were quiet then. I listened to the ping of stones in the wheelbeds. I was tired. My throat burned from the dust. We carried on driving as dark fell. I wondered how much further it was possible to go. We were already a long way from the road.

We were inside his camp before I knew it. Riaan told me he'd deliberately chosen a spot out of sight of any road or herder's track. You couldn't see the camouflaged rondavel, the cement hearth or a lookout platform suspended between the branches of an enormous Iwi tree.

Riaan put the firewood on the hearth, one leg propped up, his face a study in concentration. The last of the light was draining fast from the sky. In the darkness I could just make out a dry riverbed, and across it a sheer face of rippled ochre rocks.

Riaan issued orders: connect the generator, gather the hurricane lamps, and I obeyed. We ran around in a burst of activity, our head torches illuminating tiny patches of solid darkness.

'You're good at this, aren't you?' he said, after we'd done the basics.

'Setting up camp? Unfortunately yes.'

'Let's have a seat.' He took out two folding camp chairs and poked them into the sand. I leaned back in my chair and looked at the boxy constellations of the southern hemisphere: Pleiades, Orion, Antares, the Southern Cross. Pieter had been teaching me them, with the help of a star map from the planetarium.

'It feels heavy, here,' I said. 'Like the air is made of lead. But not in a bad way.'

'Well this part of the planet is very old. Or it could be the ghosts.'

'What ghosts?'

'A hundred thousand men were slaughtered by the Germans in this desert alone.'

In the firelight his face looked thinner, almost gaunt. It was a misapprehension, that first day in Cabo Frio, when Riaan had emerged from his Landcruiser and I thought I'd seen Pieter's face. True, there was a shadow of his father in him, but now I could see how much he looked like his mother. Like Sara, his cheekbones sat high and taut in his face, two sails furled around their masts. He had his mother's alertness, a lofty tension which, were it ever to relent, threatened to collapse with uncertain consequences.

A sound ripped open the air and with it a cold thrill settled inside me, the feeling I had these days when I sat on a plane on the runway, waiting for takeoff.

'Elephant,' Riaan said, 'A bull. Alone – well, they're almost always alone. He's unhappy about something.' He rose from the campfire with gunshot swiftness. He moved like this, I'd noticed, a series of explosions, although once he was on his feet his was a smooth, elastic stride.

We heard a vehicle pull up. Two headlights briefly swept us in their beams and were extinguished. A tall, thin man with a dignified bearing alighted from a pickup. He walked toward us, coalescing out of the darkness. I saw his eyes first, then a narrow, tense reflection of forehead. After a moment I recognised Silas from our brief encounter on the road.

He shook my hand. 'Summer is long this year.' It was true. The heat had barely relented with nightfall. We were all sweating. 'I've never seen anything like it,' Silas said. 'Ten times as much rain as in a normal summer, and twice as hot.'

We threw our bedrolls on the ground. We would sleep

underneath a large Iwi tree, Riaan said. 'Not so close to the trunk,' he said when he saw me unfurling my sleeping bag. He didn't say why not and I didn't want to ask. Silas made dinner while we finished opening up the weather havens and checking for animals – snakes, essentially – that might have got in over the last few months. We ate under the feeble light of the hurricane lamp.

Silas asked no questions about me, not even my name. He looked older than Riaan, although on examination his face was supple and unlined. It might be his bearing, so ramrod straight with long legs that swung around his body in shallow ellipses, that produced this impression.

'How did you two meet?' I asked.

Silas smiled hesitantly. 'That's a very long story.'

I waited for more, but Silas went back to his dinner. I looked at Riaan.

'Shouldn't we worry about leopards?'

'No, man,' Silas's voice was suddenly hearty. 'That won't happen.'

'Silas knows all about leopard, don't you?'

He gave a mild *hmmm*.

'Show Nick your scar.'

Silas sidled up against me. He removed his cap and lifted up the hair on the base of his neck. I had to peer with my headtorch on his nape. There I saw a long scar, narrow and ridged, running down the back of his head. It looked like a miniature railway track.

'When did this happen?'

'Oh, a long time ago now, when I was a kid. We spent our days herding, there was no school then. We had goats, sheep, some cattle. The leopard were always taking some, especially in the dry season. We were very frightened when this happened. To see that animal move – to see it kill.' He shook his head. 'We were only four dusty boys with no gun. We had dogs though, and the dogs chased the animal and kept it cornered. But then the leopard found a rock and jumped down into the dogs and killed them all. Well, one survived I think. We just watched this with awe. My friends, they had only sticks. Some had stones which they threw at the cat, but they just bounced off him.'

'And it attacked you?'

'Yes, but only a little bit. But it was very agitated, and it left me alone.' Silas stopped and angled his torso back, as if he were about to rise from the table, or strike out. I couldn't tell which.

'This is how a leopard kills you. They leap onto you, often from above. They attack from the front. They get your face in their teeth – here he opened his mouth wide, his teeth gleaming, reflected in the fire. Then they take their paw' – here he took his arm and flung it back, over his own head, and dragged his hands down his face. 'They scalp you from the back, and pull it down over your face to blind you. Then they take their hind legs and jump up to dig their claws into your chest and rip out your intestines.'

Riaan nodded a silent assent.

'Thanks, that's very reassuring, Silas. I'm glad there's no reason to worry about leopard.'

'You are welcome,' Silas said gravely.

Riaan and Silas went to wash up in the bush kitchen they had constructed out of branches of fallen fever trees. From the fire I watched them as they worked together in silence. It was obvious they had the kind of bond that is forged by experience rather than talk.

I'd had this too, or a version of it, with some of my colleagues – when you dig a hundred latrines together, or watch a volcano erupt at night knowing that the red lava streaming down its sides could, within an hour, spell your end, when you awake in the morning to find hundreds of people had died of hunger overnight. But then these colleagues went back to Copenhagen or New York and I never saw them again.

Riaan called from the kitchen. 'Okay, it's 9 o'clock, bush

midnight. Time to hit the sack.' He turned to me. 'Anything happens, give me a shout.'

'And you'll come and save me.'

Riaan yawned. 'Unless I don't wake up.'

I woke three times that night. Each time I opened my eyes into the trio of stars that make up Orion's belt. Alnitak, Alnilam, Mintaka, the constellation slowly tilting across the sky. Pieter had taught me their names, which I was able to remember because they all sounded like anagrams of one another. The second time I awoke I heard a rustle on the ground near us. I dared not move. Slowly my eyes adjusted to starlight. When I could see I sat up and scoured the darkness. Nothing at all. But I felt it: a presence. I could hear Silas and Riaan breathing. I think it was this sound, the soft inhale and exhale and the steadiness and perpetuity that it contains, the heart soldiering away in the chest, lungs blooming, that convinced me to go back to sleep.

I woke to the crackle of firewood. The outline of Fire Mountain appeared in the dawn, a fist towering above the karst of its skirts.

Riaan thrust a tin mug into my hand. He wore a scarf already tied round his forehead in anticipation of the arrival of tiny sweat-sucking bees which, I would learn, showed up for work punctually at 8.30am. Silas appeared looking as if he'd never slept – clean-shaven, his sand-coloured shirt perfectly pressed.

'Today we head north,' Riaan said. 'There's a school we run up there, but it's closed. There's been an outbreak of some kind of hysteria. Some sensitive and slightly strange kid is being persecuted. That's what I've heard, anyway. It's time to pay a visit.'

I looked around at our campfire, its bowls smeared with porridge, our cups of powdered coffee. There was a hinge buried inside an ordinary moment and the announcement of our trip. I wanted to believe it was just that, a routine inspection. I was getting further and further from my ordinary life and with distance my normal power was diminishing. Perhaps the trip to the north would teach me something. Here, I thought, you can walk lightly on the earth; we can behave like mortals, for a change.

# V

The rains had left a thin coat of grass on the ground. In between these savannah stretches red dunes stood bare-headed under the sun.

Now that we were heading north I realised I had assumed that at some point this arid landscape would simply peter out and we would arrive into foothills, or green fields, a river or the sea. But it just went on and on: orange trees, dun hills, chocolate boulders, outcroppings of russet rock. It has its own grammar, this place, I thought. You might read it if only you knew how.

When we stopped for a piss on the roadside I sat in the shade cast by the wheelbed of the Landcruiser and hung my head. I had been in hot places before, of course, but here the heat was of a different category. It was as if the heat had melted my thoughts into a sticky mass.

I realised what an epic we had set out on: we would drive four hundred kilometres in a day, then another three hundred, then come back to camp after Riaan had seen his school project by the border. Silas would accompany us in a separate vehicle for a couple of days. After we made our visit to the school his plan was to drive on to see his family, who lived in the region.

Rain had transformed the land. Around the tiny petrol stations we stopped at, and which sold only boxes of matches and warm beer, green shoots poked through the dusty soil. Beyond a sable carpet of grass undulated as far as the eye could see. The buffalo thorns were suddenly coated in white blossom and rivulets snaked through the dry riverbeds we crossed.

'You're lucky to see it this way,' Riaan said. 'There are only ten, twenty days a year like this.' He recited the names of the grasses that came after the rains; love, needle, swamp grass, and a woolly-headed species called silver three-awn.

At times we drove in silence, the only sound the grind of gravel underneath the wheels. After some hours a town appeared, again without warning. Straight away we were driving along a dusty street. Clumps of young men stood in pools of shade; their legs and arms looked too long for them, like prosthetic limbs. As we drove by they looked at us as one, glassy indifference in their eyes.

'Here we are.'

I could only see a shack – that was really too grand a term; a box of sticks stood in the full sun, in front of a thorn tree. Around it, a few dusty goats with patches the colour of dried blood hunted for shade.

'Ok, but where is "here"?'

'My friend's place,' Riaan grinned. 'He is a hundred years old.'

A figure appeared from within the box. Thin, wiry, tall, no sign of a Centenarian's stoop. I couldn't see his face, but the body convinced me Riaan was joking.

'He can't be.'

'Not that he has a birth certificate to prove it. But he was born in 1906 or 1907. His family were killed by the Germans. When he was ten years old he was moved here.'

Silas pulled up beside us. As we all walked toward the box/shack another moment condensed into something heavier than anticipation. The man on the threshold, his yellow cat-like eyes, the sun and the thorn tree behind him, the torn patches of indigo sky and iron oxide soil – all this was familiar.

Riaan turned around and that hesitant smile I saw not often

enough fixed itself upon me – a beckoning, almost tender smile. I knew he would do this, I knew the man waiting in the shadow of his shack would see it, and understand.

His friend introduced himself as Bamma or perhaps it was Gamma – I didn't quite catch the name. The shack was dark but this did nothing to staunch the heat. A tarpaulin had been rigged up over the sharp end of sticks. This was the roof. Through it I could see slits of sky.

Riaan, Silas and I took our seats on overturned plastic bottle cartons, with a piece of cardboard on top, a flimsy card table between us. Riaan's friend opened three bottles of the warm beer we'd brought with us. Their slender necks gathered at our feet like friendly geese.

Riaan, Silas and his friend switched to a language I could not understand. I listened to it, the clicking sounds they made with their tongues against their palates, the long rivers of soft vowels. I took in our surroundings. On the walls hung faded pictures cut from calendars: a palm tree on an island surrounded by azure sea, a giraffe, its giant moist eyes. The giraffe's month was June. There was no year.

I got up and left the shack, saying I needed a breath of air. Outside were outcrops of yellow resinous grass emerging from iron-red soil. The fields did not tilt but ran hard into the horizon. There, red rocks hummed with their own mute heat.

Brown fingers rested on my shoulder. It was Silas, grave as ever. 'He wants you to come back in. He has something to tell you.'

I followed Silas back into the shack. I sat down on the stool I had vacated.

Instantly the man's eyes changed. They held a look of slight hurt.

'I know,' the man said, in English, 'that you have come here for a reason.'

'Well I hope so,' I said.

The eyes narrowed. 'You are afraid to return home. But

you need not fear. This is your home. It was always known that you should end in Africa.'

I rose. 'Thank you,' I offered my hand, 'for your hospitality.' I went to stand in the shade of the truck. After a while Silas joined me.

'Where did they meet?' I asked him.

'In the war, I think.'

'Why do you think he said that to me?'

Silas shrugged. 'I don't know. But when these guys tell you something, you listen. I was taught that as a boy.'

'What do you mean, these guys?'

'They are seers. They know things that – ' Silas twirled his hand in the air in front of us, let it fall. Then he shook his head.

'Oh, fantastic, the village clairvoyant. What did he mean, I should end here.'

'I wouldn't worry about it,' Silas said. 'He probably meant "end up". I'm surprised he can even speak English.'

Riaan emerged from the shade of the hut. He lit a cigarette.

'We can't reach the border tonight,' Silas said.

Riaan blew two streams of smoke from his nostrils. 'We'll make camp then.'

At five o'clock Riaan drove us off the road and took us among the thorn bushes, using the Landcruiser to flatten them like a tank.

'We'll find a nice flat spot. We'll have the cars as an enclosure and we'll build a fire. Just you wait, it's great. Once you sleep like this, you'll never want to sleep in a bed again.'

I wanted to believe this, but I'd done enough roughing it in my life. Although in my job I was important enough to usually be allocated a bed, no matter how dire the conditions.

'Wild dog will probably be around,' he said. 'We'll hear them but they won't bother us.'

I'd never seen a wild dog but I'd seen photos of their blunt muzzles and paint-splattered hides I remembered reading somewhere that their favoured hunting technique was to rip their prey to shreds while it was still moving.

We found a low rock. We all sat there and watched the sun lower itself slow and stately into the horizon. We could see the tracks our Landcruisers had made through the long khaki floss of grass, the peppercorn pyramids of rock. As the sun went down a small breath of wind ruffled the air. The grass stood up straighter, and sighed.

'The wind does that at sunset.' Riaan swept his eyes over the view. 'I love this moment. I could live my whole life for it.'

A sound started up, a mechanical rotating, like when you can't get your car to start.

Riaan said, 'hyena.'

'They don't sound real.'

One broke cover just then. It loped in the grass, head held high, dragging its hindquarters. It looked like a moving rocking chair.

'They called this place The Land God Made in Anger,' Riaan said. 'It was uncrossable, unless you knew how to find water. So many Europeans died here. They just couldn't believe that there would be no shade and little game, just rocky fields and sand.'

'Yes,' Silas echoed. 'God was angry when he made this land. He wanted us to suffer.'

The moon ripened that night, rising closer and larger until it was an explosion.

We would sleep next to each other, with the fire on one side and the Landcruiser on the other. I would be in the middle, between Riaan and Silas – the newcomer's position, where you are less likely to get eaten.

I fell asleep thinking of the leopard padding through the night. The vision dissolved the seam of time and I was dreaming of being on a ship up the coast of Africa, hanging over the deck rail, marvelling at the dazzle of white light as small boats bearing men and guns speed toward me.

The next day we passed the hamlet of Xaia, the last real town before the border. North of Xaia the road quickly deteriorated.

Its strip of worn asphalt began to be colonised by potholes, at first one or two, then a mosaic of them.

Silas received a call on his phone. I couldn't understand what he was saying, but I saw Riaan glance across at him. The asphalt petered out and we were on gravel again, which tugged at our wheels. Then we lost signal; I watched the little bars on my phone diminish, then vanish.

'There – ' Riaan pointed to a hollow in the road, over a low ridge. I saw a pale green corrugated plastic roof, a breeze-block building, a dusty yard of sand around it, patrolled by what looked from afar like a flimsy fence.

We jolted down the road. As we approached the school there were no children to be seen. All the doors to the building were open, swinging in the wind.

We pulled to a stop inside the fence, flinging dust in all directions. We walked through the school. Flimsy padlocks dangled from the doors, cut or picked. Inside were jumbles of benches, torn books, a wooden desk that had been dismantled methodically then thrown into a heap. A single flip-flop, with blue and white stripes across the foot; a stuffed rabbit, pink fur still attached to its back but yellowed and scoured by the wind and the sand on its front. Numbers and letters painted in faded pink, yellow and green marched across the walls.

Riaan stopped and lit a cigarette. He took two drags before speaking. Under his hat his eyes squinted in all directions. 'We painted those two years ago.'

'How much money did you give to the school?'

'Thirty, maybe forty thousand. There are only three we've supported in the border region.'

'What do you think happened?'

'I don't know. I didn't expect it to be deserted.'

'Do you get the feeling we're being watched?'

'Possibly. You never know.' He turned around and looked into the distance, toward where we had come in on the road.

I walked away to find a pool of shade. The village which

surrounded the school itself was also empty. It looked as if no one had lived there in months. The droppings of whatever goats had once grazed on this parched ground were dry as chalk. Here the land was stony; rose-pink granite boulders were strewn up and down dull hills. The only trees were gnarled acacias. The sun beat down on their branches, turning them silver.

My throat ached with thirst. We had only the water stored in the Landcruiser's tank now, which had to be fetched from a tap and a pipe on the car and which tasted vaguely of lead.

In the schoolyard Riaan paced back and forth. I watched Silas approach. He made various hand gestures, sweeping his arms around like a whirligig. I wondered if they were arguing. Then I saw the graffiti; it was painted on a wall that faced the road out of the village; we hadn't seen it on the way in. *ONE INDUSTRY, ONE UNION*. Why was it in English? Who was it a message for?

Riaan came toward me. 'Silas is driving back tonight. His wife called him; one of their children is sick.'

'What's going on here?'

'I don't bloody know. And that's the truth. We'll make camp and tomorrow we'll drive back and I'll ask a few questions. If I can find anyone.'

We returned to where Silas was taking refuge from the sun under the school gutter. He was suddenly restless. As for Riaan, he was agitated, even spooked, as if we'd come upon a village of dead people.

He turned to Silas. 'We'll stay in the hyena hills.'

'Now there's a reassuring name,' I said.

'Oh, don't worry. Hyena don't really bother with people. Although if you were wounded, that would be a different story.'

We left the deserted school and drove with Silas back to Xaia on that potholed road. About ten kilometres from the school we finally saw another human being – a man in a dark blue shirt and shorts and wearing a striped knit hat. Riaan stopped the truck and got out to talk to him, but the man took one look at us and sprinted away.

Riaan walked back to the car, grim-faced. 'Working your usual charm on him I see,' Silas joked.

He shrugged and sniffed his shirt. 'I guess I should have washed.'

We parted at the petrol station; Silas headed west, Riaan and I would continue south. An echo reverberated, not so much aural as spatial, in the wake of Silas's departure. I had gotten used to being three – plus, there was a certain safety in numbers in this wild place.

At an unmarked point Riaan swung us off the road and we entered the bush. He pointed to a low mountain in the distance. 'It's over there.'

'We're going that far?'

'It's a really nice spot. Good elevation. You'll see.'

We finally drew up in the lee of the mountain, on a low plateau. Here we would sleep beside the car with two fires in either corner – good fires, Riaan instructed me, his voice sharp; they needed to keep going all night. He taught me to spot the good trees from the bad. Lavenderbush, for example, would kill us if we burned it, with its toxic latex. I learned to check for scorpions before I lifted branches onto my chest. They loved nothing more than to hang onto the dark side of branches near the moist earth.

To begin with the fires were so hot we had to take refuge on the other side of the car until they burned down. The ridges of the hills were bathed in copper and puce. Early autumn colours.

Later we sat in the green penumbra thrown by the flames. He opened a beer and passed it to me.

'You're completely at home out here,' I said.

'I don't know. There are so many beautiful places on this continent. I'd rather be in a hot, tropical place, that's the truth. Tanzania or Mozambique. But I'm not sure I'd ever get this place out of my bones.'

It was true possibly, that he was not really a creature of the desert, rather he was using it draw himself in outline more bluntly.

The moon rose. It was as if a floodlight was trained on the land and I could see as if it were daylight.

Ochre outcrops stretched into the horizon. Between them snaked game trails. Squat thorn bushes stood at intersections of these tracks, as if they had been planted there as signposts. Behind the outcroppings cheetah were active. Riaan showed them to me, handing me his binoculars. I could just make out their shapes in the moonlight, a pair, hunting together. They moved like two pieces of wire.

'How did you find this spot?'

'Our unit camped here one night. When I came back ten years later I remembered it. Or it remembered me.'

'It's strange, I felt that too, the first time I came here, I mean, to your parents' house. I thought, this place knows something about me. I thought, I'm home.'

'You have to learn to listen to that voice,' he said, his voice breezy with conviction. 'So many people think it's fanciful if you hear the land calling to you.'

'Maybe they've never experienced it. I didn't, before I came here.'

Riaan seemed to be absorbing my admission. I wondered if he were going to ask me again what convinced me to stay in his parents' house. But he rose and turned on his head torch. 'Time to pack it in,' he said.

We lay on our bedrolls and stared at the stars, that shining herd. It was like sleeping in a planetarium. Sky-antelope did backflips across the darkness, chased by question mark-shaped cheetahs and cubes of oxen.

I expected Riaan to fall asleep straight away, as he seemed to do. But he was staring at the sky with a peculiar intensity.

'I don't understand why you went into the Army,' I ventured. 'You could have gone abroad, dodged the draft.'

'I would have been conscripted anyway. Even before High School they had their eye on me. We were told – indoctrinated, really – that this was our country, given to us by God.'

'Did you believe that?'

'I did and I didn't.' He fell silent. His breathing deepened. I thought he had fallen asleep, but when I looked at him his eyes were still fixed on the stars.

'We would follow dry rivers, that's how we moved in the night. The roads were too dangerous. The lieutenants didn't really know what they were doing. They weren't native to this place. We were like children, piecing together our reality as we went along. The times we thought we were north of the border we were actually south, and vice versa. There was no GPS in those days, just old creased pilots' maps from the days before the war, they showed flight paths, but that wasn't much use to us.'

He turned onto his side and propped his head on his arm. 'The enemy had tanks, more of them than the intelligence guys had led us to believe. They had helicopter gunships. I preferred the tanks; there's something about being fired on from the air…' he paused. 'I always had an instinct to run, when they came, and that can be the worst possible thing for you to do. They could pick us off like deer because there was no cover in the desert. But I always thought that if I was going to die, I'd die moving.

'The worst was when the earth kept exploding underneath your feet – that's what it feels like, when mortars hit their targets, like depth charges. The first thing you know is not the fire, or your injury, but the sand blasting your face. Then you realise your leg is gone. Every night I was on patrol I'd have the same nightmare – in it I'd wake up and look down to see a stump where my knee had been.'

My stomach clutched itself. I had never faced that rank of fear. Dangerous situations had come my way, but I'd been protected to an extent by my position, my nationality, the colour of my skin. When I left the ship only a month before

I had sensed the danger he was talking about, possibly, and dodged it.

I looked at him, determined to say this, to tell the truth, for once, but there was a distance in his eyes which halted me. I wasn't sure he would understand, if he would forgive me my cowardice – if that is what it was – in leaving the ship, in not telling him or his parents of my failure.

He was right there, next to me, but we might as well have been on opposite sides of the continent. I couldn't follow him where he had gone in those days and nights when he'd moved through this same landscape, not knowing whether he would be alive come the morning. The distance between us became a physical thing, a piece of darkness.

I woke once more that night. I don't know what time it was when I heard the unmistakeable chatter of hyenas. Bats came to strafe our sleeping bodies, swooping low on us. They seemed to consider it a kind of game. I thought I saw a bird – a bustard or vulture, judging by its ragged wings, one of the lean raptors which flensed this land.

I dissolved into dreams. The land was burning. Trees fizzed into fire like matchsticks. Small deer-like creatures launched themselves vertically through flaming grass. In the midst of the fire I was swimming in a lake or a river. I looked up to see a man, a stranger, cradling my head, stroking my hair. I felt bathed in love.

# VI

It was Friday; we had been in port since Monday afternoon when I had joined the ship. The wind blew and blew. It was like being swatted by a plank. Even the mountain looked unmoored in the gale.

We all wandered the ship's narrow corridors, looking for ways to pass the time. I was nurturing a secret: I hadn't slept in three nights, not through insomnia as much as anxiety. There was something troubling me, a smothering heaviness I had never felt before. It didn't feel like fear. Rather the bulk of an event powered it, something which had already happened or is happening or will happen.

Of course anything could happen, in my line of work. Fear was normal, even necessary; if you weren't afraid from time to time you might end up dead. On those nights in my bunk I ran through possible disasters in my mind: the ship sinking, someone (hopefully not me) becoming unbalanced and throwing themselves overboard (this had happened once in our organisation, although before my time), the more obvious threat of attack – a siege, possibly lasting for months, if the warlord-in-residence at Kassala were to overtake the forces which had overthrown him. This was very unlikely; all our analysts agreed his weapons had been seized.

Behind my reasoned thoughts was a voice – not a voice I could actually hear, I was not that deranged – more a force, coming from very far away; it had arrived after a long journey and was finally pressing against me. It said *Get off this ship*.

During those days I pitted the murky dread I felt against my fear of career disarray and shame. I couldn't simply do as the voice commanded. Although we were still in the harbour I was seasick from trying to steady myself. I was already on the ocean, an internal tempestuous sea.

Then news came that finally the wind was forecast to relent. We would set off on the Sunday morning.

On that Friday night I was awake all night, my heart pounding, my brain shrieking. When I woke up at Saturday I rose from my bunk, barely aware of what I was doing. My lungs felt hollow, as if I couldn't get enough oxygen. I felt it again, the hand against my back, pushing me forward.

Later that morning I stood alone in a sun-baked parking lot. There, what looked like hundreds of people sat underneath meagre trees in whose branches they had strung plastic bags containing all their belongings. Young lean men stood with their arms crossed over their chests.

The parking lot was where men who had stowed away on ships in other countries were deposited, and where newly arrived immigrants congregated to try and get a piece of paper which would allow them to work.

The immigration building provided a windbreak. I remained in its shade, going over in my mind what had happened that morning.

I had gone up onto the bridge and spoken to the captain. I needed his authority to leave the ship. I'd said I had a family emergency and had to return to the UK immediately. I was handing over responsibility for logistics to Ernst. I would get in touch with my line manager in London. I asked him for my passport. He handed it to me without a word.

I didn't say goodbye to anyone apart from the captain and to Ernst, who looked dazed by how quickly his fate had spun on a dime. He behaved impeccably, shaking my hand, promising to email me once they were underway. I left the ship like a criminal or a celebrity, a baseball cap pulled down over my eyes, sunglasses on.

Now in the parking lot, time had melted. I didn't know how long it had been since I had left the ship; it could have been minutes or hours.

I dragged my bag to the shade of the delivery entrance of the immigration offices. I came upon stacks of newly bound passports, shiny and plastic-looking, bound in bundles in the back of a security van parked there. The driver looked at me suspiciously until I took off my baseball cap and sunglasses and he saw that I was a white man.

*I will need to find a hotel.* Then I remembered Ruth's email. *I know you won't have time, but if you do you must meet Sara and Pieter. He's my father's brother. A very famous writer, there.* In that single word, 'there', lurked an admonition. He was not famous enough to be famous anywhere else, or he was famous in an inconsequential country. She'd sent their number in the email. *They have a big house, you could stay with them if you get time.*

I searched through my work email on my phone. The messages were already there, their subject lines bullying or concerned, depending on the sender. *Report Immediately. What happened?* And then, in a message a month old now and ten slow-loading screens away, was Ruth's, titled *Contact*.

'Hey, got a few cents to spare?' A wild-eyed man appeared beside me, his skin the colour of charcoal. He fixed one of his rotating eyes on my bag, another on my phone. I gave him money and he walked away, scowling at me over his shoulder.

A smooth, urbane woman's voice answered. I kept my voice light, as if I had just arrived on holiday.

'Oh yes,' the woman – Sara – said, with a distracted air. 'Ruth mentioned you to us.'

I didn't believe her, but I was grateful anyway. She gave me directions to the house. 'We're so looking forward to meeting you.'

'Me too,' I said.

Only when I stepped away from the shade into the sun did

I realise how dizzy I was. Stars rotated in wild ellipses around my eyes. More charcoal men wearing knitted hats had noticed me by now. As one, they advanced toward me. Everything started to take twice as long to happen as it should, or there was a gap in my perception. The world had frozen and I was paralysed. I could only watch it happen.

The security van pulled up and its blacked-out window glided down. 'I'm not allowed to take passengers, but you'd better get in,' the driver who eyed me earlier said from within his bulbous helmet. 'You're about to be robbed.'

I threw myself and my bag in and closed the door just as the knitted hat men poured into the space I had just occupied, and we sped away.

Nine months before I left for the Kassala job, I went to Barcelona to visit Mercedes.

I stayed with her in her flat in the Eixample. It was summer and the daytime temperature was 35 degrees. Like anyone with sense we cowered inside during the day, parked in front of fans, only venturing out at 7pm, when the sun was low in the sky.

Those nights we went to bars in the Raval; the bars had changed since I was last there: El Indio and El Chino were still there but so were newcomers who seemed to be vying with each other for the title of bar with the most obscure name: Boysenbery in the Carrer de l'Hospital, Bit-Bit in Carrer del Carme. We went to the Mad Bull Bar, the Taverna Incognita. Everyone we met was an architect. Or they were architects, before *la crisis*. The economic crisis had been ongoing for so long now people said the word, crisis, with a flimsy, resigned familiarity.

In the mornings we woke groggy, just before her first clients were due to arrive. She did readings on the telephone now, mostly, she told me – she could take pictures of the cards and email or text them to her clients – but some still insisted on coming in person.

'Listen, Nicolas, I don't want to hustle you out but…'

'But it would be easier if I weren't here. I get the picture.'

'The clients don't like it when – when there's a man around. It upsets them.'

'Do most of them have man troubles?'

'A lot of them are looking for a man, and if they think I've got one it makes them jealous. It's easier for them if they think I am in the same boat.'

'Do men ever come to see you?'

She thought for a second. 'Maybe one in fifty clients is a man.'

'So men don't want to know about the future?'

'It's not about the future.' The word dripped from her mouth. I hadn't seen her in a year and I'd forgotten she avoided the word, if at all possible. 'It's about introspection. Men don't tend to look inside for answers; they want explanations from the external world.'

'So men are rationalists. They don't believe in invisible forces.'

She gave me a penetrating look. 'I'm sorry about having to kick you out during readings. I wouldn't normally work in the summer. I wouldn't normally do this at all, except for la crisis. I'm sorry it's so chaotic.'

'Compared with my work this is not chaos.'

'I know,' she said. 'We haven't even had a chance to talk about that yet.'

The telephone rang. '*Cómo estamos?*' Mercedes' voice was high and fluting. Her voice changed when she was working. She probably imagined she sounded lofty and knowing, but I heard a cajoling note.

She paced up and down around the long, dark flat with the phone stuck to her ear, a radically thin, still-young woman with an androgynous haircut. I wondered what her clients thought when they met her for the first time – she looked more like a barista than a psychic. Her telephone voice floated toward me: 'I see a group, well a small group – a kind of coterie of people – who are behind this, pushing for their own ends.'

I'd been sleeping in a small loft constructed above the desk where she kept her cards, candles and other esoterica. On the desk was a basket of sweets. Inside it, a little piece of card poked out: *Take one!* I hadn't had breakfast, not even a cup of coffee, but I worried the sweets might have divinatory properties.

Finally she put the phone down. 'Okay, let's have a look.'

'What do you mean?'

'It's time to get some perspective on what you're doing with your life.'

'I told you, I'm afraid of the future.'

She winced at the word. 'Think of it like a bird's eye view. As if you are flying above your life and suddenly you are able to see where the mountains and the rivers are and how they connect.'

Afterwards, she looked at the picture that had emerged on the table for what felt like a long time. Outside, the traffic poured along the boulevard in the greased heat. We heard the on-off sirens of the Mossos d'Esquadra.

I tried to read what she saw in the cards, which were upside down. They had pictures of men and women in godlike poses. I saw chariots and lightning bolts and a young blond man with what looked like a deer nudging itself against his leg.

'What do you see?'

'Well, literally it shows a hammer, as when you strike something.' She slammed her fist into the palm of her other hand. 'It means a turnaround, in about nine months' time. Or it can also mean a "go" point. As if someone fires a pistol, like at the starting line of races, and you are off.' She drew her eyes level with mine. They were dark and unusually liquid; changed, or charged, perhaps, with knowledge. 'It means you'll take a sudden decision.'

'What kind of decision?'

'It's not telling me.' Her eyes dropped back to the pictures on the cards. 'Whatever it is, it will be the right thing to do.'

That night I lay in my bed on the platform above her consulting desk listening to sirens careen up and down Gran Via, thinking how the pictures on her cards looked relatively harmless, like posters for Hollywood blockbusters with their lightning strikes and horses and rainbows.

'What about the truth?' I had asked her, before she took the cards away. 'Do you always tell the person what the cards say?'

'Always.' She said. 'Sometimes there is bad news. But I give it to them in a way which emphasises what they can do about it.'

'But what if they can do nothing about it? Like, the cards say you will have a car crash and be injured and will live in pain. Do you say, don't get in a car for the next year?'

'I might. But that might also freak them out. Plus it's impractical.'

'So do you tell them, or not?'

She pursed her lips. 'I find a way to tell them. I have to.'

'Says who?'

'It's like a code of conduct you sign up to, when you learn to do this.'

She shifted in her seat. She was beginning to feel cornered, perhaps, by my questioning. She knew I didn't approve of what she did for a living. She knew I thought it was fraudulent – not that she was a fraud, not exactly, in my mind there was a distinction – but that I kept my counsel because she was my friend.

'It's not possible to know the future, Mercedes.'

'How do you know that, Nicolas? You know nothing of this realm. We all know the future. We dream it, all the time. We just suppress the knowledge.'

I flung my hand in the direction of the cards – 'Why do you keep calling them *it*? *It* says this, *it* says that. Who is behind this it? You got the top mark in our Masters year, you must know.'

'If I knew the answer to that I'd be very rich or dead.'

'Or both.'

At other times, in a different atmosphere between us, she would have laughed.

She got up, so suddenly the chair moaned beneath her, as if reluctant to let her go. 'All these years we've known each other did I ever question your values, your profession? Did I ever say, you are working for vultures who follow the latest catastrophe around the angel of death, just so that they can feel useful to the world, just so they can feather their middle-class nests in Paris or London. Did I ever say that?'

'I never knew you thought that way.'

'Exactly. I showed respect for you. For our friendship. Most of all I showed respect for what you had chosen to do for a living. And you come here – you pitch up here, actually, with two minutes' warning off some plane from God knows where suffering from a nameless affliction you won't tell me about, and the first thing you do is criticise what I've had to do for a living.' Her eyes flared. 'Notice I didn't say *chosen* to do. I've had to. You wouldn't know anything about that. Your parents are rich, they can always bail you out. You're like all people who congratulate themselves on being principled; inflexible and inhumane.'

Her eyes narrowed and something constricted inside me. She was one of my oldest friends. We had only known each other for ten years, but in my itinerant life ten years was a lifetime. I might be about to lose her. Perhaps I was even pushing her away, so that she could join that pool of impermanence that was my past.

'I don't mean to criticise it,' I backtracked. 'I'm afraid of it. I don't like it. Whatever *it* is.'

She closed the door to her room. I waited for her to return, to say something. Eventually I saw the sliver of light underneath her doorframe turn to darkness.

That night I had no idea whether I would remain in her flat, as I wanted, or whether I would be in some terrible hostel within days, eating stale toast on the buffet breakfast.

Beneath me on her desk, neatly folded into their black velvet bag, were blaring kings in their scaly armour, sinister castles by rivers, bickering wolves and the lightning bolt and giant hammer Mercedes had seen in the outcome position of my reading. That night I imagine a soft wind ruffling through the cards, scattering them, like the sudden desert wind I will encounter here, that comes as the temperature dips before sunrise, not an exhalation across the land but as if the sun were siphoning all air and heat from the world to fuel its arrival.

I woke to find Riaan tending to the campfire. The logs were so dry they burned without the usual spit and sizzle, rising in a single column of smoke.

As I rose from my bedroll I saw footprints in the sand around the fire. I studied them: five digits, all kidney-shaped.

'Hyena,' he said.

'They were right here?'

'It was a busy night in the combat zone. Didn't you hear the lion?'

'I was out like a light. I must be getting used to this.' I sat with my sleeping bag pooled around my waist. It was still cool. 'So what do we do?'

'Well I'm not bloody giving up.' Riaan lit a cigarette, fishing a flame out of the fire on a twig. 'I'm going to find out what's happened at the school. We'll have to go back to Xaia and find an official. If that doesn't work, maybe to Kashema.'

We packed up and got in the car. Soon bony mountains appeared on the horizon. We drove through sorrel grass into passes studded by miniature mesas of megalithic rock. We found the main road and turned on to it, driving beside amber hills. Sand-coloured antelope revealed themselves in their folds, before bolting at the sight of us.

We reached Kashema at three in the afternoon. Riaan sprang out of the Landcruiser and disappeared into the office of the regional protectorate before I had even left the car. I followed him into a dark room that smelled of dust. A man in beige fatigues sat behind a ship-sized desk with nothing on it – no papers, telephone, not even a bar divulging his name.

I heard finishing-up sounds behind me. Riaan left the building without signalling to me. I trotted after him, casting a glance at the seated official. He averted his eyes and looked out the window, suddenly fascinated by something happening there.

We reached the truck, parked in a pool of shade. We propped ourselves against it, leaning into the sudden coolness.

'Just as I thought.' Riaan avoided my eyes. In him, worry looked like anger, and anger like worry. 'It's Justice.'

'You mean the law?'

'It's his name, the kid. He's very clever. A kind of genius in fact. I've never met him, but the headmaster told me about him. He's only eleven or twelve but he's more intelligent than the teachers. He can do everything – maths, chemistry – as if he knows it already. So, the local evangelicals decided he was a witch and closed the school down.'

A heaviness moved through me. 'Oh.'

'Oh indeed. They've taken him to some prayer camp. I know where it is, more or less.'

The hard gravel of the parking lot shimmered heat upwards, baking us. I wiped sweat from my neck, where it itched.

'What do you want to do?'

'We can't leave him there. They'll kill him. Or at the very least abuse him. We'll have to get him.'

'You want to take him out of there, to rescue him?'

'It's worth a try. We can take him to a place I know run by nuns while Silas locates his family.'

'Are there many evangelicals here?'

'All over the place, now, since AIDS. Sometimes they're a front for the SLA.'

'What's that?'

'The local liberation movement.'

'What do they want?'

'To form a country out of this godforsaken strip of land.'

'Still? Why?'

'It's a long story.' He looked tired, then. 'I don't know that I understand it myself. I'll tell you tomorrow.'

We drove until it was nearly dark. Riaan veered off the road, once again in a place with no markers, no promise of a road or a flat, stoneless piece of ground to camp on, following some instinct. Soon we did come to a piece of level ground shaded by a broad-branched tree. We laid out our bedrolls, made the fire and went to sleep.

Later – I don't know what time it was – I woke suddenly to find Riaan sitting up, alert. The sound came again, a tear in the fabric of night.

'Eight kilometres away, give or take,' he said.

'Does a lion's roar carry that far?'

'Ten, max. Don't worry, they're heading the other way.'

I couldn't get back to sleep. My heart refused to stop pounding. I could only hear the sawing sound of the lions. But there had been a plea, too, inside it, a strangely supplicant note. *Are you there?* They seemed to be saying, calling for each other. The reply came from further away, affirming, even soothing. *Yes, I'm here*.

# VII

*Welcome to Agbelengor.* The sign, dirt-scarred, rushed to meet us. Underneath this text was an amateur drawing, in white, of a pair of hands clasped together. Then, painted in unsteady capitals: *PRAYER CAMP.*

We pulled up underneath a tree. I counted five low buildings painted in blue and white, hemmed by a rim of orange dust. Inside we could see the egg-shaped heads of children, row on row, bowed at desks. Paths snaked between the buildings. The compound was unusually neat – no spare bicycle wheels or spent car tyres leaned up against the buildings, no piles of plastic bottles lurking behind trees.

Very soon we were confronted with the pastor himself, who received us with a wide smile.

'Welcome gentlemen. We are so pleased you have come all the way from the snowy north.'

Riaan was Norwegian, I was Dutch. That is what we had agreed. Riaan had called the pastor, impersonating a faith-based NGO from the north. He'd made the call the day before, standing inside the dark confines of a roadside stall, making all the people waiting there for their mobiles to charge speak in the background in officious voices.

He had just landed in the capital, he reported. He and his associate were coming to Agbelengor with chequebook in hand, but first we wanted to inspect the prayer camp.

We trailed the pastor into an office. Above the desk a three-blade overhead fan scraped unevenly, missing its fourth rotor. Only two books sat on the pastor's bookshelf: *Holy Bible* and *Bismarck: a Biography*.

'We are glad you have come,' the pastor said. He wedged himself in behind his desk, his eyes huge, magnified in coke bottle lenses. His hands were entwined in a prim knot in front of him. His face was a sunken pillow – it had once been the face of a plump man, but something had siphoned the air from it.

'We're very glad to support your organisation,' I said. 'But we would like some information first.'

'Anything, gentlemen.' The pastor's smile had a goofy, childish lilt. He was nearly bald, his forehead ovoid and polished.

'We've heard about the case of the boy you took from school,' I said. 'Our congregation is very concerned.'

'What happened at the school where he studied?' Riaan said.

'The people didn't want to be in a school any longer where there has been a witch.' The pastor said this matter-of-factly. 'So they deserted the place, and went back to their villages. It was God's will. We left with the boy, and the school was abandoned. I did not see it myself.'

I glanced out the window. A beige sedan was parked there, with a long bonnet and boot like a snouted fish, the kind of car that hasn't been seen in Europe for thirty years. I could only just read a sticker on the side of it: *Farming God's Way*.

'The boy is a spectral thief,' the pastor went on. 'He is a soul-eater. Or he commands the soul-eaters.' He gave a shrug, as if the difference between the two was inconsequential. 'At night we have seen him around the camp. He walks in the shape of a dog. Plus, the child eats in his dreams.'

'Perhaps he is hungry,' I said.

The pastor made a noise with his mouth, a sort of titch. 'Eating in your dreams is the sign of a witch.'

'But that's nonsense.'

'This boy has killed his mother, maimed his father,' he countered. 'When his aunt took him in she died within three months.'

'Of what?'

'Witchcraft!'

'You may as well point to that tree and say that it is causing this child's family to fail.' I pointed to the mango tree which draped lustrous shade over the compound. The pastor turned and eyed the tree with a new suspicion.

'I'd like to speak to the boy.'

'Yes, yes, of course.' The pastor's voice was breezy. 'But first you must rest.'

We were taken to our room by a young woman who would not look at us, avoiding not only our eyes but our entire bodies. She treated us as airy phantoms, waving us here and there.

On the way we passed neat rooms with narrow pews, a kind of fusion of a chapel and a classroom. The compound had a sense of purposefulness about it. We passed several young men, each trim and dressed in a neat white shirt, a black bible clutched under his arm.

The young woman showed us two severe beds, placed far enough apart that were we to hold out our arms we would not be able to touch one another's hand. There was nothing else in the room apart from a chair in the corner and a sombre wooden cross on the wall, equidistant between the beds. There was no pretence at ethnic simplicity – no earth floors, woven tapestries, no exposed beams and thatched roofs. It was the same décor I'd seen in other religious compounds: linoleum, formica, plastic, all the colour of petrol.

I put my bag down, claiming the bed nearest the door. 'I'm a bit claustrophobic,' I said, by way of apology.

'No problem. I sleep like a log wherever I go.'

I sat down on the unyielding bed. 'A log on a plank.'

'If it's that bad I'll just get out my bedroll and sleep on the floor.'

We turned our backs to each other to change. In the desert we had been at ease, undressing and sleeping in bedrolls only a couple of metres apart. But now that we were enclosed within walls I was suddenly shy.

On the chair in the corner was an ancient ghetto blaster, precariously balanced. In our brief interview the pastor had told us of its purpose.

'Demons are active at night,' he said. 'In your room we will play Christian music, to deter them from entering your dreams.'

'Don't worry,' I said. 'I brought ear plugs. Enough for two.'

'Thanks, man. I guess we'd better play along with this spiritual nightwatch.'

We slept badly. The liturgical mutterings woke me; my earplugs had fallen out at some point in the night. I recognised the voice on the taped recording. It was the pastor himself, saying *Here on earth life does not go to plan*.

The next morning I woke to find Riaan already dressed and sitting on the edge of his bed, facing the wall. His head was bowed. From behind he looked as if he were praying.

'What's wrong?'

'You go talk to the pastor. I don't trust myself. You're the more rational of us. Find out where they're keeping the kid. Then we'll make a plan.'

I sat up, a headache foaming between my eyes. 'Look, Riaan, I don't know this whole thing is such a good idea. What if they phone the church in Norway to check our credentials? They've all got cell phones.'

'People don't think of doing that here. They still think the white man never lies.' He met my eyes for the first time that morning. Two dark commas of shadows flanked his mouth. 'We're here now. We might as well go through with it.'

It was late afternoon by the time the pastor finished preaching. I presented myself at his office. He was dressed in an oversized suit that armoured him like a car made of cloth. He greeted me with an air of distraction. We sat on opposite sides of his desk, empty apart from a standing crucifix and a pad of paper.

'You can reverse a bad fortune,' he said. 'You must make an *ebo*, a sacrifice. You must undertake *ese*, which means decisions, hard work. Then maybe you can change. How many children do you have?'

The question took me by surprise. 'None.'

'You must be careful, or you will have a bad destiny.'

'What's that?'

'When you do not have a wife, or children, or cattle. When you refuse to live a good life. Also – ' the pastor's face darkened, 'moral sickness. When a man loves a man, or a woman a woman. That happens when the spirit of a woman enters a man, without him knowing. This makes him desire another man. When the spirit is banished, he is cured.'

He nodded before speaking again, as if carrying on an urgent dialogue with himself. When he spoke, his voice had changed. It was pensive, tight.

'The child is unusual.'

'How so?'

'Let me give you an example,' he said. 'The other day the boy went to the matron and pointed to three of our goats. He said, you must put these goats inside tonight. The matron asked him why. At first he wouldn't say. But he saw she was going to ignore his advice. The boy said, if you don't put them in a lion will eat them tonight. And that's exactly what happened. We never heard anything. They were silent lions. But in the morning we found the goats torn to shreds.'

'But that must happen often.'

'Never! There are no lions around here. It's too dry for them.' He fixed me with a blank look. Within it was a note of fear. 'How can you explain that?'

'Maybe Justice had seen lions around, or their tracks.

He's a farm boy. He might recognise the signs. Or maybe he just' – I threw up my hands – 'sensed it.'

'A lady who works for us here, he told her she must go home because her father was ill. Sure enough, the next day she received a message he had died.' The pastor sat forward. 'So you see why people think he is unusual.'

'They're frightened of him.'

He nodded. 'I am frightened of him myself.'

The pastor was less of an ogre than I'd believed. Perhaps he was just afraid, as he said. The only thing he could think to do was to make a penitent out of the boy, to punish him for his greater power.

I looked out of the window. The slashes of shadows under trees, along eaves and gullies, black as pitch, were growing. My mind rushed backwards, too quickly almost for me to keep up, to what Mercedes had told me about the future that night, when I had accused her of dabbling in it.

'Anyone who *dabbles* is a fool,' she'd said. If you do, it will come and find you.' Again, the *it*. Who or what could it be? A god, a demon, a celestial computer programmer, a secret society of enlightened beings dressed in flowing white robes?

She always had an ability, she'd told me. This was early on in our friendship, six or eight months into the degree at the university where we studied, a haven of sensible offspring of United Nations functionaries and developing country ministers of the interior, ambitious flinty people who would likely never take a risk in their lives. And among them, a bohemian Spaniard with a penchant for ripped jeans and depressing European arthouse films, which she dragged me to every weekend.

She'd kept her pastime secret from me long enough to determine whether she could trust me. When she told me I hung my head. 'I can't imagine anything worse than seeing the future.'

'It's not that bad.'

'How do you maintain hope?' I asked.

'Hope is always there.' The way she said this, floaty and sage, rang another warning bell. I hadn't realised how much I'd been living on a diet of hope all my life – that life would be better, that I would become more intelligent, that I would find love and stop being such a control freak, that I would have a family who I would love with more passion than my parents had been able to muster. To think that hope could suddenly disappear, with one throw of the cards, like a bucket of ice tipped over your head.

The raucous evening birds called outside the pastor's office. I looked up to find him staring at me. I was aware of a light, dim at first, but slowly increasing in pressure, at the back of my skull. I raised my hand to my head.

'What's the matter?'

'A headache coming on, that's all.'

'Be careful here, there is a lot of illness. There is some malaria.'

I knew this, although I'd assumed it was too dry, this far north.

'I'll take you to meet the boy now.'

We walked to a low structure only a few metres from the pastor's office.

'Here he is.'

My first thought was: *Where?* Then I looked down to find a child who looked no more than eight years old, although Riaan had told me he was twelve. An utterly ordinary looking child: head too big for his shoulders, dark saucer eyes, a note of confusion there.

'Child, what do you have to say for yourself.' The pastor's voice made the child flinch.

The boy dropped his eyes to his feet. 'Hello, mister.' His voice was barely more than a whisper. He was so unmistakeably a child, his bony shoulders a coat hanger for his thin shirt, his hands limp at his sides, clutching a rubber ball. The pastor said something to him I couldn't hear and he ran off.

In our room that night Riaan and I were quiet. The night itself was silent. We heard only the sound of the wind beating the sparse grass.

Riaan stood and went to the window and drew the thin curtain aside. We surveyed the low-ceilinged, dark buildings, scattered about the neat compound.

'Have you noticed there are no goats, no chickens, roosters, nothing.'

'They must be kept out of sight.'

'Where do you think they're keeping him?' I whispered.

'They'd have him sleep with the animals, or on the ground.' He turned to me. 'You see now why we had to come here. Why we had to try.'

'Yes,' I nodded. 'I see.'

The following afternoon we went in search of Justice. We found him sweeping straw from the pig's quarters. Flies swarmed around the boy in a cloud.

We approached him. He tried to hide behind his broom, which, while taller than him, was thinner, if only by an inch or two.

Riaan spoke with him while I stood sentinel. The heat drilled into my head, and I felt the affliction that had come upon me the day before building again; a headache, a thick malaise that spread to every part of my body.

Riaan left the boy shuffling straw behind him.

'What did you say to him?' My voice echoed in my head. My vision had started to produce tiny zig-zag patterns, like on the screens of old cathode ray televisions in the first instant they were turned on or off.

'I told him we were going to take him out of here. I don't think the door is even locked. We'll do it at four in the morning. That will give us an hour and a half to make tracks.' Riaan peered at me.

'Why are you looking at me like that?'

'You're as pale as a sheet.'

A rivulet of cold sweat trickled down my back. I shivered.

'Come on,' Riaan clutched my arm. 'You need to lie down.'

I wake clothed in sweat. A burning white spot bleats at the centre of my mind. It isn't only the heat – there is a deeper force buried within it, far inside me. As if something were falling through me with a dark purpose, an urge toward disorder.

All day I battle fever. I am not aware that is what it is – fever – as no word can cohere in my brain. In fact I'm unaware of anything other than the lashing waves of heat. Riaan's face flares like a match in the darkness. The pastor's voice gurgles through the room. *A child is born with heaven. It is a creation in process. We enter into a river – the river of time, the river of life.*

'Hey man. So glad to have you back.'

Riaan sat forward in the chair. His brow was furrowed. He wore a striped shirt I had never seen before. I wonder if I were hallucinating it, with the zig-zag patterns of the fever. I wondered if fevers could damage your optic nerve.

'What happened?'

'You were away with the fairies.'

'It wasn't a fever. They poisoned me.'

'Maybe, but unlikely. They would have hit us both. When we get back we need to get you looked at by a doctor, just to rule out malaria.'

'What day is it?'

'Tuesday.'

'We need to get out of here tonight.'

He frowned. 'Why tonight.'

'I don't know. But we've got to leave.' The knowledge had a familiar clarity. It was of the same order of instinct that drove me off the ship.

'Are we really going to do this?' I said. 'We take Justice out of evangelical prayer camp and hand him to Catholic nuns. Do the words frying pan and fire ring any bells?'

'He'll be safe at the convent, they'll treat him well,' Riaan said. 'At least he won't be sleeping in a stable. His family will come and get him.'

'And then what, he'll spend the rest of his life tending goats?'

'He'll tend goats for a while, and then I'll get him a scholarship to a school in Nova Friburgo. He'll go to the capital for university and become a doctor.'

'As in, hey presto, here's your dream on a plate?'

He gave me a cool look. 'Why are you so certain everything has to have a tragic ending?'

'I think it's cruel to expose people who have no power and no future to possibilities they can't actually attain. Dreams don't create human beings, they destroy them.'

'Don't I know it.' His voice was dark and slippery, like a sand dune in the cool of night.

He walked to the window and stood with his back to me. From behind, his body took on a new shape. He was not muscled or bulky, yet he gave the impression of great power. It wasn't so much his physique as the way he moved that suggested vigour, impatience, and another, nameless quality held taut, in suspension, until it could be unleashed.

We spent our last day in the camp in prayer sessions. In our room our bags remained unpacked, in case they were watching us. We parked ourselves under separate trees, Riaan and I, riffling the pages of bibles, pretending to read.

*I am about to abduct a child who has himself been abducted by a religious sect.* I read this sentence to myself as if I were reading it off the page of the bible which allowed itself to be held unconvincingly between my fingers.

I stood abruptly, the chair falling backward beneath me. I stared at the neat paths of the compound, its whitewashed buildings whose purpose was obscure, the tattered windmill that twirled in the hot breeze, under the hard brilliance of the noon-day sun. How many days had it been since I had come to visit Riaan? The fever had wiped time from within me. It was less alarming than soothing, to be so claimed by experience.

There was something odd about Justice, that much was certain. I remembered a psychology article I had read for work, once. The writer held that children who are unwanted or who come into the world unexpectedly are less embodied than other people. They struggle to find their vocation, to settle and have a family. They are more likely to cast themselves to the wind of fate, lacking the direction built by self-belief. Bad destiny, in other words. The wind picked up and the tree I stood underneath shook its leaves in admonishment. The pastor's warning rippled through me.

# VIII

'What are you doing?' I twisted around to look through the rear windscreen, sure I would see headlights. We had come to an abrupt halt only a few kilometres from the gate.

'Trying not to kill that nightjar.' Riaan switched off the headlights and inched the Landcruiser forward. On the road ahead of us there was a soft flurry as a bird levitated itself into the sky, the neat white chevrons on its wings arcing into the darkness.

'For Christ's sake. They could be right behind us.'

'It's bad luck to run over a nightjar.'

'It's also bad luck if a bunch of Christians catch us and bash us to death with their bibles.'

I hadn't allowed myself to think of what would happen if we were pursued, let alone if we were caught. No one in the prayer camp had a gun, as far as we knew, but they had knives. We hadn't failed to notice the thirty or so young men who were the pastor's devotees and who hung around the compound, whittling wood into religious statuary.

The headlights were flicked back on. The bird was gone. 'The light blinds them,' Riaan explained. 'They can't move.'

The boy was asleep on the backseat, a ragged bundle underneath a blanket. He had come with us without a single word, as if he'd been expecting us to burst into the stall where he slept on a bed of straw in the dead of night all along. He'd simply risen, reached for a tattered purple rucksack, and followed us.

After another few kilometres, Riaan stopped the car abruptly and leapt out. I heard the sound of sweeping. He returned after throwing something on the floor of the back seat. This turned out to be a broom.

'If you erase the first few hundred metres from where you turn off the road they don't catch on. Old Army trick.'

After that, at every junction Riaan jumped out with the broom, while I drove slowly ahead. He jogged behind, sweeping frantically like a curler on an ice rink.

We drove all night, taking turns at the wheel. At dawn I heard the boy stir. His head appeared beside my elbow. He was looking intently out of the windscreen at the sky. 'When I was here before there were clouds.'

'Were you on this road?'

'No.' The child withdrew, back into the seat. I glanced back at him in the rear-view mirror. 'We would fly through the clouds.'

'Who is we?'

'Other people, many of them. A hundred or more.' The child nodded, his face deadly serious. 'We fell to earth and I died.'

'When was this?'

'I can't remember.'

'Were you a bird?'

'No, I was in an airplane.'

'What kind of plane?'

'A modern plane. One with jets.'

How could a child who had been raised in a village, then in a mission outpost, know about jet engines? 'Do you mean the planes you see in the sky?'

'Yes, in the sky.' The boy's mouth moved from side to side. I heard murmurs, as if he were speaking to someone else. 'It wasn't here,' he said to me. 'But in a country with jungle. It swallowed us.'

'And you say you died?'

Justice's saucer eyes were pensive. 'You don't think I'm a witch?'

'No I don't.'

The child didn't smile, or look relieved. Then he put his small hand on my bare shoulder. His skin was cool and rough.

We made a brief stop to relieve ourselves. The child clambered up onto a rock turned amber in the morning sun. He looked out into the red cut land. There was something unordinary about his gaze. He wasn't merely looking. He was reading the land, gathering information from it.

'I want to go to university,' he had said, as we walked back to meet Riaan and the truck. The child's voice was firm. He broke the word into three syllables: *uni-ver-sity.*

'Then you'll have to study hard.'

'Will you take me to your country?'

I looked down into the child's serious eyes. 'No. But I will watch over you.'

Then he fell asleep again in the back seat. I looked at him in the rear-view mirror. *Once someone has seen your face asleep they know something about you. It's as if they can steal your soul.* Had someone said this to me? I realised it was a line from Pieter's novel, *Mercy Street*. Faces asleep have always struck me; they are an arbour of secrets. Riaan's face changed character in repose. By day he looked capable, unfazed. But asleep he grimaced; short sudden spasms rippled across his face, as if receiving a blow.

'There it is,' Riaan said.

'What?' I could see only the sage and khaki bush, and a low road which curved up into the sky. But in another second or two I saw a low-slung outbuilding, like a mining shack perhaps, flanked by a crane or tower. As it came into view we saw this was a thin spire. The structure was a large wooden house. Silver sand piled up against a wall. At the entrance a squat structure stood, made entirely of some grey stone, a rounded cross perched on the top. It looked Celtic.

No one came to meet us, at first. Then, slowly, small bodies dressed entirely in black emerged from the shadows, like beetles. These turned out to be nuns.

Riaan spoke to them quickly. I stood to the side with my hand on Justice's shoulder. His face showed no sign of nervousness but I could feel him trembling under my hand.

Justice watched the spectacle of the nuns wide-eyed. He looked up at me. 'I am going to go to Atlanta,' he said, his voice solemn.

'What?'

'Atlanta, USA.'

I didn't bother asking him, why there? He'd probably seen it on someone's T-shirt. Who knew. Children were always saying random things.

I remember my last sight of him, wedged in between two of the beetle nuns, his tiny back, vertebrae visible through his thin shirt. Riaan and I called goodbye to him, but he did not look back.

He is perched on the bonnet of the truck; his legs dangle over the wheel base. I sit in the passenger seat with the door flung open.

The day is waning. The sky is wheat. In the distance is a low shadow on the horizon – Fire Mountain, Riaan's camp in its flanks.

'It's good to see it again.'

'I know,' he says. 'I always feel I'm home when it comes into view.'

'Thank you for staying with me.'

'When?'

'When I was sick.'

He takes a swig of beer. 'What did you think I was going to do, leave you there?'

'I wasn't sure.'

'I think you're too suspicious, man.'

His voice is steely. I decide to say no more. For some reason the pastor springs back into my mind; he will dangle there for many weeks after our rescue of Justice.

We are sitting in his office, waiting for my second interview with Justice. He is telling me about the tastes of spirits.

'They love mangoes, perfume. They like to come to market with us. They look at all the bowls of ceramic clay, the textiles. They are curious that we can buy so many things, also envious of our ability to choose. They can no longer choose anything for themselves.'

'Who commands them, then?' I ask.

'The light or the dark. The day or the night. Depending on their character.'

These discussions – strange, swirling, perambulating debates in which I believe not one iota, come back to me in the coming days and weeks. As if we had had been involved, truly, in a duel of truth.

I realise how much I had been relying on a certain version of the world – open to accident, chance, random occurrence – in which there was no immanence, only that stark force we call luck. Maybe I was wrong, and it really was possible to go to market with spirits, or see them under the mango tree, enjoying the smell, or riding a donkey because they are tired. Maybe a spirit really could be picked up by a person as innocently as you would buy a calabash of tomatoes.

That day we drive south for many kilometres. It is already night when we pull off the road to find a campsite. Our headlights cut two swathes through yellow grass, disturbing scrubhares who uncoil, eyes gleaming, into the air. We swish through the long grass which spills over the running boards, a tiny ship in an inland sea.

We sleep on the ground. I am used to it now and do not wake once all night. Towards morning I have a dream. Justice has grown up to become a doctor. I go to him for treatment in Atlanta. I don't know what is wrong with me, but they have to operate.

Justice starts to administer anaesthetic. Dream-adult Justice is an elegant man, all stringy limbs.

'And that man?' he asks.

'What man?'

'The man. The one who helped you save me. He loved you. You must leave him, or you will die together.'

Then dream-Justice passes the mask over my face, and I black out.

# IX

'A friend of mine owns a lodge near here,' Riaan gestured to where we'd begun to see small villages, followed by an electricity transformer – something we hadn't seen since leaving Nova Friburgo and which now looked alien, even futuristic. 'We can stay there tonight. We're due a bit of comfort.'

After five hours of silver road and a thorn tree, a shattered fence, two cheetahs and a desultory lioness who did not even move off the road as we crept by her, we reached the place.

'I thought you said it was near.'

Riaan turned off the engine. 'Five hours is near.'

The owner was a fellow ex-hunter. I forget his name now; he was older than Riaan, one of those people whose age you could tell only by his knees, which had become two brown puddings, as the knees of men over fifty seem to do. The hat he wore was identical to Riaan's: once it had been a chocolate colour of suede, but now it was rubbed to a shiny watery brown. This man had none of Riaan's delicacy yet they shared an indefinite quality, the way the man looked old, then in the next instant young, how he seemed to be shuttling between versions of himself.

The three of us sat in the lodge bar, which was deserted. A tinny radio pumped out last year's hits. The nights were unseasonably hot, his friend told us. 'By this point in the year you're normally huddling around the campfire.'

We stayed drinking for a few hours, until my eyes struggled to remain open. We said goodnight and walked the short distance from the bar to our tent. As we rounded the corner of the main building, beyond the reach of the generator-fed lights, two green eyes glinted in the night.

Riaan froze. 'Don't move.' A low growl emanated from him. I didn't know it was possible for a human to make that noise – heavy, serrated.

The eyes circled us.

'Keep still.'

We waited. The eyes did not reappear. He touched my shoulder; that was the signal. We walked, very calmly, and unzipped the vestibule made of tent canvas that led to our room. Riaan's hand was steady. Mine was shaking.

We flopped on the bed, side by side. Breaths raked my lungs.

I thought of the animal we had seen, its mottled coat, the wide, powerful jaw and paws big enough for an animal double its size. The cat had moved so sinuously, pouring itself from the ground where it crouched, eyeing us, to a standing position.

'That'll teach me not to have my rifle on me,' he said. 'Leopards like lodges. There's always scraps around. One ate an eleven year-old boy not too far from here. A tourist. Didn't you hear about it?'

I shook my head. My blood buzzed with the quinine mixer as much as the gin. I'd lost count of the gin and tonics we'd drunk – six, maybe seven. Thoughts swirled in my head: tomorrow we would reach camp. Perhaps we would stay there for a few days, no more. We would return to Nova Friburgo, and Riaan to Tanya. I would fly back to Pieter and Sara's, then to London. The future rushed toward me.

'This was the place Mark nearly died.'

I wasn't sure I'd heard him properly. 'Who?'

'A friend of mine in the Army.' His eyes stared fixedly at the canvas ceiling.

'What happened?'

'We had a puff adder in the trench, can you believe it?

Our worst nightmare. Apart from being shot by the enemy of course.' He made a sound not unlike the pastor's *titch*. 'Of course somebody was going to get bit. You can't really handle those snakes. They strike at 300 kilometres an hour. That's faster than a bloody plane taking off.'

'Hang on, who was Mark?'

'My friend. We were in the same division. He discovered the snake. He was so terrified he couldn't move. If someone didn't get it out it was bound to bite him. That's why my finger is like this –' he held up his damaged fingertip, as flat as a plank – 'and the next thing I knew I was in a truck. They took me to Quelimane, where there was a helicopter to take me to the capital. We landed in front of the bloody hospital, right in the flowerbed, everything flattened, and the last thing I remember before I blacked out was rose petals, flying everywhere, all around me, like confetti. Like I was bloody getting married.' He laughed.

'What happened to him?'

'He lived. I lived. Not such a tragedy. We were in the same battalion for nearly a year. It took us two, three months to get to know each other. We were all wary of friendships – we'd been taught to fight and relate as a corps, and we didn't want to get too attached to one person.'

'In case they were killed.'

'Everyone saw what happened to the guy who survived, when his best friend was killed.'

'Did you see him again?'

'Oh yes. After I was discharged we met up again. We would go for a drink, or to the beach. But life changed, once you were out of the Army. It wasn't the same.'

A vision, cold and pure in its completeness, came to me, of cold nights in the desert trenches, months of guns and rain, he and Mark talking about the things they would do when, if, they got out alive. They would go surfing, they would eat oysters. But six months or a year passes and they get out alive and manage to do those things together, yet they feel awkward, cheated – no, as if they are cheating someone. They become aware of keeping a surreptitious distance from one another as they'd never had to do in the Army. After a few of these victory meetings, when they are both still alive and both still have their lives ahead of them, they stop keeping in touch, first in an unaware, I'm-busy way, then more deliberately. Something – an unwelcome energy, close to resentment, unstable – has crept between them. They take it to be shame, which is only a component of the actual feeling, and slink away.

We lay in silence. Bush sounds I could not decode entered the tent – a scratching, coming from the ground. The looping, mournful whoop of hyena.

He propped himself up on his elbow and peered at me.

'What is it?'

'It's just so strange.'

I looked away. It was me, rather than Riaan, who couldn't face it.

'I've only ever wanted a woman.'

I might have said, *me too*, or, *I know*. I don't remember. The time for talking was suddenly over.

I remember I waited, or he waited. We could both hear a sound. It was a muted, almost inaudible hum – the sound of blood travelling through our veins.

He rose from the bed, twisted his torso, and bent toward me. I had only just enough time to put my glass down on the bedside table before it was toppled out of my hand. I heard him murmur *please*, or a word which sounded like this, a supplicant word that needs no answer, but then that too was swallowed by time.

His mouth filled mine and it felt like my mouth. Everything that was his felt like mine. His tongue probing the ridges in my palate, the press of his thigh on my leg, the roar of oaths in my ears, the teeth that left half-moon scars on my neck. The hot pearl sting of his lips.

He put his hands around my neck and choked me. I could not breathe. I trusted him – trusted that he meant me no harm.

The need that struck my body then was absolute and also foreign. I flipped him over, suddenly powerful, with one arm. The bed groaned from the shock. I was trying to forge him, to let the desert into his body, to squeeze out the cool particles of his soul. Somehow I knew what to do.

Afterwards we did not kiss or entwine fingers or do any of the things lovers do. We rolled onto our backs and were silent, staring at the ceiling. There was a bark cloth Riaan had told me was from a place far to the north in the tropics, tacked up over the window as a curtain. It was made of raffia, which rustled stiffly in the night wind.

I asked, 'Why me?'

He dropped his eyes onto me. His gaze always had a swooping grace, like a raptor, a hawk. 'I think we want those characteristics in other people that we most lack in ourselves. If someone were to put you and I together, as a single person, we'd be unbeatable.'

I opened my eyes. He was sitting in the chair opposite the bed, fully dressed. His elbows were propped up on his knees, his chin cupped in his hand. He was staring at me with those porcelain eyes.

It was morning. 'How long have you been up?'

'Since 5.48. The time I wake up every morning in the bush.'

'Why are you dressed? Why are you smoking? I thought you said you were going to quit.'

'Did I?'

'Last night, in the bar.'

'Oh yes. I forgot.' He plucked the cigarette from his mouth and gave it an accusing look.

'You were going to drive off and leave me here.' My mouth felt like dust.

'Yes.'

'But you didn't.'

'No, I didn't.'

'What are we going to do?'

He looked at me – quizzically is the word I think. It was neither hostile nor benign; like an animal Riaan was capable of a self-contained neutrality.

'Well, you're going to get dressed, hopefully, and we're going to have some breakfast. They might even have real coffee.'

The dread left my lungs and I breathed in, then out, in a horsey wheeze.

'What's the matter?'

I shook my head slowly. I couldn't speak. I managed to say, 'You were going to leave.'

He shook his head slowly. 'But I didn't.'

The dread flooded back into me. He hadn't, but I sensed it was only a reprieve.

Thuds erupt from the ground. Not all of them explode; it is the ones that land with a dull lugging sound near his feet which frighten him more than the ones that go off. The silence, the seconds, counting *now, now, now*. The explosion that never arrives is more terrifying than the one that does.

For days they have walked through temporary forests. The trees are in leaf, because it is spring. The papery leaves rasp against their rucksacks. The topside of each leaf is green, the underside silver, which shimmers where the light catches it. It is these waves and glints of silver that helicopter pilots on both sides of the conflict are trained to spot from the air, and fire into.

He has the impression he is walking through a forest of conspirators, of whispering ghosts. These trees are their betrayers but there is no choice, they must be crossed. Three days later they all come out the other side intact. It is here that the mortar fire catches up with them.

Helicopters come at dawn, to execute survivors from the air. He learns the hiding places in the rocky outcrops, which fissures will swallow a man. But for the most part there is no cover. They can be shot like animals in the red brew of morning.

At nineteen he doesn't fear death, or it is not exactly fear. He doesn't know what he feels: there is a blunt edge to the possibility of dying, it is a wedge of solid but transparent black. He'd like to try his strength on that edge. He doesn't believe it could really cut him. He is *unbreakable*. That is the word Riaan uses, in his mind – rather than *indestructible*.

But the way they are living now there is no future. Only the next step, and the next blow as mortar fire hits is mark. And this futurelessness is one element in why this time in his life will feel more alive, and vivid, and important, than almost anything that comes afterward. When it is over he will have been cut off from something vital to his existence but yet which has no name. Other people call it *danger,* or *war,* or *the military*. But it is actually a black beckoning on an internal horizon which, once set, will remain with him for the rest of his life.

The liberation army on the other side of the border are better armed than they had been led to expect. His superiors had lied to them, this is the fact. He should be in university falling asleep in lectures, seducing lank-haired girls, staging political protest marches, but no, he is here and he will die in this russet land.

He lifts himself off the ground. *I'm still alive*. The same thought I will think every morning rising from the same ground fourteen years later, only no one is trying to kill me at night, or the next day. No black metal bees of death buzz in the sky, fixing my brain in the hairline trigger sight of an automatic rifle. Maybe that is why Riaan sleeps so deeply in this land, because it once tried to kill him, but he survived.

His hair has lightened under the onslaught of sun, now

it is the dark blonde of good honey. But open sores cake his feet. His lips are cracked so deeply they will remain quilted with fissures.

This is the day he meets Kamma, who he takes me to see fourteen years later in that dark shack. A face pops out of the bush and he finds himself staring at a black man wearing the fatigues of the Liberation Army. They are both so shocked they smile.

'What are you doing here?' the man asks.

'I don't know. I was sent here. Last night I took cover on those rocks – ' he points to a flat mesa not a hundred metres away – 'and got separated from my unit.'

Kamma is twenty years older than this youngster. He thinks: *God send this boy back to his mother.*

'Over there, that outcropping. No, not the one to the right, the one to the left, which looks like a monkey's bottom. Yes, that one. You will find your unit camped behind there.'

'Is it mined, the way?'

Kamma clicks his tongue in reprimand. 'Do you think I would send a young man into a minefield?'

With his eyes Riaan counters, *But this is a war.*

*No*, Kamma shakes his head, and speaks in the silent language they have forged. *I would not do it*.

Riaan will tell me about this silent conversation, the one that saved his life. That is why many years later, at a conference organised by the Annexation War Reconciliation Committee, they would meet again and become friends. Kamma would be like a father to him in his first years working in the desert, teaching him everything he knew about tracking and survival, and he would have a father's instinct – far more than Pieter – for the people Riaan would love, which is why he will eye me with odd neutral suspicion on that day Riaan brings me to his shack to meet him.

Riaan will never forget how this land became not his enemy but the enemy of his survival. The ponderous hunters and their brittle wives he would guide through it would see the stirring power of the plains, wheatgrass foaming, the small cautious antelope, the red shale of the mountains. *How beautiful,* they will say, over and over. That this thorny landscape fed only goats a bitter meal, that just underneath the sand lay fragments of bullets and shells, that this land had once tried to squash Riaan's bones to the ground, was his secret.

Other people are always aware, on some level, of these carefully guarded pacts with the self, which manifests itself in such subtle ways, such as the astringency and snap with which Riaan moved in this place, the reserve in his gaze, and also an impression that he was looking for something or someone, always, that he was on a rescue mission. So that for the women and men he guided during those years he was outwardly gregarious, talkative, flamboyant – a character. But they would all agree how, after days and even sometimes weeks in Riaan's company, they parted feeling he would not remember them at all.

# X

The nights were getting cooler. In the day the light still fell from the sky in metallic sheets. But at sunset it turned furtive and wove sideways across the desert.

We arrived back in camp to find the land had changed, too; it was gathering its energies for the dry winter.

We had trouble lighting the fire in the wind that night, but at last we'd got it going. Riaan was unusually quiet. He seemed to be considering something, turning it over and over in his mind. Indecision sat so unhappily with his normally decisive nature, it coated him in some sort of glaze.

'I heard from Pa. He sent me a text. They're worried about the house. The mountain is dry – dry as kindling he says. It could go up any minute.'

'But there are firefighters, aren't there? They seem pretty organised.'

'I'm not sure how much use they are once a fire gets going.'

'Do your parents have insurance?'

'Yes, but you're never sure if they're going to pay out. It's not like Europe.'

'I didn't say it was.'

He gave me a narrow look. I tried to change the topic, to avoid the restlessness coiled within him. 'How is he? How are they both?'

'He didn't say. But he mentioned his novel still isn't

working. I don't need to tell you it's not worth going back there if he's in a mood.'

'I don't think Pieter – your father – has moods as much as states of mind.'

'That's right, he has two states in fact: my book is going well, or doing well now that it has been published. Or my book is not going well, or my book has sunk without a trace.'

'That's never happened to him.'

Riaan snorted. 'He thinks it has.'

'I finished *Shame, Mercy Street, The Glass House*. I'm reading the essays now, *Memory and Desire*.'

That warning flash – flint or tourmaline – passed through his eyes. 'Oh yes? And what do you think?'

'If I could interpret the world like that, I'd feel at home in it.'

He turned his face away from me. With a long stick he poked at the fire until it spit at him.

'What do you think of his work?'

At this, he was silent for a long time. 'I don't know how to think about it,' he said finally. 'At times I think it's because he is more than one person, so he writes to give life to these alter-egos of his. At times I think it's an atonement, but I don't know for what. Or it could be a moral experiment, a way to process the history we were all born into, here, simply by arriving on this earth in this country.' He paused and stared into the fire. 'He once told me that if he didn't write, he would have been locked up long ago. I don't know if he meant he'd be a criminal or a nutter. Maybe both.' He gave a dry laugh. 'Maybe it's just self-preservation. Other people drink to forget, and he writes.'

I thought of Pieter, his easy company, his bonhomie, his meditative temperament. There was an internal reality behind this diorama that was kept well hidden, possibly to Pieter as much as anyone else; it was a part of himself he was not much in contact with. Maybe Riaan was right and the hidden element was history, specifically the history of this country.

Before he was old enough to have done anything he'd need to forget or elide, Pieter had inherited a deed or many deeds from history. In order to erase their energy he had to make them live again first, in the form of his books.

'Or maybe it's multiple personality disorder,' Riaan went on. 'Culturally sanctioned schizophrenia, even.'

'Do you really think that?'

'What I really think is that my father is a pathological liar. All writers are. They use their writing to legitimise this. Not only that, they're given awards and prizes for being liars.'

'Sometimes you have to lie in order to tell the truth.'

He laughed. 'That's what my father would say.'

I should have been angry with Riaan. But I was troubled by that plasma-like ability I'd seen in Pieter to absorb anything that came into his sphere as information, to feed off it. Behind this vaguely cannibalistic quality was a more difficult to define threat: that he could turn this apex predator instinct inward, on himself.

'Did you ever want to be a writer?' I asked.

'No, that was Stephen. He wrote a book. A collection of poetry. Although I love to read. I just wanted to live. That was all I wanted.' His voice rippled with conviction. 'When you are about to die – if you're lucky enough have time to perceive you're about to die – and there you are, on your deathbed, do you think you will remember all those hours at your desk?' His gaze then had chilled, as it sometimes did. Cool, tendentious.

A warning ruffled through me like the sundown wind. I had a sense of what he was about to say; not its content, but its spirit. I stiffened.

'Are you attracted to my father?'

A spasm went through me. 'No.'

I got up from the camp chair and began to pace – aimlessly, kicking up sand. 'I thought you were different, but you're just like everyone else.'

A flicker came from deep within his eyes. 'How is that?'

'You're a despot,' I wheezed. 'That's what people are, little *despots*.'

'Why, because I asked you an obvious question?'

'It's an obscene question. You're jealous of your father, you compete with him. Don't drag me into that.' I very nearly said, *I am not your father.*

He went to sit on the other side of the fire. From time to time I caught sight of his face. He looked lost in thought. Wherever he had gone, I had cast him there with my words. I wanted to have an effect on him more than I wanted him to love or to approve of me. I am a kind of revenge, I thought. But who has sent me? To avenge what?

This was nothing I had felt before: to be drawn toward a person with my soul, but for my body to resist, not out of prudery or propriety or anything at all to do with what we call sexuality, but from fear – fear that it would be sullied, whatever lived between us. Every touch between men might be only a modified blow. Women can be affectionate with each other without raising suspicion of physical desire, but ask any man how hard it is to touch another.

I woke to a hand over my mouth. I saw a glint in the moonlight and remembered where I was.

Riaan had raised himself onto his knees. In his right hand was a long sword, curved – a scabbard. Where had that come from?

He remained crouching. His eyes scanned the darkness around us. I levered myself off my bedroll and assumed his position. He took me by the elbow and brought me to my feet.

A soft thud on the ground behind us. I felt it before I heard it. Then I heard a barely audible sound – a coiled *pad, pad, pad*.

We whipped around to find two emerald eyes hanging in the darkness. Beyond them, a lean spotted body stretched away into the night, its tail swaying like a cobra. Then a growl, like a very loud stomach rumble, but at any second the sound threatened to tear the air. The leopard's face gave nothing away – no fear, no reconciliation with its situation.

Riaan growled again, more urgent. At this, the cat's ears went back. Its mouth narrowed, then opened to show purple gums and teeth that in the moonlight looked more like jewels. I felt no fear. In fact I felt drawn toward those gums and teeth, smooth and clean as a baby's bottom.

Riaan's hand was still around my wrist, encircling it in a vice. If he moved it one way or the other, my wrist would break.

The animal backed away. Its gaze never wavered, nor did it disappear. It simply rejoined the night.

I looked for it. Where had it gone? Had it gone to attack from behind? Would the last thing I felt be the thump of the weight on my back, the punctures of the claws, the scalp as it was peeled from my head?

Riaan went to the fire and picked up a burning stick. He threw more wood on the pile. 'Sorry about that. I thought they were long gone from this area.' His voice sounded like water. He was completely calm. 'They must have discovered that goats have come back. There's been only cattle here until lately.'

'Do you think it was going to attack?'

'Hard to say.' He stepped into the fire to knock an ember with his boot. 'One thing is for sure, he wasn't expecting to find two guys trussed up like giant sausages on the ground. That would make a tasty snack.'

I sat down in a camp chair. My head was still heavy from our argument. We had gone to bed without speaking, the first time we'd left the day on bad terms.

'I suppose that's the end of sleep for us tonight.'

'The smart thing to do is to stay awake until dawn,' he said. 'Everything loses interest at first light – leopard, hyena, lion. You can drive a herd of cattle right by them at sunrise and they'll hardly sniff their hides.'

He came around to my side of the fire and pulled his rifle

out from where it had lain beside his bedroll. He examined the muzzle, then blew a puff of air into it.

'Why didn't you use that?'

'Not enough time to aim and fire. The leopard charges at 90 kilometres an hour. That's faster than the lion.' He fixed his eyes on me. 'That makes two leopard encounters in a week. You must attract them.'

We remained awake, watching shooting stars hurtle across the sky. After a while I could tell these apart from the long looping tracks of satellites and the blink of long-haul flights. The stars were bunched together, focussed, the eye of a distant watcher. We are all huddled on this planet, I thought, trying to protect ourselves from the flensing intelligence behind that eye. Maybe that is why Riaan had come to the desert, as mavericks and unwanted sons used to go to sea: they can withstand the exposure.

I could feel how this land might be an antidote to that probing eye in the sky, how it offered a certain protection with its yellow skies and waves of plains. There was no distant roar of traffic, no headlights or contrails of planes overhead to remind us of the shuttling, indifferent passages of others, the smooth comfort of knowing we are part of a pattern of people going here, going there. We were on our own, there, sandwiched between the stars and the earth.

At dawn we gathered our bedrolls. We followed the cat's tracks for a while.

'It's long gone,' he pronounced. 'Look – ' he pointed to a track. 'It's jumped over there' – he indicated where the trail picked up again, on the other side of two boulders. 'Ten metres, easy. You should see these cats in action. They're a cross between a gymnast and a sprinter. The most athletic animal in the bush. They're impossible to tame. People have tried to keep them as pets, but they have a very particular nature.' His accent flensed these words into upright, alert syllables. *Par-ti-cu-lar.*

All day we struggled to keep awake. Riaan needed to clear some brush. He left me to watch over the new solar panels he'd had delivered in our absence. He was going to do the switch from diesel to solar by himself, without expert help. Solar panels were still considered new technology in disaster relief, at least for large settlements, so they were beyond my expertise but I'd seen colleagues, specialists really, rig them up in the field.

That night we barely had enough energy to eat. By eight o'clock we were asleep. We awoke some hours later – I couldn't see my watch in the dark – to drops on our faces. Within seconds it was a downpour. We gathered up our bedrolls, sleeping bags, backpacks and the cooking pots and were in the truck within two minutes. Even so, we were already soaked.

'Hard to get sleep around here, between leopards and rain,' I said.

There was room for two bedrolls, just. We lay on our backs, listening to the rain.

What had happened between us in his friend's lodge seemed to belong to a different dimension. I had never moved away from an experience so quickly before. There was a frightening dimension to our evasion, as if we had been temporarily insane.

'What about you?' he asked, out of the darkness. 'Why aren't you married?'

'Women have always been more interested in me than I have in them.'

'How do you know?'

He thought my answer arrogant. Maybe it was.

There had always been women, I told Riaan, in the library, in graduate school, in my block of flats in Bloomsbury, at work. The English women I met were milky and diffident, they didn't seem to care at all whether they fell in love, got married, or what happened to them. Or rather I took their languidness for indifference but discovered I was wrong.

These women were actually supernaturally tough and remote. I could see how other men would want to crack their shields, if only to get a response, but I lacked the guts.

In the field, there were better opportunities: a flinty Bulgarian woman doctor, and Karen, my Hawaiian girlfriend of several years who was part Hawaiian, part Japanese and part Chinese. Then Mariana; she was the closest I had come to really being in love.

'What happened to her?' he asked.

'Two years ago we were working in Azerbaijan and she was charged by a herd of horned goats. She tripped over a stone and hit her head. She lay unconscious in the hospital for three days. If she'd been in a first world country she would have lived. She was thirty-three.'

I opened my eyes. I was not aware of having closed them. Riaan was staring at me.

Since Mariana, I realised, I hadn't kissed anyone. Until Riaan. How long stretched between those two kisses, how much boredom? That is what life is made of: acres of boredom, kisses scattered across it like the corpses of rare birds.

'That's tough,' he said.

'Well there's the irony of it; there we are working on the frontline and she dies from a herd of goats.'

We were silent for a while. The rain pounded on the roof as if it wanted to be let in.

'What about men?'

'There are no men. There have never been any men. I've had friends. There was Adam, we met at university. We were close for a long time.'

'What was he like?'

'He was an excellent athlete. We spent a lot of time playing squash and swimming but I couldn't really keep up. We planned a trip to Europe together, but he changed his mind at the last minute and instead went to Australia. He never arrived. He made it to Raratonga, then disappeared. This was before email. I couldn't find him, although I tried.'

'Disappeared in Raratonga. Killed by goats in Azerbaijan. You do have some stories.'

'They're not *stories*.'

I turned away, seized by a fear that they might just be that. That I might be only a story, that I was offering up sorrows as anecdote. Perhaps this is what happens as we get older – years of pain are compressed into a slick phrase to share in the desert rain.

We said nothing more. I was harsh with him, much more than I thought I was capable of. He was disintegrating in my hands, fraying to muscle and ligament and filament. It was not only desire but a frenzied tenderness; a need to give love, stronger and more alarming than mere lust. My fingertips burned for him. Not just for the touch of his skin but for the idea of him. I was trying to lay my hands on this substance, but it eluded me. I couldn't extract thought from touch.

We allowed ourselves to sink into an absolute place, then, a dimension where I felt at the very heart of being – not mine, nor his, but of being itself. I can't describe such a place. You need to have been there to understand.

# XI

We work hard. There is barely time to go to the street market and sample Lebanese kibbeh or organic Mexican burritos. We are all addicted to our screens and the rivers of names and numbers tumbling down them, an unending cascade. Our telephones summon us to board meetings, crisis meeting, Department, Region, Section meetings.

Gemma enters the frame about that time, a few months ago. At first I am dimly aware of her existence, although I notice the air seems to part, Red Sea-like, for her when she walks down the corridor. She is in Policy. Her colleagues are women with hard mouths and curiously soft men who wear yellow shirts more often than not. Gemma looks at me and it is different, somehow, from when other women do. I have always been told I am diffident, a hard-to-get man. Gemma gives me a look that is not at all admiring, rather as if something is out of place. A look of consternation.

We eat our couscous in the 'break out' area. We have broken out, but are still captives of our desks, monitors, Skype conversations with our staff on the ground, KLM air miles, insomnia. Everyone in my team keeps a wheelie case underneath their desk, filled with hiking shoes, underwear and toothpaste. We carry our passports with us every day, hauling them from home to work on the Tube, on our bicycles, while normal people struggle to find them under piles of paper for their annual holiday to Cyprus.

Eight times now since joining the organisation I have

come to the office on the Tube in the morning only to find myself on a plane at Heathrow in the evening, headed to Kinshasa, to Marrakesh, to Nairobi. I arrive blinking at Terminal Five, a latecomer to my own situation, mustering the resolve to project myself into the reality which I will encounter the following morning: women in abeyas, monkeys leering at me from the trees, dysentery.

My home in London had been notional for many years – a barren flat, home in word only. I had no plants and no cat because I would kill them if I did. I had no idea what was on television, even what season it was. I would arrive back from Mozambique in April, say, where the nights had been thinning into winter, to find see small mewling pink things like miniature kittens peeping out from the trees and think: What's that?

Home/field – this was the duality we lived with. When in the field we pined for the comforts and safeties of home. When at home we paced out of boredom, wanting the next checkpoint to be brazened through, the next dose of Coartem to beat our latest bout of malaria.

Where is your wife, your children? This was the question the people I helped asked, on the rare occasions when I met them personally, not *why*, or *who*? As if geographic location could solve the issue. I took to keeping a picture of my 'wife'. It was a picture of Ruth, actually, now that I remember – Pieter and Sara's niece. The 'children' I borrowed from my colleague Rory.

When I showed these pictures people's faces shut like small doors with satisfaction. They are well? Everyone enquired, their brows knit. What they meant was, how can they be well, when you are not there? Yes, I said. They are safe. The word, safe, brought the unmistakable mist of nostalgia to their faces. They had once been safe.

I looked at the photos – Ruth, of Tilly and David, Rory's kids – and felt something of the anchorage they would have given me. A tugging, somewhere at the base of my heart, light and insistent. I remembered an old word, one you only encounter in French or legalese: *liens*. The word lurks within her name. Elise, when I first met her. She told me about the death of her mother, her abuse by her relatives. I *always knew something terrible was going to happen to me. I was just waiting to find out what it would be.*

Gemma came to the pub the night before we left for Kassala. We didn't usually hold leaving drinks before going on mission – we were too superstitious for that. But the Kassala mission would last for months. Everyone understood our need to get in a few drinks at least, before joining a largely dry posting. We were considered hardcore in those purple corridors. We were going to the worst place in the world, where the prospect of murder, kidnap, and worse was very possible.

Three of us were flying out the next day. Everyone had come to the pub in force. It was a mild night in early December. The smokers huddled outside in the darkness in their shirtsleeves. The pub was crowded. The wooden floor groaned. The door flung open and shut, wafts of cigarette smoke in its wake.

'You don't have go to,' she said. Gemma had – has – glossy, dark hair. She flung this over her shoulder, as if to reinforce her comment. 'I mean, you've proven yourself.'

I thought, what an extraordinary thing to say. She spoke as if she knew me. 'That's why I have to go,' I said. 'I'm probably the only person who can go in there right now.'

I ran over in my mind what I knew about her: She was a Middle Eastern specialist. We had been in several meetings before I was deployed. She advised me on what passed for politics in the country – factions, warlords, thuggery disguised as religious faith. I saw her in the corridors after these meetings and we always smiled. After that I began to see her everywhere. She lodged herself in my mind. It was a year and a half since Mariana had died. I still dreamt of her. While you are dreaming of one dead lover you surely cannot take another.

Gemma was not exactly unattainable, but it was as if she hid behind a veil of potential rebuke. It would be very hard to get things right with her, or for her. The sense of task she carried about her ought to have been exhausting but it invigorated me. She was a person who made you try harder – to be more intelligent, more refined, more analytical than you thought yourself capable.

Everyone left a cordon of respect around Gemma and I that night. They angled themselves very subtly from the force field we threw – that unmistakeable aura of attraction which people detect very quickly, and of which they are both afraid and jealous.

I watched her that night. She was a generous talker. She engaged everyone she spoke with straight away. Twice she made the same gesture – once with me, once with Mussa, her boss – of putting her face in her hands, whether in shame or in delight it was not clear, until her eyes emerged from her fingers, laughing and bright.

She knew I was watching her. Sliding glances told me so. She might even have known I was making a decision of some sort: I decided I liked her because she was capable of bashfulness. It's an underrated quality, one we are often capable of when we are young, still in thrall to life, still mesmerised by its arbitrariness, by our latent capacities, amazed that we are selves at all.

I thought: when I get back I am going to pursue this woman.

Now that I am disgraced at work, I wonder if she will wait for me. I realise now, too late, that I loved my job there, the sixty-eight nationalities that work under its roof, a mini-United Nations, the seriousness and purpose, the over-used microwaves in the kitchen, the dreaded break-out room, the seminars by visiting professors from Sciences-Po and think-tank directors from Boston, the FAO and UNDP apparatchiks who seek our opinion, the FCO briefings by terrifying women unfailingly named Lucinda. Gemma and I have that in common: we are committed to solving problems which have no solution. This is not just hubris or ruthless careerism but a riposte to death – our own deaths and those we are surrounded by. It is all we can do.

We stayed at camp for ten days and ten nights. The rock doves began cooing an hour and a half before dawn and purple birds arrived to roost in the trees. Each day was dawning a minute later, Riaan told me. The planet was spinning toward winter.

We washed in open basins from which we temporarily evicted frogspawn, pulling them out in thick gelatinous wedges to let them soak in clean water, then returning them for the night. I was becoming acclimatised. I no longer considered the heat to be a tormentor. I began to recognise details of the days – the harsh, insistent call of the desert cisticola, the copper springbok that passed through the red river sand bed with their mountain goat antlers. We talked all the time. With Riaan, I never had to think, what shall I say now? We failed to annoy each other. We had a stash of beer which although warm we drank quickly and guiltlessly.

It was a Sunday when we finally left camp and drove an hour to town so that Riaan could get a signal to call Tanya and his father. I listened to him explain that we were assembling the solar power unit, which was true, and that we were enjoying being in the bush together, which was true, and that I didn't want to leave just yet, which was also true.

But to hear him make excuses was the first contact in a long time either Riaan or I had had with deceit. Until that moment in town – the same town we had visited only three weeks before, with the Bergville supermarket, the decommissioned uranium mine and the dank bar where he'd spoken to the Chinese prospectors, or whoever they were – everything we had done together felt honest and true. The introduction of even a small measure of lies soured the air between us, and we drove back to camp in silence.

There, we threw ourselves into tasks: tinkering with the solar unit, lugging electric cables up to the top of the outcrop where the windmill would one day be placed, scouring the insides of the rainwater butts. Little by little, our exertions also scrubbed away the taint of evasion, and I remember those days as long clear hours in the desert.

The nights were different. They began at sundown with building a fire, cooking, drinking beer, sitting back in our portable camp chairs and looking at the stars, but they ended in a crisis of touch.

# XII

Tanya stood leaning into the counter, petting one of their dogs. She had one of those physiques people call rangy. We were in the kitchen of their modern, glassy house. Every corner had views to the ocean. It was the first time Riaan had brought me home.

Tanya gave me a public, gracious smile. 'So good to see you again.' She gave me her hand, which I took – she had a firm grip. 'Riaan told me you had an amazing time in the desert.'

Her voice was mellifluous, educated. By now I could pick out the particular timbre of the well-born of this part of the world, those children of doctors and economists and governmental ministers and architects. They were not complacent, despite their wealth and privilege. I had never met people like this before, whose instincts had been sharpened rather than dulled by their power, their luck.

'It was certainly eventful,' I said. I smiled to show I meant no harm, but Tanya had heard or intuited something that gave her pause. She flicked her eyes in my direction, but said nothing.

'Riaan could use a few friends,' she said, draping her arm across his shoulders but not drawing him toward her. 'It's been lonely here at times for him – for us both.'

I looked at him for an explanation. 'I've never doubted my connection to the landscape, but meeting like-minded people – that's not been so easy.'

'But you meet so many people here,' I said. He had told me how people he'd never heard of looked them up when they came to town – wildlife cameramen here to make documentaries about the desert, friends of friends from Europe on luxury safaris, Swiss or Swedish or Norwegian (as they always seemed to be) agriculture experts.

'But they always leave.'

Tanya glanced at Riaan, then me. 'When do you leave, Nick?'

'The day after tomorrow. I'll go back to Pieter and Sara's, then to London.'

'Well you must stay for dinner, then,' she said. 'I'm off myself tomorrow to Quelimane. Just for a couple of days.'

'What's in Quelimane?'

'A job, I hope.' She gave me a friendly wink.

Riaan brushed past Tanya to fetch something from the refrigerator. He treated her with an almost undetectable delicacy, as if there was a force field around her. He skirted her edges, he did not resort to seigneurial gestures: pats on the shoulder, grazing her cheek with kisses. I saw how he dreaded losing her confidence, her understanding.

That night I stayed in their guest room, a garage they had converted and the only place in the house from which the sea was not visible. The ocean was very close. All night it pounded in my ears.

When I got up the next morning Tanya had already left. Over breakfast Riaan told me that she would start her new job in June. She had been trying to get meaningful work (the phrase was hers, delivered to me via Riaan) in the NGO sector for over a year. Finally she had secured a position in sustainable agriculture, working with indigenous women from nomadic groups who wanted to plant seasonal crops. She would have to stay in Quelimane during the week but would return home each weekend.

'They don't know it yet but she won't be there for long,' he said.

A buzzing, like a tiny fly, started up in the back of my head. 'Why?'

'Tanya is pregnant.'

I nodded. The words had been coming for a long time, I thought, like a train from a distant city. The moment of arrival could be put off no longer.

With three words I had been transposed to an alternate present in which we were friends. We sit by the fire and drink beer, we look up into the stars, we cook dinner together, we talk about women we have loved and who did or did not love us well enough, and then we go to our bedrolls, our separate tents and separate rooms.

I thought of the day in Cabo Frio when Rodrigo the ex-mass murderer took our photo. Until then I had been suspicious of Riaan, and him of me, too. We had made an effort to get on with each other because we wanted to please Pieter and Sara, but I was afraid of him. I knew he was one of those people who attract worshippers, partly out of fear. Perhaps that is our weakness: to worship a person or creed we have to fear it first.

Riaan squinting, the thought coming to me, as if generated somewhere else, *Now he will look at me*. The instant frenzy of tenderness. I knew its nature straight away but the context was wrong. It had nothing to do with *women* or *men*. It was simply different from anything I have felt before: hard-edged, desperate. There was a grain of violence in it.

There had been no *falling* in love. There was no descent or plummet, no transition at all. That we are capable of such changes of state seems to me the worst danger – no, treachery.

Now our futures would diverge. There was nothing I could say that would reassure him, or me. I ran my fingers up and down his spine, from his shoulders to the small of his back, feeling the ridges there, the tensile backbone of him. He let me do this, but did not speak.

Riaan walked me to my hotel that night. I was back in the casino with the safari-suited German gamblers and Dutch adventurers. I thought, but did not say: *My home is with you*. I had been cast out.

He left me at the door to the hotel, an archway flanked by two serious desert palms.

'Will you tell my parents?'

I must have stared at him. He took the back of his hand and brought it toward me. I refused to flinch. If he were to hit me, I would just take it.

He stopped just short of my cheek. He flipped his hand around, and brushed the hair out of my eyes.

I caught his forearm in my hand. The muscles there felt like ropes – thin, tensile ropes. I drew a breath. I don't know what I was going to do – to yell at him that he should leave, to ask him to stay with me, to say, *don't fucking leave me here*.

He said, in a near whisper, *no*. Before I knew it, he was walking down the deserted street.

'Riaan,' I called after him, even though I knew he wouldn't stop.

I went back inside and tried to pick up a glass to have a drink from the mini-bar but my hand shook too hard to hold it. I sat down on the bed. The room swayed.

I lay back on the bed and fell asleep.

At some point during those last days in Nova Friburgo, Pieter calls from the city, but he speaks only to Riaan, he does not ask to speak to me. He says there has been no rain in the month I have been away, that the mountain is crisping in the heat. But there have always been fires there, Riaan tells me, they kill the snakes, weevils, bacteria, they green up the grass. It requires no people, bushburning, only a strike of lightning. But there is promiscuous and proscribed burning, and they are not the same thing, he says. The word *promiscuous* is elegantly flensed by Riaan's accent, so that it sounds voluptuous, divided against itself. Riaan tells me that the mountain's escarpments, its antique shale, wait for the fire. Afterwards, cruel carpets of flowers will bloom into an autumnal spring.

On my last night Las Brisas, the bar on the beach, is crowded. Another cannonball sunset hangs over the ocean. I see some of the same faces I saw on the first night Riaan took me there. They are perhaps surprised to see us together, still.

'You look alike,' an older man with a beard, tells me. 'I didn't see it before.' I look down at my body, as if to check if it is still there. At first glance we look nothing like each other, Riaan and I, me with my dark hair and brown eyes, his shale-coloured hair, those preternaturally blue eyes. But we are both very tanned now, and thinner, and the casual observer might see a stray hunger in our limbs.

We are all sitting around a table; later three or four of us go to the bar to order a round of drinks. The next moment I miss, because I am trying to concentrate on remembering a complicated drinks order – gin and tonics, weissbier, rum and cokes, red wine – and suddenly everyone is laughing.

'What's so funny?'

'Did you see the barmaid, when she set eyes on you?'

I shake my head, genuinely confused. 'No.'

'Well she nearly fell over, she couldn't serve you fast enough.' Another of Riaan's friends, a man our own age, says, a competitive shear in his voice.

'You're not as attractive as you think you are.'

I feel a sting against my cheek. I turn to find that Riaan has said this.

'And you're not as cruel as you're requiring yourself to be.'

The conversation around us seems to fall silent, or perhaps this happens only in my mind. I steal looks at Riaan, who sits far from me, at another table, laughing too loudly with his friends, who look like roaring, post-prandial lions. I can see the abrupt tan line on his arms, from where his short-sleeved shirt stops mid-way between the shoulder and the elbow. How vulnerable his skin looks, in its white incarnation.

I slip away and walk the twenty minutes from the bar to the hotel through cold empty streets.

Two hours later, when I am packing, I hear a knock on the door.

'It's me.'

'I know.'

'Open the door.'

An immense weariness overtakes me. I feel dizzy.

'It was a lie, what I said.'

'Sometimes lies are necessary to tell the truth.' I quote my own line back to him. 'I don't have a lot of self-respect, Riaan, but I'm trying to hold onto at least a remnant of it. Don't take that away from me.'

With that he must have turned and left. I couldn't watch him do this, but I heard the door shut and his footsteps fade into the night.

*Xaia 115; Benguela Bay, 360.* The road signs all show epic distances. He swings the steering wheel round as if it is a life gone wrong. I have one hand on the dashboard, my knuckles pressed tight into the hard plastic. *Now I'm going to show you something, man.* A brotherly invitation, issued constantly, an expression of trust. The morning was pure unfiltered sun, not the gritty light you expect in a desert, even if the sand blew everywhere, into the crevasses of our shorts, our boots, the brims of our identical braided leather hats.

The night we arrive at the farm where we become lovers just before sunset. The land is thornveld, the sky emerald. We get out of the car, and as we walk together to the lodge now being consumed by darkness, our forearms brush. Not for long, but neither of us moves away. The cool is instantaneous. As the sun disappears the air chills. It ruffles between us, exploring the electricity. Look, he points to the sky, where the stars are emerging just now. *I call that constellation the leopard. Can you see him?* I look and look but my eyes can't weave together the outlines of a lean spotted cat with a too-long tail. *Yes*, I say. *I see him*.

*We can just be friends. No one will know, can't be secretive, can't let her down, she is counting on me. Don't love men, not attracted, not gay. Don't understand why I am attracted to you, am not in love with you*. There is no *I* in any of these fragments because whether he or I said these things now seems irrelevant.

We are driving into camp. Headlights fork the dark: two streams of light shutter behind us as we pass. The vultures and jackal that patrol that interim realm between the hearth and the darkness scatter. His shoulders are slightly hunched in the combative posture he adopts when driving. His face is illuminated now and then in profile as the moon cuts across it. Those startling blue eyes which have in them the conviction of a man who was forced to confront the danger and squalor of adult life early, without any kind of compensation for his lost youth. He could have died at eighteen, but here he sat next to me. The only truth that exists in the world for me is what moves between us and links us at that moment, a strange instinct, not only sexual but powered by an infinite nameless yearning. Within an hour we will have made our camp, built our fire, and the yearning will be transformed into touch. In that moment I think, this is just experience. I will go on in life, after this. I will survive its loss. I am resolute.

My flight was in the evening. To kill time I went to the bookshop and talked to the same assistant I'd spoken to a month before in another lifetime when I thought I'd be returning to the city the next day, and would never know the desert, or Riaan.

Then I had lunch in a cafeteria, rye bread, salted meat, hothouse lettuce and bland cheese. The food was like dust in my mouth. I kept my eyes on the door, expecting Riaan to walk through it at any minute. Before my taxi came to pick me up, I went for a walk on the beach and watched the sun lever itself into the ocean for the last time.

I was driven to the airport by a spirited woman named Xola, passing a lofty giant dune, sandstorm warning signs, over narrow highways fringed by battered kelp on the one side and a 300 kilometre-wide desert on the other.

I felt no fear on takeoff, it was as if I were indifferent to whether we rose or slammed onto the ground in a kerosene fireball. But the plane clawed into the air, over the lights of the ships in the harbour, the only light in that black carpet of sea and desert, and flew south.

# Part III

# I

*The mountains stray into the ocean. There is no departure point, no leave-taking; they simply dissolve into the cold sea.*

*He drives roads that hug precipices, nets against rockfalls on one side, the crashing descent to the ocean on the other. From time to time on this road boulders fall and crush cars and their occupants.*

*The city's light is unique, the product of an interstitial latitude, neither temperate nor tropic. He would never be able to leave it, the jade shards of glass that fall from the sky in the day, the protracted evenings, how darkness fills a room like liquid poured into a glass. He is a habitué of such rooms, waiting until the last minute to turn the light on, when he can no longer see.*

*Yes, if he were to leave this country he would wither. Peninsula dwelling people are different, he thinks. They understand the tenuousness of life.*

'Pieter?' I hovered outside the door. When I did not hear his voice, I pushed the door slightly. It was ajar.

The light was off. A half-finished cup of coffee sat on his desk. The typed page glared at me, illuminated by his desk light. The running header at the top of the page said *Fire on the Mountain*. I saw him. He sat in a chair by the window, half in darkness, his back to me.

He swivelled around. 'When did you get back?'

'This afternoon.'

'What's happened to you?' He was staring at me.

'What do you mean?'

'You're so tanned you're almost black.'

I looked at my hands. 'Does it look strange?'

'No,' he said, and the wariness that had sprung up in his eyes dissolved. 'You're still the same handsome guy you always were. I'm sure you've broken a lot of hearts in the desert.'

We looked at each other for perhaps a moment too long. I was still staring at my hands, as if they might hold the clue to my transformation.

The city is parched. There has been no rain for months now. In the windless afternoons a great stillness settles on the flanks of the mountains. The birds are too hot to cry out.

This landscape makes me think more sharply, almost as if it has given me a new mind. *Mountains make weather*. I read this on the page when I went into Pieter's office, looking for him. He'd written: *They rinse and clarify, like language*.

By the end of my first week back in the city I begin to doubt what had happened in the desert, doubt the existence of the place itself. I only know it was real by the sand that falls out of the cuffs of my long-sleeved shirt and the smell of woodsmoke on my shorts before I throw them into Pieter and Sara's washing machine. Before I do I put them to my nose and inhale them. I smell mangoes, carbon, and that nameless smell of the desert: sand and flint. Each streak of dirt or slight tear bore a story: axle grease when I'd helped Riaan fix the chassis on the Landcruiser after he judged it had become slightly misaligned, the thread-pricks where thornbushes had lashed at my arm as we flattened our way through them.

On the mountain the forest fire alert dial is set in the purple V of the pie-chart, the one after red: Imminent Danger of Bushfire. Birds with long tails squabble over water all day and night. The grass is tobacco-coloured, battered by the heat, the trees bent by wind, dry branches are turned platinum in the sun and squeak when you walk by. The cobras are desperate. On the mountain paths they sit, awaiting water and prey, lily-shaped hoods open, heads erect over the bush like periscopes.

In the night I watch the city from outside Pieter and Sara's guest flat, standing in the garden that looks over the bay with a view so commanding it is as if I can see the whole world. I had forgotten how the hills glitter and their lights stutter in the wind. I remember the gales when I first arrived three months ago, those five days of wind when the ship could not leave and I had time to register the future and make my exit, before it closed around me.

CONFIDENTIAL.

For the first time in a month I opened my laptop. It sat on the desk, blinking into the darkened room. I stared at the capital letters, wondering why everything legal had to be conveyed in the typographical equivalent of shouting.

I clicked and re-read the message I left unanswered a month ago, before I left for Nova Friburgo. It had not been what I was expecting, which was a redundancy notice, demands for compensation of the expenses of sending me here, or at the very least notice of some disciplinary procedure or other.

The email began with a ponderously worded press embargo and a personal disclosure agreement which warned if I leaked the information contained in the message to the press, I would be sued.

Ten nautical miles off the coast of Kassala our ship was attacked by insurgents. The armed marshals who now routinely accompany our ships fought back; the attackers were outnumbered but managed to kill ten of our number and wound another seven. Among the dead were Carlos and Ernst; the latter was shot in the heart. There was no news of how Carlos was killed. Several people huddled in the engine room for twenty hours. All surviving colleagues and the ship's personnel had been evacuated from the ship by the military and taken to an aircraft carrier in the Gulf.

The ship I spent those terrible days on in the harbour now sat at anchor, stripped and deserted. The story has not made the press because several governments are sitting on it; the use of armed escorts for humanitarian aid missions was still controversial, and often secret. In London, our office was closed for an official, if unspecified, day of 'reconciliation'. I looked at the date for the planned day of mourning: today.

When I read the message before leaving for the desert I sat in front of my computer for a long time. When I found the strength to stand I saw a rose-and-ashes sunset settle over the harbour. The colour seemed to have a message for me, one of reprieve but also warning: *next time you may not be so lucky.*

I have no way of knowing if I would have been one of the casualties. As far as I can tell you were caught in the crossfire or you weren't. Ernst was twenty-three, or was it twenty-four? It was his first job in international relief. Before I skulked off the ship he'd helped me with my luggage. He was so looking forward to seeing the ocean unimpeded by land, for the first time in his life.

'It know it will be so beautiful,' he said, looking not at the city and mountain which now shimmered in the heat in front of us, but at the southern ocean, beyond the bay's perimeter. 'I will want to stay there forever.'

# 11

I woke early to go for a run and found the door to the house open – unusual in this city where no one leaves doors open unless guarded by dogs.

I finished my run by driving myself up the steep steps that lead to Pieter and Sara's house, through the banana leaves and weeds that tendril across them and must be hacked back by municipal gardeners who materialised every two weeks.

In the house a sand-coloured hold-all crouched in the hallway. Pieter's voice called from the kitchen. 'Look who's here.' There was a note of taunt in it that made me pause.

A figure sat at the kitchen table with his back to me. He looked so outlandish, sitting in that well-appointed kitchen with its track lighting and its artisan pottery, I nearly laughed.

He turned around. 'Hello Nicklaas.'

I had to put one hand on the counter. Only with great effort did I manage not to say *I thought I'd never see you again*.

'When did you arrive?'

'Early this morning. You were out running. Are you okay?' In Riaan's voice was a tone neither of us wanted his father too hear.

'Fine. I'm a bit hot, that's all. I've just run up and down those stairs five times.'

Riaan stood up with a jolt. 'That's bloody tough in this heat. You need some water.'

'He's become a marathon runner since he got back,' Pieter said. Lately a new note had crept into Pieter's voice, one which I was keen to dislodge. It said: we are not tired of you, but when will you go? How much longer can you stay here, avoiding whatever it is you are avoiding?

I stared as Riaan wrapped his long limbs around the counter, as he leaned to the water tap. It all felt very unreal.

Why had he taken this risk? His father was the most accomplished writer of his generation. His father would know straight away. I had the impression we were both of us already fixated on Pieter, watching him for signs of understanding even if we weren't sure what form they would take: a subtle dilation of the pupils, a downward turn at the edges of his lips, as if he'd swallowed the seed of a lemon.

'You didn't tell me you were coming,' was all I could manage.

'It was a spur of the moment thing. I wanted to tell Pa and Ma about Tanya. Plus I needed to see some green – you understand that now. I'm flying back the day after tomorrow. I have to go back to deal with the school. It's pretty much as we thought: they were driven away by the SLA. Justice is fine, by the way, although the nuns are also a bit freaked out by him. They wonder if he's an angel. Not bad, eh, to go from being a witch to an angel in a matter of a month?'

'The day after tomorrow?' The words sat like lead in my lungs.

'I must leave you two,' Pieter said. 'I have to go to a meeting. A journalist wants to interview me about my new book.'

'That's great Pa,' Riaan said. 'But I thought you weren't anywhere near finishing it.'

'I'm not, but the idea is topical, it seems, they want a writerly take on climate change, as they put it, why summers have become so dry, what would happen if a major forest fire broke out on the mountain.'

'I know what would happen,' Riaan said darkly. 'All these Croatian millionaires or Russian gas tycoons who are your neighbours would watch their glass palaces explode.'

I sat down at the table, across from Riaan. Pieter was gathering his papers, clicking his briefcase shut. He turned, almost as an afterthought, to say goodbye. He was dressed in a white shirt, crisp jeans, a belt with stitching at the edges. Sunglasses were perched on his head. He didn't look sixty-five at all.

'See you later, then.' His eye rested on his son, a question mark in his gaze.

When Pieter had left we remained at the table. The clock ticked like thunder in the background. 'That old clock,' Riaan shook his head. 'It's always losing time. I keep telling Pa to get a new one, but he seems wedded to it.'

After all he and I had talked about, after all we had done together, here we were discussing the kitchen clock.

He felt the horror of this, too, maybe, because he hung his head. 'I wasn't even sure you'd still be here,' he said.

'I couldn't get a flight until next week.'

'Won't you stay?'

'I've been here for three months. My visa's running out.'

'Oh that's easy enough to fix.'

'I don't know what I'm doing here anymore. When I'm with you, life makes sense. I can be where you are, and that's enough. But here, jogging around the streets, living in your parents' house…'

'Why is that so hard?'

'Because I've never had a holiday, in all my working life. I don't know what to do with myself if I'm not working. So it's a particular shame I've screwed up my career.'

Riaan's eyes brightened. 'What will you do?'

'In London? Find work, I suppose. That ought to be interesting. My name is mud, now.'

'Tell them you had a breakdown. People in your line of work must have them all the time.'

'It's what they think anyway,' I said.

'My parents want us to go out for dinner with them tonight.'

'I don't think I can eat anything, Riaan. I feel so sick.'

He sprang up and began to pace in the kitchen. 'I can't stand it there, I can't stand it here.' He tugged at his hair. 'I feel like I'm going crazy.'

He kept pacing back and forth. The familiarity of this scene crashed into me: Riaan and I talking in Pieter and Sara's kitchen, him pacing, an air of desperation, a sheared feeling in my lungs, as if I were breathing fire. I realised I'd seen this exact moment all in a dream in the desert one night. In the dream I was afraid what Riaan would do. I'd ejected myself from it by imploring myself, over and over again, *wake up, wake up!*

He whipped around. 'Come back with me. We can work together. Or you can work as a mining geologist, can't you? Come and live in Nova Friburgo. We will figure something out.'

I could see the appeal. He would have Tanya, they would soon be three. He would have me.

'I think people already know.'

'What people?'

'Because of the way you treated me in Las Brisas. Both times. I think Tanya knows.'

'She knows what?' In his eyes was a wild glint.

'She knows something is wrong, that's all.' I gathered my resolve before I asked the question. I was so close to jettisoning it, to never having thought it. 'Can you really live a life of betrayal? These are the things I love about you, your passion, your honesty. I would be the person who took those qualities away from you. Eventually you would hate me.'

He sat down in a heap. 'For the first time I think my life wants to destroy me. As if it's a separate thing, as if it's not mine at all to live.'

'I know. I've felt it too.'

This is what all those days since I returned to Pieter and Sara's had been about, running, running, pushing myself to the limit, vomiting nightly when I had tried to eat. Outrunning the hand of fate, or perhaps the hand of God, who knew? The hand that had nudged me off the ship so that I could know Riaan.

I knew this country now. I knew that between where we sat in Pieter and Sara's kitchen and where we had been in the desert stretched sorrel hills that turn sable in twilight, oxbows of the great rivers that plough the furrows of the aridity, long-abandoned homesteads flooded by sand. Until this morning I had thought it was only this giant country that stood between us.

That night Pieter and Sara took us out to dinner on the waterfront. They ceded Riaan and I waterside seats, so that we could gaze upon the harbour lights. The yachts threw a cold light onto the harbour. In the distance the mountain was floodlit with a bluish tint. I remember Pieter telling me when I first arrived how these were turned on when some dignitary was in town, or the President was sitting in parliament.

We told Pieter and Sara the stories of our adventure: the ransacked school, our encounters with two leopards, the nights of rain, our daring rescue of Justice, the dry riverbeds that flowed at last with water, our struggles with the solar panels and the vegetable garden we planted, which would surely get scavenged before it could die of drought. We gave a convincing performance, holding his parents rapt. But we both had to muster an energy within us. We related all our stories with the forced gusto of people who within hours or short days will be in airports, who are already fading out of the picture.

Afterwards Pieter and Sara went home; we said we wanted to stay for a drink. We found a bar, a kind of sunken ship-themed space beneath a cavernous hotel catering to rich foreign tourists. There we drank wine and ran up a bill.

I hadn't seen Riaan in a city, I realised – only in Cabo Frio and Nova Friburgo, and in the bush. Why did he look so different here? In cities, surrounded by infinite representations of ourselves, we shapeshift effortlessly. Riaan lacked this mutability; he was only what he was. His hair was a shade too long, his jeans were of a cut popular a few years ago. His light blue shirt, through which his brown chest beamed like a shield, looked worn.

He saw me studying him. He shivered, although it was not cold. 'When I came back from the war this wasn't same city you see now. This mall didn't exist, for one. It was just a sleepy town at the end of the world. I spent the week shivering. I hadn't felt cold for a year. Here the temperature must have been 20, 21 degrees, but I was freezing. I used to stare and stare at the trees. To me they looked extra-terrestrial.'

'What did you do, when you first came back?'

'I went to university, then did my Masters. I went overseas for a while, to London.'

'You didn't tell me about that.'

'Not much to tell. I went, I came back.' He fell quiet. 'I looked for my friends from the Army, those who made it. I found Mark again. He'd got a girlfriend. She was nice, if a bit meek. We went out for drinks.' His gaze travelled over the yachts. They were still, supposedly, tied to their moorings, but by some trick they looked to always be in motion.

He said, 'I'm not much of a fan of secrets.'

'Secrets divide you against yourself.'

'That's right. They divide you in compartments. They pit one part of you against another. You can't be honest with yourself, so you can't be honest with anyone.'

He looked at me then, really looked at me, for the first time that evening. When we were having dinner with Pieter and Sara he'd given the appearance of meeting my eye, but really he had slid his gaze over me, then taking it elsewhere, raking the room for what – for a beautiful woman? There were no shortage of those in the bar where we sat, thin goddesses, their tanned, salt-scrubbed faces lighthouse-bright.

'You blame me,' I said. 'You think I've forced you into that territory of secrets.'

'You haven't, but you're the catalyst.'

I searched his eyes for any hint of fellow feeling. But his gaze did not soften. He needed someone to shoulder the responsibility for what had happened.

I had been waiting to ask him a question. In the desert the moment had never seemed right. I wasn't even sure I remembered the image correctly, until I saw it again after I returned. When I had gone to Pieter's office the day I'd returned, this was what I'd been looking for. The man by the white truck, the dirt road so smooth it looked cast in ceramic, the man's crushed berry eyes, the look of hungry valour on his face.

'When I first came here your father showed me a drawing you did when you where a child, of a man beside a white truck,' I said. 'Pieter said you went through a phase of drawing that man, over and over.'

'That's right.' His voice was cool. He was still holding me at bay. I told myself I hoped for nothing. He twisted his body away from me. 'I was twelve, maybe. I stopped drawing soon after that, but for a while I was pretty good. My parents encouraged me. That man – ' he still would not look at me directly – 'just came to me. I thought I might have seen him in a film. My mother thought I was drawing myself, as I would be when I was older. She called it an ego-projection.'

'But he – the man – doesn't look anything like you. In fact he looks exactly like me.'

'I thought that as soon as I saw you.' He looked down at his hands. His gaze seemed to settle on his crushed fingertip. 'I haven't got an explanation, if that's what you're looking for.'

I sank back in my chair. From time to time women in the bar made studied sorties past us. I watched his eye snag on these women with an automatic curiosity. The stab of jealousy in my stomach sickened me.

'No one person would ever be enough for you, would they?'

He gave me one of those long evaluating stares. 'Is one person enough for anyone?'

It seemed too much of a capitulation to say, you would be for me. If you were mine I would never look elsewhere. What would be the point? In love affairs – this tired term made me queasy, *love affair* – there was always one person who is more powerful simply because they are less captive.

'If you had me there, next to you, whenever you wanted me, would you still want me?'

'No one can know the answer to those questions, Nick. You just have to live and see what happens.'

Our silence attracted curious looks from three women ranged around the bar. Just as on New Year's Eve at Cabo Frio they seemed to decide something about us, independent of each other, and look away.

'What will you do when you go back?' he asked.

'I have to go to Spain, to Barcelona. My best friend lives there.'

'What's his name?'

'*Her*. She's called Mercedes. I think well in Barcelona. It will be summer there, soon.'

'Will you take me, one day?'

I tried to imagine Riaan in that boisterous city of preened men. 'Of course,' I said.

He sighed with impatience, as if everything we had just said had been a game. 'I want you to come back with me. To Nova Friburgo. I so need a friend.'

'Is that what I am, a friend?'

He stared at me. 'You might be the best friend I ever had.'

'And do what? Come to dinner with you and Tanya every weekend, because you're the only people I know in town. Watch your child be born? The only thing I have left is my honesty. I think you admire this in me. But you also can't resist the urge to exploit it.'

I thought he would rise and leave the bar then. Instead he put his face in his hands. 'You're forcing me to make an impossible choice.'

'No one's forcing you to do anything.'

'Will you stay with me tonight?'

'No.'

Back at the house, we drew the curtains in my flat. The bedroom was directly below Pieter and Sara's, so we had to be quiet. Riaan clamped his hand over my mouth, we lunged into each other, and all you could hear was the scrape of air in our lungs.

# III

After Riaan left Pieter and I were alone in the house. Sara went away to visit her mother in Malanga. In five days' time I would leave the country.

Pieter made us a dinner of pasta. We drank wine and listened to the wind, which had increased steadily during the day. The winds which reached us were hot and weirdly electric. The roof rattled. In the garden trees were whipped into agonised postures by the gale.

'You saw my work in progress, the other day,' he said.

'Only a few pages.'

'What did you think?'

'I thought it was… intensely imagined. But possibly claustrophobic, over the long run.'

He pursed his lips – in Pieter a sign of pleasure rather than censure.

'What will happen to these people in your book?'

'Characters are not playthings, if that's what you think.'

'No, I see them more like experiments. The way we might also be the experiments of super-intelligent beings, for example.'

'Except I can't lay claim to any special intelligence.' His face clouded over. 'There are fissures. That's what I think. I send these people on expeditions to explore them.'

'What fissures?'

'Ruptures in the waking dream. When things leak through moments. Cracks in the façade of reality. I feel them, more than think about them, and once I know I have that feeling, as if they are leaking into me, I'm intrigued enough to write. It's as if two dimensions of reality are suddenly forced together; they're a bad fit, so I have to reconcile them.' He paused. 'Don't you think there's an uncanny dimension to life?'

Instantly the ship floated back into view, and with it the remote intelligence, the lighthouse mind that had sought me out within its decks and cabins, and nudged me off my intended course. I still hadn't told Pieter what had brought me to his shores; after my initial evasion there seemed to be no way back to the truth.

'I've been having dreams. For the first time in my life they're coming true.'

Pieter sat forward in his seat. 'What's that? Your dreams are happening?'

'Right down to what people say. They're like flashes of déjà vu, all the time now. I know what's going to happen next, exactly.'

'That means something important is coming.'

I wanted to say, I know. But I was spooked. Mercedes had told me long ago that we only have conscious access to the future shortly before we die. Or, more precisely, that to know the future is to hasten your death.

We sat in silence listening to the wind rip through the trees. Since I had returned from the north Pieter seemed smaller than when I'd met him – less of a towering figure overshadowed by his reputation. I wondered if it were really true that his son, Stephen, who I had never met – would likely never meet, now – had an equal talent, and Pieter had strangled it.

Riaan, we knew what had happened to him; he'd exiled himself into wild man territory so as not to have to compete with his father. In that place Riaan tries to nourish his dreams, he moves forward into that enticing horizon which grows no closer, no matter how many hours he drives in the desert night. He does not live on several different levels at once, as his father does: levels of the real, the possible, the fantastic, the absurd, the symbolic and the metaphoric. He does not deal in that shabby currency of things gone wrong, of turning points, of tragic failures. But he could go there, if only his father, and his father's reputation, did not stand in the way. His name will never grace the national newspaper, as his father's does. The internet search engine will not return 402,458 results, as it does for his father. His father is on the bookshelves, in the history books, his father is everywhere.

The wind hit the kitchen window so hard I started. 'You'll get used to it,' Pieter said. 'When you live here.'

'Do you think I will ever live here?' The hope that sprang up in me then surprised me.

'Of course you will.' His voice become distant. His proclamation was arbitrary, I realised, not oracular. He began to talk about his months spent abroad on fellowships, attached to distant universities.

'If only I'd stayed in California,' he said. 'The Pacific – I'd never seen that ocean in my life. The sunsets are unbelievable. I loved the ease, the self-indulgence programmed into the place. But I realised it would be disastrous for me as a writer to live there. Those kinds of places – Australia, California, New Zealand – they suck all the anger out of you. You can't be a writer and live in a place like that.'

'Are anger and creativity connected for you?'

He gave me an impatient look.

'I don't know, Pieter. I'm not a writer. I just live.'

'But you'll write about this – about your trip here. About Riaan.'

'I have no plans to do that.'

He nodded. 'You will. Someone will.'

He cleared away the plates and we went to bed.

I woke to shouts, then a crash that sounded like cymbals falling onto the floor. The alarm clock said 3.17. I got up and opened the door to the main part of the house.

Framed in the window of the dining room was a wall of flame. At its base it was the livid red of Chinese silk. The tops of the flames were incandescent, almost transparent. They were scratching the sky for oxygen, ragged and gasping. The fire was perhaps a kilometre or two away.

Sirens peeled the night open. Pieter came racing down the stairs, still putting on his shoes, hopping on one leg.

'We need to get on the roof,' he barked. 'Help me with the extension ladder.'

We were in the garage – I have no recollection of having walked or run there, perhaps we flew – and then we were in the back of the kitchen, and somehow I had my head torch on, and Pieter was rigging up the pipe from the swimming pool outtake. He threw the hose up to me and I managed to catch its heavy coils and not allow myself to be dislodged from the ladder. It was a long way down.

From the ladder I saw that the mountain was scarred with rivers of fire. They flowed from the north, the direction of the wind. One of the rivers paused right behind the house, on the other side of the swimming pool. The flames leapt back as one, as if they were a living creature, as they encountered a sudden lack of trees to feed them.

'Get down. I'm coming after you. There's no point...' Pieter's words were eaten in a vortex. 'Don't breathe!'

A plume of smoke enveloped us, acrid and burning, and then just as quickly disappeared. The air smelled not of cinders and ash but of sap and grease of melting: trees, the fat in the small deer that lived on the mountain, the lizards and the guinea fowl which could not take flight quickly enough and were incinerated two inches above the ground as they tried to lever themselves into the air.

The fire lunged forward. Pieter and I jumped, as one, into the swimming pool, fully clothed. I surfaced, gasping. The heat was on my face.

'We have to burn it – everything,' I gasped. 'The garden.'

'What?'

'It's the only way.' I leapt out of the swimming pool; at the same moment a branch as big as my body and cloaked in flame was tossed across my path. I managed to reach the garage without being hit. A petrol can stood in the corner. Pieter had drained it from the tank the night before, as the city's dry season directives commanded, so the car would not explode. I tore pieces of material – I would not be able to say what it was, rags or pieces of sail, treasured towels, and soaked them in petrol. I lit these with a burning branch and flung them into the garden.

Pieter levered himself out of the swimming pool. He stood, fully clothed and dripping, staring at me. His face was gaunt with shock.

The wind blew a sliver of the wall of fire in his direction. 'Get inside,' I shouted. 'Get inside the fucking house!'

The fire – my fire – brushed the grass in ragged streaks, seemed to hover above it, then ignited. Snakes exploded out of the bush: two yellow cobras flashing across the grass. I watched them slip into the swimming pool. Other small animals, creatures I couldn't identify, exited the shadows where they'd been taking refuge in a scurrying tide.

Pieter stood next to me in the kitchen, dripping and sodden. His face was punctured. I couldn't blame him; he had just watched me raze his grass, the garden furniture, the pear trees that have taken nearly two decades to grow.

I tugged at his wet shoulder and forced him to the floor. We lay there chest-down on the cool tile, rags sodden with the remaining water from the water butt tied over our mouths. Our throats were too dry to speak. Pieter's eyes said: *What have you done?* I sent him back a message: *Trust me*.

It would dawn on him once his mind was released from the claw of shock. I had burned the fire's fuel. When the thirty foot high wall of flame reached the boundary of Pieter and Sara's back garden, it hesitated. There was nothing for it to eat or drink. So it folded back, shivering on itself, then fanned out in a giant red arc around the house. Just as it looked as if the fire would consume us it made a leap around the house, then carried on down the mountain.

At dawn we sit in the kitchen with blankets around our shoulders.

Pieter is framed in the door, reading glasses perched on his head. His eyes are red from smoke.

'How did you know to do that, to set fire to the grass?'

'If you create a vortex through burning everything in its path, then the larger fire has nothing to feed on and it moves on.'

'Why didn't anyone ever tell me that?'

'Firefighters don't want ordinary citizens to know about it, it's too dangerous.'

'Sara hasn't gone to visit her mother,' Pieter says. 'She's gone to the coast. She needs medication, a rest.'

I blink. My eyes itch from ash. It's a hasty confession, and unnecessary. Does he think that now the house has almost been consumed by flames I would somehow find out about her whereabouts?

'I hope she's alright,' I say.

'Her patients are all in serious distress. She takes it on board, you can't not. Then there's the stress of living with me.'

I expected to see the wry smile he usually delivered, but his expression was sombre. I always suspected that Pieter and Sara were married through something more ripe and dangerous than ordinary love. There was a secret at the heart of their marriage. I couldn't guess what it was.

By that night new smells emerged. A stench of dead flesh in the flowerbeds revealed the corpses of mice and a delicate unburnt corpse of a small red deer that had died of smoke inhalation.

We sat with a bottle of gin between us. In the fridge was a two-litre bottle of diet tonic water and more ice than we needed. Electricity came courtesy of the backup generator. The news told us there would be no electricity on the mountain for a couple of weeks; all the transformers had exploded in the fire.

As we drank, Pieter began to tell me a story. It seemed to emerge out of a dense silence inside him, a presence I had perhaps perceived from the first moment I had met him and had mistaken for a secret. Although, as he told his story, it became that, too.

'She was a friend – not a girlfriend – of Riaan's,' he said. 'She was twenty-two years younger than me when I met her. Kristina. Her friends called her Kiki. Riaan brought her home with a few other friends – a mix of men and women, or *girls* and *boys*, as I thought of them. That was one of the first years I felt old. I couldn't have been more than forty. No, I was forty-two, that's it.

'I came into the garden to say hello; they were talking and drinking beer. I took no notice of her at first. Then I saw the book she was reading – she had placed it, perhaps strategically, on top of her bag. *Mercy Street*. I saw how affected, how silenced she was by meeting the man who had written it. But she also knew Riaan well enough to say nothing and to not behave as if she were awed by his father.' Pieter shook his head. 'She was discreet. It was all there in a single look we exchanged while I stood barefoot in the grass. I remember the grass had just been cut and the sharp edges tickled my feet. I kept hopping from side to side. She must have thought I was nervous. I was.'

He fixed me with a steady look, very similar to how Riaan would look at me, but without the note of challenge at its core. 'A man always knows, from how a woman looks at him.'

'Does he?'

'You tell me.' He put his glass down and it rapped on the table like a rebuke.

'She slipped her telephone number, written on a tiny scrap of paper, into my hand as she shook it at the end of the night. Did she really expect me, a married man, the father of her friend, to call her?'

Pieter paused long enough for me to think he expected an answer to the question.

'I let three, four, five days go by. I did my sums. Nineteen. Was nineteen a girl or a woman? What harm could there be in meeting a fan of my work for a coffee, for a drink?

'We met in hotel rooms, they weren't cheap, but a hotel room always cheapens love. I would sit in the chair in the corner by the window – there was always a chair in the corner by the window – and watch as darkness slid across her arms, her legs. She had downy hair on her arms, like a child. That was the only time in my life I have ever loved beyond thought. There was no thought involved.'

'What happened to her?'

'She married another of Riaan's friends, someone her own age. I didn't have the guts to tell Sara, let alone to leave her, so I watched the woman I loved marry someone else.' Pieter folded his arms unhappily across his chest.

'Does Riaan know?'

'No. Never. You must never tell him.'

'He hates secrets.' I said.

'Don't we all.' Pieter leant forward. I could smell the arid berry tang of gin on his breath. 'How well do you know Riaan?'

'Not as well as you.'

'Do you love him?'

The word was out of my mouth before I even thought it. 'Yes.'

Pieter nodded, as if he'd only been waiting for confirmation. 'Does he love you?'

'No. Yes. I don't know. If he does, it doesn't change anything.'

Pieter nodded again. This time it meant, *good*. This was what he wanted, I realised, that someone else be in love, and for it to not change anything.

# IV

*He shoves me face down onto the bed. He reaches underneath my stomach and undoes my belt. I am pinned underneath him. He is trying to get not into me but through me, trying to reach somewhere on the other side. The thrust of him is so powerful I feel he will rent me in two.*

*He stays on top of me. I can barely breathe but this too I like, the feeling of being crushed by him, of having the air pushed out of me.*

*His mouth is in my ear, whispering something.*

*What? I breathe. A vertigo whirlpools inside me. One day this will be a memory, and the distance between our bodies will rush in my ears like the wind. I see myself in cold cities, in train stations buying tickets, in offices at photocopiers, all the stations of the cross of my old life, the life I led before I came to this burning country and I am so, so afraid.*

*Now he is beneath me, his golden body, his long limbs, the downy hair in the small of his back, the beads of sweat there. I press my knee between his thighs to prise open his legs. The truth is, it's not* a man, *it is Riaan. I am doing what I want to do to my lover. And that is all that it means, and all that happens.*

Two days after the fire it finally rained. The ocean turned muddy and opaque. When the sun came out again the light was swords glinting off barren trees and the singed grasslands. At night the burnt trees squeaked in the wind. Above the house, the mountain was lined with their skeletons; at sunset they formed a line of silhouetted sentries.

I still heard it, the voice that first tugged at me, luring me into the city I was about to leave, those first few days on the ship. *Stay here* – I suppose that was what it was saying, all along. Certain places speak to us this way, it's not uncommon. If it weren't for the shameful turnaround I'd made on the ship this would be a story of ordinary seduction.

I wonder what will happen to the city of Pieter's novella? In his story, climate change is creating stronger and stronger winds, and what used to be ordinary summer gales have cyclone strength. I look at the houses that perch on the mountain like nesting albatrosses, at the three cylindrical high rises called Protea Towers which nestle in the crook of the mountain. Will their windows smash, their roofs take flight? The wind will feed the fires, which also used to be seasonal but which now threaten a local apocalypse. The wind and fire will be followed by drought, the warming ocean will starve the humpback whales of krill. The city's days are numbered, and that is why I want to stay here, to be able to say I saw it in all its glory, before the future took hold.

The day before I leave Pieter holds a lunch to see me off. Sara has returned. If I mention her week away she moves the conversation swiftly into the future, to my return, to England, to their next foreign trip when they will certainly see me in London, we will all go to dinner on the South Bank, they love it there.

What has changed about Sara in my eye? She is a beautiful woman, with her grass-green eyes, her milky limbs. I'd thought she had gotten away with something, somehow, by having the life I'd believed she'd had. But in reality the life I imagined for her had been damaged, perhaps irreparably, a long time ago.

'I can't believe it,' she says, walking around the house in a daze. 'I can't believe we nearly lost all this.' I realise that Riaan has her voice, or she has his, pitched an octave higher. There is a shear in both their voices, a note of tear and uncertainty which gives them gravitas.

I see her taking in the stained glass panels near the ceiling, the ones that turned the afternoon light that decanted itself into the living room the gold and orange of cold fires. I see her imagining it melted into a ball on the floor, the roof a charred ribcage of timber. She walks inside the vision of her ruined house like a haunted child.

Before lunch I go into my bedroom to start packing. I see I have left my laptop screen open. My screensaver has failed to come on, as has the time-out lock, so I don't need to log back in to see what is written there, I only need touch the keyboard for the text to emerge.

I have been trying to write about what we did together, what we really did, Riaan and I, to each other's bodies. I am not Pieter, I am not a writer, I lack the language to say what it is I really feel for Riaan, but I needed to write it down. If I could I would have it all engraved in stone somewhere and plant it in a lost corner of the desert, for someone to excavate one day.

Then behind this thought, a sense of something violated. A half-processed memory of a man standing in front of a laptop screen in the middle of the night, or perhaps in the morning – some interstitial time when I am neither awake nor asleep, reading what I have written there. It is one of those dreams in which you want to cry out but discover you have no voice.

Pieter leaves his novella *Fire on the Mountain* for me to read in plain view, I know now that he is never happier than when he sees his novel in my hands. I am certain he has come into my room and read what was blinking at him on the screen like a hieroglyphic siren. That is why he asked me if I loved Riaan. So I also have the gratification of being read, even if it comes from a grave error, and an avoidable one.

*Pieter Lisson, Pieter Lisson*. Back in England I will say

his name again and again. What is its secret? The hiss in the 's', maybe, its symmetry of the vowels on either side of those serpentine sounds. Not a name of empty intrigue, nor a Lothario's name, not brutal nor effete. A name built to be in print. How strange, that it should be Pieter's name, and not Riaan's, that should resonate in my head, like a slogan or a song.

Standing in my bedroom I look at my body and see signs of the months I have been here: my watch strap is disintegrating. I have Riaan's dramatic tan lines on my arms, my legs. How new and white the skin looks on one side of the frontier and on the other, how used.

He walks toward me on the grass, still singed by flame. It is the end of the driest summer on record and tomorrow I am heading home, back to spring in England.

I see the leanness of his body, how his shirts won't stay tucked into his jeans, no matter how tightly he draws his belt. His narrow feet and graceful ankles. His feline stride.

It is a hot day, this farewell lunch, and Pieter comes walking barefoot across the grass, past the swimming pool. Patches of sweat soak his sky blue shirt, detailed with small white stitches. He has several buttons open from the neck.

'You're halfway to taking your shirt off,' Sara says.

'Well I would, but I don't want to scare away the ladies.'

'Or we'll fall on you and attack you!' Sara's cousin grins.

'Don't do it,' I say, 'it's not worth the risk.'

Pieter returns to the dark cool of the house. We sit underneath the sculpted lime tree, which the fire half spared. The side that faces the mountain is blackened. Its front cupola hangs over us, forlorn and tattered. The swimming pool has been replenished but is full of charred twigs and leaves. The mountain is ribbed by swathes of blackened grass. The purple Ibis have returned, though, perching on the rooftops of the glassy mansions that surround us, casting their soft graphite eyes over the scene, as if to survey the damage.

The heat has the sharpness of afternoon but has reached its apex. In an hour, at four o'clock, it will subside into a thin, fine heat of autumn.

I look up and see Pieter walking out of the darkened arch of the kitchen. There is a deliberate note in his gait. He comes up behind the elderly uncle and hovers, facing me. The uncle with the hearing aid takes no notice of him. I stare at Pieter, giving him what I know is a plaintive look. This may be the last time I ever see him.

Pieter hovers above the aged uncle. 'Cheers,' Pieter says, to me. His voice is distant, even acrid.

Then he turns around and walks inside the house, dark and close with the heat of the last day of summer.

# V

Moments ripple across the surface of time.

Riaan at the swimming pool in Ocean Point, poised on the diving board. Riaan photographed in mid-air as he lunged toward the water. That clay feeling of time in the late afternoon. As if time is first being moulded before being set for a larger purpose.

He enters the water like an arrow. He was always graceful.

He would hug me, until he suddenly stopped, at twelve. He would envelop me in great unending hugs, pressing himself into my ribcage so hard I could not breathe.

Riaan coming home from school having been temporarily expelled for criticising 'the history of the fatherland, which is a matter of record, not the opinion of thirteen year-old boys', as the headmaster had written to me. Not so, I wrote back, and quoted eleven massacres on record, the deaths of interned slaves, the wholesale slaughter of game in the first a hundred and fifty years of colonisation so that not even a paltry gazelle remained on the mountain by 1800, and quoted some poems I had written about on this subject ten years before and which had won the Varley prize, the most prestigious literary award in the country.

We sent him to a boy's school, but had to take him out after a year. He quickly became a cult. Other boys tumbled into an instant stinging hatred of him, of the kind that shocked the haters far more than Riaan, or fell in love with him, as he required most people to do.

The headmaster came to tell me personally, arriving sweating and nervous in a dark car, that he was 'disruptive to the culture of the school', although he 'recognised Riaan's powerful personal qualities.' Something made me take pity on the man. I ushered him out of the house, blinking, into the garden. 'Don't worry,' I said. 'We can't afford the fees much longer anyway,' which was true.

I remember Riaan at the fundraising barbecue for the lower income neighbourhoods our Rotary Club held every February, sweating over the grill, deep-frying calamari, being spat in the face by hot grease from sausages. When the older men would flake out at 10pm – just as business was getting rowdy, with queues of teenagers in their best Saturday outfits, ravenous, penny-pinching, comparing prices – he would keep going until one or two, when he would suddenly slump onto the grass.

We saw who he was, instantly. The dark holograms of anger that swirled from him. Around him the air was electrified but unhappy. People were fascinated by this, but we were afraid for him, of who he might become. Riaan was a dimensionless creature, not unlike the land he came from, copper-skinned, one of those scorched people who say: *Leave the place burning*.

Nicholas and I talk about him, on those nights before the fire comes. I divulge my suspicion of my son to him. I say, Riaan, there he comes, charging over the horizon of your life with his 4x4 and his enormous dogs which stand sentinel around him like those half-lion half-jackal creatures which guarded the gates to ancient Assyrian cities. While his light is turned upon you, you bask, certain there can be no other place as thrilling, as intense. But the beacon is indiscriminate: it turns on the next person with equal interest and intensity.

And Nicholas will ask me, *How can you say that about your own son?*

*I can only say that because he is my son.*

But there is another reason that Nick could not guess.

People who spend their time with invented personages, constructing entire worlds with only an effort of will – writers – don't take kindly to feeling impotent, not in control, as Riaan could make you feel. Passing judgment is a way to resurrect the putrid authority of the writer.

The son always spirals away from the inclinations of the father: what he likes, what he does for a living, his talents, his passions. I didn't expect much else. It is as if it's ordained this way. It could be part of natural selection; the conformists are weeded out, ensuring that only the questing adventuring rebels survive to propagate the species.

I expected that as time passed we would know each other, or at the very least Riaan and I would be friends. I expected that there would come a time when he would stop resisting me, when he would love me with the abandon and tenderness of that ten year-old boy he had once been.

But he remains for years in that landscape whose dimensions could accommodate without consuming him. We spend so much time apart we no longer know each other. When he comes home I stare at him, this simulacra of my younger self, trying not to resent how he shows me up as over-complex, burdened, old.

He has taken that decision so many of us have: to stay, to go. At twenty-four he came back from London chastened. Until he went overseas he hadn't realised how much he was a product of this country whose political past he detested. *I don't know who I am there, Pa*, he said, of England. This is not a country that produces immigrants, but exiles; even if you choose to leave for a job in Deutsche Bank or Columbia University that is what you are, forever: an exile. You give up one identity but you will never replace it with another. All because you come from a country that is not only a place but which has the density of an idea.

During the two years he spent in England he did not return for holidays. He was so homesick he actually felt physically ill, he told me. The rainy summers produced ashen crescents underneath his eyes. It wasn't only the golden mornings and the vacant skies he missed, he said, but the names of things. We have six or ten languages, depending how you count them, to draw upon here, for birds, the trees, insects, from English, Spanish, Dutch, Portuguese and the African languages.

I sense all this from afar, even though he hardly writes or telephones. This is the curse of being a writer; if you are any good you are psychic. You can feel the moment coming before it arrives, feel peoples' thoughts congealing until it is unclear whether they are your thoughts, theirs, or something dreamed up by a distant overlord who you are channelling.

Even if Riaan does not luxuriate in words as I do, he will feel that insistent nudge to create something, and which will be for him as it is for me so intimately linked to happiness. He will not be content to live on a diet of action, to lead a compass-less charge of days into days. He will be more than the sum of his parts: hunter, schoolboy, rugby-player, charmer, beloved son, dreamer, penitent, saviour, listener, environmentalist, soldier, desert-dweller.

It took Nick to give him a dose of astonishment, which is what he has been living for: days of hunger and spirit. Days of that intense surprise which reveal the fiction of the idea of a coherent personality, of character, to us. We think we know who we are, but then we make an avoidable mistake, or are overtaken by a breakdown, or eaten alive by an unfathomable desire, and we realise not only do we not know who we are, but we don't know what we will do from one moment to the next. Riaan always understood this, and created himself anew in each moment. This was his thrust: to live through days that take him to the edge of himself, to the edge of possibility. Unhoped-for. To be a lover of another man. To be chosen.

No, this is not the book my publisher wanted. This elegy for my son written through another man's eyes.

The first time I saw him he had passed out in the living room of our guest flat. He lay there on his back, a swatch of dark hair over his eye. Sara had told me she was worried about him, that something didn't seem quite right about his story of how he had come here. We knew Ruth would have told us to expect a guest. We knew something unexpected had happened to him. We were only waiting for him to confess.

When he came to and looked into my eyes I saw a very handsome young man, so much so that it made me suspicious of him in a different way – men that good-looking do not get to be thirty-two or thirty-three and still unpaired for no reason. I flipped through the usual suspects: vanity, egotism (not quite the same animal), the emotional ruthlessness in which the English excel. When I got to know him better I saw he had kind eyes, a crushed note within them, like grapes readied for the harvest underneath stomping feet. He had a sturdy capability about him I liked and which I imagined he had developed on the job, as much as it was an innate quality.

Now I sit in my study, where Nick and I would talk while the light drained itself from the sky. In Nick I gained what every writer desires: a reader. Twice I caught him in my office, reading my work on the laptop screen, printed out in draft piles. Within four months he had read everything I had written – nine books in all – and crucially he would tell me what he thought about it. He was not burdened by thinking himself a literary man or an intellectual, so he could be candid about my writing.

He liked the complicity between my characters and the darker dimensions (his words again) of experience: how easily betrayal and treachery came to those who had been forced by history to betray themselves. People know what values mean in a country like this, he said, where everyone is automatically compromised by events that happened in some cases long before their birth. Few countries are chosen by history to tell as important a story as yours, he told me: of violence, oppression, of seemingly destined collapse, but ultimate triumph.

'But Pieter, you don't let your characters speak for themselves enough,' he said. 'They have a mantle hanging over them. They know too much about their own predicament. In real life people know nothing about what happens to them. They can analyse other people's lives but when they try to understand their own lives they are at sea. You have to be more generous. Why not let these people live, rather than driving them remorselessly into the dark destiny you've decided they deserve.'

The email arrives from the northern autumn. Sender: Anthony Edwards. A textbook name for an English editor, the surname which could be a first name, the bland reversibility of it.

I have known him for twenty years but I always think of him with both his first and last names. He is a reedy blond man, a dandy – as evidence I quote his Gieves and Hawkes suits, his manicured nails, his pastel shirts. As long as I have worked with him he has suggested I consider changing the endings of my books to something marginally less bleak. He often exhorts me to explain inexplicable things to the people he calls 'my audience'.

'You have to think of your audience, both here and in the States. People in the UK know nothing about your country. They don't have the patience to look up terms in a foreign language. They don't have an automatic knowledge of racial categories, either – thankfully.'

I know full well how my audience sees this country: a distant, over-ripened, corrosive place, an ex-dystopia in modern times. Readers in other countries can afford to be lazy with their economies of scale, their pounds sterling, an actually functioning central government. God forbid they should have to make an effort to understand any of this, along with colloquial words, dialects, the names of tree and flower. I can remember a time when writers were neither schoolmasters nor cultural ambassadors, when writing difficult books was expected – more than that, it was their duty.

'Why do you want me to change the ending?'

'Because you are missing out on an opportunity.'

'For what?'

'To tell the world what really happened. This is your story, after all.'

Anthony Edwards has long been urging me to *tell the world* about my life. He has been waiting for a memoir: my political struggles, censorship, the women I have loved, the unceasing struggle to write something profound about this country and its suspect founding myths instead of the cheapened currency of love affairs in which my creative work has traded.

Several times over the years I have tried to write this kind of book. But it has been written by other writers who were far closer to the events that changed the country. Try as I might, it always transforms itself into fiction. I don't know why. I have no control over that sly eliding. I can only assume that fiction is the only thing I can write because the unadulterated truth does not interest me. Or I simply don't believe in the truth, that it exists. Perhaps I never did.

Like many writers I knew what I couldn't do; my limitations defined what I ended up writing. I could only write about what happened to me, that was the real problem. I didn't have the imaginative largesse or the sheer intelligence to scan and distil the concerns of an age, for example, to channel undercurrents, conjure a cast of outlandishly fictional characters. These were always for me manipulative gargoyles of false humanity, fetishes of the writers themselves in whose creation they could luxuriate, convincing themselves of their imaginative genius. I wrote for a pedestrian, even suburban, reason: to try to work out what I experienced and observed because I could not live with the inexplicable incoherence of actual life. My novels all came out in the same form, despite what I had planned: slim bars of bitter chocolate.

'Pieter, as your editor and your friend, it's my duty to tell you that this book as you've written it so far is too exposing.'

I don't say, but you're not my friend at all. You're not even an editor. You go to lunch with people. I remember Max

Ignesi, Fergus McCarthy – both gone, but not retired, nor dead, as far as I know, just downsized or rationalised out of existence by the publishing conglomerates that run the show, now. They knew how to restructure a book, how to re-align character with history. Those editors were writers who didn't want to write. With them, I could really talk. Now all they want to talk about is, will it sell? Will it win a prize?

'Exposing of what?' I ask. Now that there is only myself to guard I find I am uninterested in self-protection. I have a line I deliver, sometimes, at overseas colloquia or when I am invited to give speeches to the graduating class in English departments in this country: *What is a writer?* I ask, and pause theatrically. *The writer is a creature unhealthily obsessed with the moment before things went wrong*. A hush always ensues. The students or good burghers at the function are bemused. They think: *Let me not turn out to be an eccentric, tweedy egoist in disguise, delivering flaccid aphorisms on a plate*. Not the moment itself, I go on to explain, nor that whining question *why – why* did it go wrong? Everyone knows there is no *why*. No, it's a writerly trait to want to portray the moment before the fall. This is the moment we will all hold in our minds like a house set solidly into a mountain, this is the true nature of the golden terror of happiness. The shy, unrecorded moment, a moment of poise, an interval between rough seasons.

Anthony's only answer is a sigh, broken into compartments by the ether across which we speak. He is thinking: If this guy weren't such an international big shot, I'd never be having this conversation. There's a pile of first novels by luscious twenty-six year-olds pining to be read on my desk, and I'm talking to this curmudgeon in a city thirteen thousand kilometres away who might sell ten thousand copies on the back of his latest literary prize and whose books are about nothing more than fathers yearning for sons they never had, or daughters betraying their mothers by ignoring their sound advice not to fall in love with the latest floating Casanova.

'There's another thing,' he says, and pauses – always bad news. 'I'm not sure that the story stands up as it might have done a few years ago.'

'Stands up to what?'

'Well, it's hardly against the law any more, a relationship between two men. Even in your country. As I'm sure you're aware,' he adds, after a moment.

'I'm perfectly aware,' I say. I see how young men press against other young men on the waterfront, in clubs, in malls, of this newly tolerant country. Their love no longer has to run the gauntlet of the law, court martial, exile. Now, like any love, it only needs strain against the lukewarm forces of familiarity, boredom, indifference, disgust.

'It's not about that, it's about internal laws. Who we allow ourselves to love, who we refute.'

'Also,' Anthony speaks again, 'I'm not sure you can be a character in your own novel without some explanation. Readers will be confused. Why don't you at least change your name?'

'I don't know why everyone seems to believe this will make a difference.'

This elicits a mellifluous laugh, which is not something Anthony Edwards does often. 'Perhaps people are more credulous than you think. It's about believability, Pieter. After all these years you know that. If you introduce an element of the real – and here we have several; your name, your son, your story – then you have to follow through on the bargain. You have to tell people what really happened.'

For four months now since the accident I have stayed up all night, retracing their steps, imagining I knew my son, imagining I knew Nick, imagining their love. I coaxed all this out of the squalor of my thoughts, after I received the news. Eventually one thought stood head and shoulders above the others: either I write about this, or it will destroy me.

This will be my last book. Anthony Edwards doesn't

know this – he would drop me from his list if I divulged it. He had been expecting *Fire on the Mountain*, a torrid novel about a love affair between a man and a woman in the hottest summer on record, the windiest too, the summer the Protea Towers had all their windows blown out and the residents had to be removed, for their own safety.

Instead I have delivered this wounded novel. Edwards will have to go to the marketing department and say, I'm sorry, I know, but this Pieter fellow you've barely heard of in a distant postcolony is so august now – he's won every prize going on the continent. With a little more success he will be one of those insolent old grandees, García Márquez, Saramago, Lessing, bad-tempered visionaries whose success has bought them independence from the thought police of commerce.

I will argue to Anthony Edwards, Nick is one of those narrators whose lack of awareness is as captivating as what they know. He is a bystander in his own life. He is one of the legion of men who have come into the planet at an uneventful interregnum, who are besieged by the hesitant, loping dislocation of being born into not quite the right time for their persona to triumph, and who look for someone to blame for their exile.

By the time he comes to live with us, he is waterlogged by life. Nick doesn't know that he stands on the edge of a sort of breakdown. His premonition on the ship has saved his life, but for what reason? And then he meets Riaan. This is the person – he knows this instantly – who will break his heart. The fact that Riaan is another man is not irrelevant, but Nick is shocked to find that gender is not that meaningful after all. Neither is sex for that matter, which is less an act than a skewed mirror version of ordinary, which is to say reasoned, life. In the fascinatingly altered mirror image you see a person's true animus, spirit. His soul.

At the beginning their friendship is forced because it is expected. They are the same age, between them there is mistrust, a barely swallowed rivalry. This is unusual for Nick;

in his normal life he has easy-going relations with men. But then a moment arrives – the moment when Rodrigo takes our photograph. I witnessed it. Together, in the same moment, they tuned into the same frequency. They had been broadcasting on separate bandwidths, but suddenly they were as one.

It will take Nick some time to understand that Riaan's relationship to his inner life is different from his. For Riaan the inner self is a watery, indistinct realm which he has not learned to map and tame as Nick has, instructed as he has been by the strictures of the so-called civilised world. He can appear cruel at times, but actually he is afraid. Emotions are dangerous and destructive. Why allow such treacherous things as feelings to be seen, let alone to rule the day? The violence of Riaan's refusal energises Nick. He needs it, banishment. In fact he has been waiting for a worthy form of resistance to appear, all his life.

Anthony has one more piece of advice. 'Pieter, I'm sure I don't need to tell you this, but you don't come out very well in this book.'

'I'm tired of everyone coming out smelling like roses. Let them smell a rat, if that's what they want to smell.'

A silence. 'I can't claim to know what it has cost you to write this, Pieter.'

No, probably not, I think, but do not say.

Now the mountain is clothed in the mists we so desperately needed in the summer. Winter is here, a season of periodic black squalls interspersed with days of metal sun. On my desk is the paperwork, still: life insurance, his will.

The road where it happened has a number: N-249. Riaan never wore a seatbelt. Nick, who had arrived in the morning from Spain, where he had gone to stay with his friend Mercedes to listen to himself and wait for direction, occupied the passenger seat, his eyes full of the landscape he never thought he would see again. Tanya, who stayed at home in Nova Friburgo, was six months pregnant. Nick and Riaan were heading upcountry, from base camp to Xaia, where they would pick up equipment for the solar panels that would power a new school.

The gravel roads where Riaan lives are designed to be driven at up to 100 kilometres an hour. Even so, for a car or a truck to hit a loose patch is not uncommon. You lose traction and steering. Riaan was an expert driver of these roads, so something must have happened to confound all his skills. He was tired, maybe nervous, or his instincts dulled by happiness now that he had Nick, now that he had everything he wanted. It was an hour before a driver passed and saw the tyre tracks and followed them to the ditch where Riaan's truck teetered on its crushed roof.

To lose a son is – I would like to say I know what it is, that it is like this or that. Like crossing a frozen river, or I am the river, frozen also, but I will never be crossed. The hole inside me is the future. And now that there is no future inside me, in the form of Riaan, what do I call this substance I am moving through and which used to replenish me each day?

There is one moment I cannot locate, the moment I decide that it is time to abandon the book I had been writing and tell this story. Was it before the accident? Had I already decided to write it?

The story begins like this: a man waiting for his fear of falling from the sky to diminish. We don't know each other yet, but he is descending on a plane in the skies above the house where Sara and I live on the mountain, he is coming to my city and he will live in my house. He is afraid, this man who once faced everything: wind, war, rain, displacement, cold, genocide or its aftermath, heat, because he has begun to receive messages from a future which has no room for him. He is a geologist by training but has left that behind to work in emergency disaster relief. He came to the city of the wind thinking he would be here three days and stayed for three months.

The sun goes down on his first evening here and he knows

this is his home. His body knows it, even if his mind must yet be persuaded. The singing of the future is separating the air into separate songs: now sand-dusk, now bruise, then a sinking as colour is sliced away: tangerine, lava, the black grip of night. He can already see their month in the desert, in a world lit only by fire. The part of his mind which has already lived this life leans into this future, even as the part of his mind which is Nick is still unconvinced. It is all so unlikely, what happens to us. At the end of our lives we think, who will believe this story? I don't even believe it, and I lived through it.

Mercedes shuffles the cards. The sounds outside her window are those of Barcelona in summer: the shriek of ambulances tearing down Gran Via, the voices of neighbours sitting long into the night on adjacent patios, the city traffic only petering out at 4am. Today will be 38 degrees.

For the first time in a very long time she is afraid of the cards, or rather of how she will translate the message of this mirror realm. That's how Nick thinks of it; he can see the cards really are speaking to him, through her. They are tuning into another planet, another Earth perhaps, where for some reason everything that we experience has already been played out, or is happening simultaneously, and the cards broadcast these back to us, as in a film.

She can feel the future foaming into life like the dun grasslands of the desert that has so captured her friend's heart. She can feel the dreamer's dream hardening.

Mercedes will endeavour to give her friend the illusion of choice. The truth is, the exact end is not yet decided. Long ago she saw that Nick would die by accident. There would be a renting of flesh from bone. She isn't sure how. Perhaps this is why he is suddenly afraid of flying.

She does know that this dreamer will go on dreaming long after we have evaporated and he will not remember us after all. We are not God's children, but numbers coming hard and fast one after the other, based on an old mathematical formula brewing new people into existence like the child now clinging to Tanya's womb.

She cannot shake her unease. Nick, she knows, is gaining access to the future. He has told her as much, and she knows this happens only near the end. It is as if the film or the dream of a future emptied of ourselves is only allowed to be screened then, once we are fading out of its narrative.

She lays down the cards and it hits her, a slap: there is more than one death here. The chariot, hammer and sickle in the 8th position – a vehicle, an accident.

She nearly says it out loud. She knows Nick believes that Riaan will go on and on, that Riaan is his brother, lover, father. He wants to be alive to see his son or daughter come long and lean into the world. Nick can already feel Riaan's pride as he watches his child walk on that vertical beach raked by cold waves, watches his child work out his or her relationship to destiny against that hard horizon.

A phrase of her grandmother's floats into Mercedes' mind: *Never go back to a place where you have been happy.*

Nick might shrug and tell her, everyone says that. But how do you know until you try?

There are so many different fires – the fire that branded a lava path on the flanks of the mountain and which nearly consumed our house, the fire that ignited between Nick and Riaan and which refused to be dampened or starved, the burnt meteor of the sunset over the ocean in Nova Friburgo, the cold white flare of the shooting star Nick sees when he wakes in the desert at four in the morning, followed at dawn by something more miraculous, the emerald flash of sunrise, its instant blare and then the death of its dark aurorae. It is the rainy season, the tail end of it. Night paws the land. Tomorrow they will drive north, but for the moment he and Riaan will sleep underneath the Iwi tree, faces upturned and exposed to the skies and the crushing intentions of the stars. Rain comes again that night, and the desert springs to life.

*Note on names and places*

The place names in this novel do not correspond to any one country or place which exists, although some of the names are from particular countries (there is a Nova Friburgo in Brazil and a Quelimane in Mozambique for example). The Iwi tree does not exist, although this word means 'atonement' in Hawaiian.

# Acknowledgements

My thanks for their kind hospitality and support in the writing of this novel goes to the following friends: Steven and Denise Boers, Pieter Leroux and Ingrid Fiske. Julia Bell, Meg Vandermerwe and Nick Dennys read previous versions of this novel and gave me valuable input and advice. The AW Mellon Foundation supported some of the research and writing time while I held fellowships at the Universities of Cape Town and the Western Cape in South Africa. I am indebted to my agent, Veronique Baxter at David Higham Associates in London, and to Lauren Parsons at Legend Press. I would also like to thank Biblioasis editions in Canada, who shortlisted an earlier version of the manuscript for their prize for the 2012 Metcalf-Rooke award for best unpublished manuscript.